THE LION'S PATH

THE LION'S PATH

A Novel of World War II

By

C.J. Kelly

iUniverse, Inc.
New York Bloomington

Th e Lion's Path

A Novel of World War II

iUniverse books may be ordered through booksellers or by contacting:

iUniverse
1663 Liberty Drive
Bloomington, IN 47403
www.iuniverse.com
1-800-Authors (1-800-288-4677)

ISBN: 978-1-4401-0973-7 (sc)
ISBN: 978-1-4401-0974-4 (ebook)

Howitzer photos obtained from US War Department Technical Manual TM-9-1325 105mm Howitzer M2, M2A1, September 1944.

Printed in the United States of America

iUniverse rev. date: 10/16/2009

To the men of the 106th Infantry Division

And

333rd Field Artillery Battalion,

Thank You.

"Leave the Artillerymen alone, they are an obstinate lot…"

Napoleon Bonaparte

"Our artillery…the Germans feared it almost more than anything we had."

Ernie Pyle, Brave Men, 1944

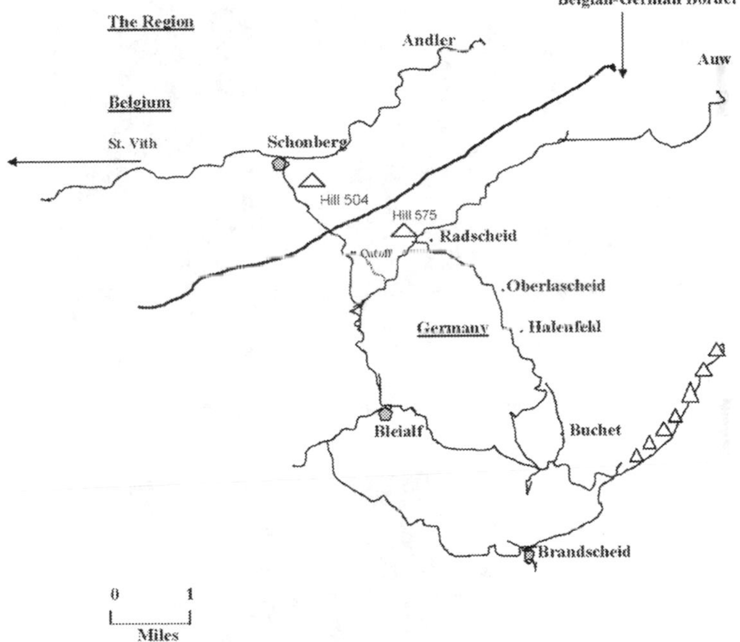
The Region
Belgian-German Border
Andler
Auw
Belgium
St. Vith
Schonberg
Hill 504
Hill 575
. Radscheid
.Oberlascheid
Germany
. Halenfeld
Bleialf
Buchet
Brandscheid
0
1
Miles
Source: The Author

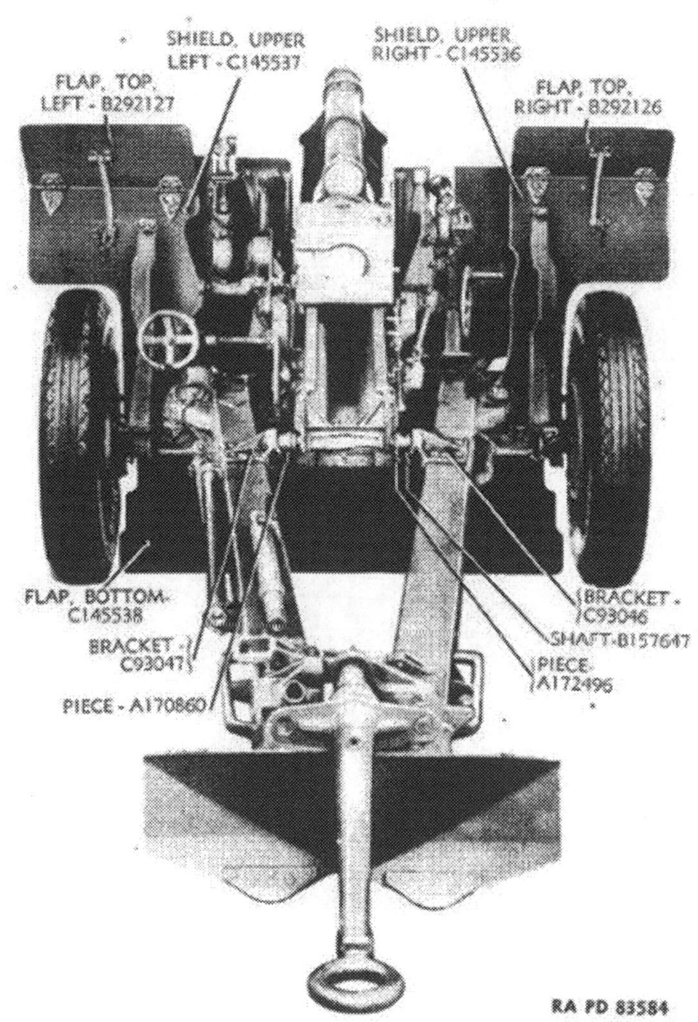
SHIELD, UPPER LEFT - C145537
SHIELD, UPPER RIGHT - C145536
FLAP, TOP, LEFT - B292127
FLAP, TOP, RIGHT - B292126
FLAP, BOTTOM-C145538
BRACKET - C93047
PIECE - A170860
BRACKET - C93046
SHAFT-B157647
PIECE-A172496
RA PD 83584

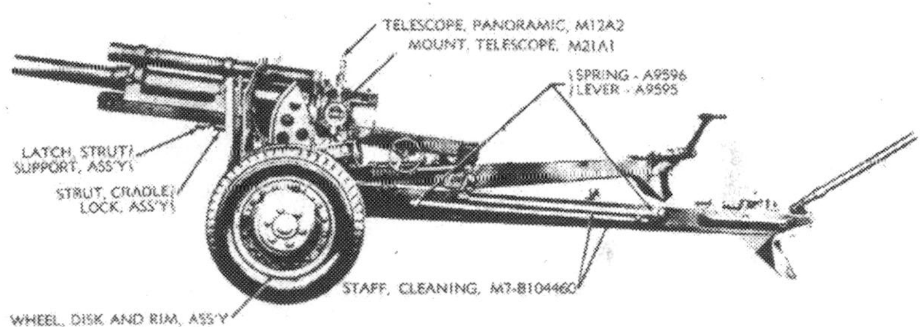
TELESCOPE, PANORAMIC, M12A2
MOUNT, TELESCOPE, M21A1
SPRING - A9596
LEVER - A9595
LATCH, STRUT SUPPORT, ASS'Y
STRUT, CRADLE LOCK, ASS'Y
STAFF, CLEANING, M7-B104460
WHEEL, DISK AND RIM, ASS'Y

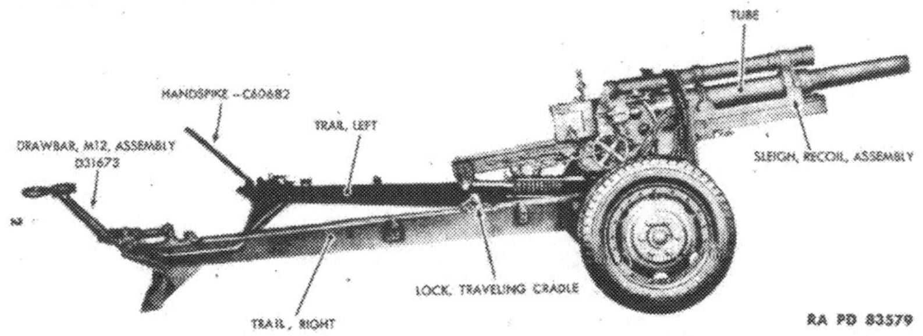
TUBE
HANDSPIKE - C60682
TRAIL, LEFT
DRAWBAR, M12, ASSEMBLY B31673
SLEIGH, RECOIL, ASSEMBLY
LOCK, TRAVELING CRADLE
TRAIL, RIGHT

RA PD 83579

PREFACE

IN THE FALL OF 1944, the Western Allies led by the United States and Britain, were confident of a speedy victory against Germany. With the Russians moving in from the East, Germany was being squeezed on two fronts. There was even talk of victory by Christmas. Some top commanders had even placed friendly wagers amongst themselves on what date the war would end. But by December, the front was static and the winter weather had arrived. The Germans dug in along the remaining barriers of the Siegfried line and were supposedly waiting for the big blow to arrive, most likely in the Ruhr, the industrial heartland of the Reich. The victories of the summer and early fall by the Allies were distant memories and the war had become a slow battle of attrition against an increasingly desperate enemy. So along this 'ghost front', as it was now being called, things became routine. Rumors about Glen Miller appearing in Paris were heard everywhere. Marlene Dietrich and Dinah Shore were coming too. Ernie Pyle left for the Pacific. If the reporters were leaving, there might not be much to do for a while. The Germans, with no real diversions of any kind, kept themselves busy reinforcing fortified positions that the Allies would have to overcome.

There had been harbingers of trouble all along the Allied front. The failed attempt in September to dash across the Rhine through Holland ended in the almost total annihilation of the British 1st Airborne at Arnhem. Later that fall, Montgomery's forces failed to secure the vital port of Antwerp until November, causing vast delays in supplying the Western Armies approaching Germany. Overconfidence led American commanders to launch an attack through the rugged Huertgen Forest on the border of Germany in September. It ended in a bloody stalemate five months later, with a high cost in lives.

In addition, there was the conflict between Allied commanders. General Dwight D. Eisenhower had been trying to keep the peace between his principal commanders: British General Montgomery and American Omar Bradley. This tension was further heightened by the machinations of General George Patton, commander of the American Third Army, and a long-time Montgomery antagonist. Each had their own view of how the war should be won. They fought each other as hard they fought the Germans.

The high casualty rates they suffered since landing on June 6, 1944 shocked the Western Allies. Control of the skies had long since been wrested from the Luftwaffe. Years of bombing Germany's industrial areas should have destroyed its ability to make war. Still, the Germans continued to fight. As a result of this miscalculation, a manpower shortage developed. Many American divisions waiting in the states had been stripped of their experienced personnel, taken as replacements for units decimated after Normandy. New recruits had been rushed through basic training and were going to have to learn on the job. In many cases, they died trying. Large numbers of African-American units were finally being put into action. Previously relegated to support roles, they were now represented in all branches of the Army.

Against this backdrop, the 106th Infantry Division arrived on the continent, making their way to the Schnee Eifel on the eastern edge of the Ardennes Forest, a rugged, hilly region in the tri-border area of Belgium, Germany and Luxembourg. The area had a Christmas card look with its narrow winding roads, mist-shrouded, snowy hills, interspersed with dense forests of fir and pine. The locals in their area, who were of mostly German descent with a sprinkling of French- speaking and Flemish Belgians, were indifferent at best. The ethnic mix brought on overlapping loyalties during the war.

The Division, made up of three infantry regiments, four artillery battalions and various other support units, was formed in 1943 and spent eighteen months getting ready to go overseas. Not only did the enlisted men lack any combat experience, but most of its officers did as well. Even General Jones, the division commander had never heard a shot fired in anger; neither had Eisenhower for that matter. The Golden Lions, as men of the Division were known, spent the winter training in the mountains of Tennessee and the summer of 1944 sweltering at Camp Atterbury, Indiana. It was assumed that by receiving the toughest training the Army could offer, that it would more than make up for any lack of experience. It was during that summer, that the Division lost almost 6,000 of its original enlisted complement to replacement depots. New men were brought in and commanders hurriedly tried to get them up to speed before deployment.

Once they arrived in Europe, they were told that they would have time to get acclimated to combat conditions. Their responsibility covered an area of over twenty miles, well beyond what Army regulations stated for a division. Despite the fact that two thirds of the division would be located inside the German border, the men of the 2nd Division, whom they were replacing, joked that they were going to have it easy. In reality, the men would have very little time to adjust to their new surroundings. A week after arriving, the Germans struck, setting off what would become known as the Battle of the Bulge.

1

Friday, Dec. 15, 1944, 1930 Hours, Bleialf-Schonberg Road, Ardennes Forest, Belgian-German Border.

A SNOW-LADEN WIND BLEW ACROSS the face of Lieutenant Brendan Green as he drove his jeep back to his battery's perimeter, in what had become a fairly harrowing drive through the darkness. No matter how much he slowed down, the jeep still slipped and swerved around the narrow turns. He had lost track of time while visiting one of the forward observer posts and was sure his battery commander would be wondering about his absence. Using the jeep's 'cat's eyes', the narrow headlamps used as blackout lights, was not even advised this close to the front. So squinting into the darkness he drove on, keeping his Thompson handy. More afraid of getting shot by his own men than the Germans, he eventually turned on his regular headlights.

Nearing his turnoff, a faint light appeared up ahead and he was able to make out two figures silhouetted against the snow. The much taller one was shouting and waving; hearing it was difficult over the whine of the jeep in low gear.

"Hold it up! Stop, now!"

Green slammed on the brakes, angry at himself for not remembering these guys from before. Everything got quiet, except for his idling engine and the slow, cautious steps of what he hoped were just two jumpy MPs as they approached the jeep.

The two men came closer, one on each side; their carbines were pointed right at him. Then the tall one crouched down to get a good look at him, flashing the beam right into Green's eyes.

"I'm Lieutenant Green. I passed you guys a few hours ago," he tried to sound as matter of fact while blinded by the light.

"That must have been the other guys." His voice was gruff and definitely much older than his partner. Green assumed he was the sergeant. "We changed over at 1800."

"Okay. Sorry 'bout that. Look, I'm with the 590th."

"You're Green, you said? Artillery guy, right? I think you passed through on Thursday."

"It's *Lieutenant* Green," he replied slowly, emphasizing his annoyance. "Able Battery to be exact. And yeah, I've been going back and forth a lot."

He did something he hated to do, pull rank in the hope of hurrying the process along as the snow flurries began swirling around. With a couple of holes in the canvas covering and a sideways wind, he was starting to get pretty wet. The sergeant's stern tone began to lessen as he peaked around the jeep, finally noticing the markings on the front bumper, '590/A'.

"Where ya headed?"

There was still a slight tone of accusation in the question.

"Back to Oberlascheid. That's where my battery is set up."

"*Ober* what?"

"Look Sergeant, blink and you would miss it. It's just down the road from Radscheid, where the Battalion HQ is. That's why I'm turning right here."

"I know Radscheid, sir. Alright. Sorry for the delay. It's these Kraut names. Just makin' sure."

"I understand. You're just doing your job. Try to stay warm."

"Lots of coffee, sir. You do the same."

With a quick return of salute and a sigh of relief, he was on his way, albeit wetter than before.

The weather was nothing new. Since arriving on the continent a week ago with the rest of the 106th Infantry Division, it had been nothing but cold, snow, sleet, rain and mud. After the Battery got settled in, Green made it a point to make contact with other units in the Division, including going forward to the frontline. The little trips started out to relieve some of his boredom and ingrained restlessness. But they turned valuable because of the information he garnered. As far as he was concerned, his battery might be called on to do anything, even acting like riflemen if need be, so they better get to know the area.

Green was the battery's executive officer. With over ninety enlisted personnel, and only four officers, the executive's post was a stressful one. Besides having to survey in the guns, he was in charge of maintenance, communications, payroll, general personnel issues and even the kitchen. He could delegate, but when all was said and done, the C.O. was going to ask him what went wrong, if anything did. Each battery had four sections and each gun crew had seven men. The other men in the battery performed a variety of duties: drivers, wire men, ammunition handlers, radio operators, and clerks.

To his relief, his ride was almost over. He slowed down, careful not to alarm the young soldiers manning the perimeter and quickly shouted the correct password without waiting to be challenged. The village of Oberlascheid was basically a cluster of about a dozen houses astride the road with large open fields surrounding it. As he approached the old farmhouse that served as section one's shelter, he noticed something amiss. A small flicker of light could be seen just for a second. No one noticed as he pulled up and slowly walked toward the back door.

"Davis, Greeley, where are your weapons?", he asked feigning incredulousness.

"Inside *Lootenant*," a surprised Private Leonard Davis, of Georgia, replied referring to the neatly stacked pile of gear in the corner.

"Didn't you hear me coming?"

"Pro'bly suh, sorry. I heard a jeep."

"Davis, what am I going to do with you? What about you, Greeley?"

"Suh, we figga it was you, but you do look like every other soldier in the outfit."

At a compact 5'9" and 165 pounds, Green was what the Army would call average size. Before the war, he had barely reached 140 pounds. Army life and the war had combined to age him beyond his twenty-two years. His dark blond hair was already receding. There seemed to be a perpetual hunter's squint to his hazel eyes from years of looking through field glasses. The wind and sun had turned his once fair complexion rather ruddy, with a long, gully-like scar near his jaw line, a result of his Kasserine experience. He referred to it as his 'wadi.' Besides his scar, the only other distinct characteristic was his bulbous nose, slightly bent to the right, after being hit by a baseball in high school.

"Is your personal weapon ready for use, Davis," the Lieutenant shot back.

"Suh, I think they ready for inspection"

"Really? Okay, I will take your word for it now. Maybe we can set up a little range somewhere in the next few days and find out."

"*Lootenant*," Davis answered, pouring on his homespun charm by exaggerating his Southern pronunciation, "suh, lookit, we in the artillery, we drop the big stuff on them Krauts."

"Do you really want me to respond to that?"

Davis just looked down and smiled.

"Suh?"

"What's up, Davis?"

"Ya think we can git Thompsons like you suh?"

"I doubt that's gonna happen. To be honest, this is not exactly Artillery issue. I had to sneak this one over. That's between you and me, got it?"

Green smiled, and knew that last request would never be followed.

How Green obtained the Thompson, when it was not issued to artillerymen, was sort of a mystery to everyone in the Battalion. Some speculated that it may have had something to do with his Silver Star. He had seen combat, knew what being under fire meant. If he wanted the Thompson, he could have it. Rumors abound that he had taken it apart in the States and snuck it over on the boat. During training, he always carried the ubiquitous M-1 Carbine, issued to every artilleryman. But once he got overseas, he showed up with a Thompson. If anyone asked, he always said he found it lying around. After a while, everyone stopped asking. It drew attention to him in many ways, something he hated, but he couldn't imagine going back to a combat zone without one. Whether it was a security blanket or a tribute to his former combat experience, he could not answer.

"My lips are sealed, right Hank?"

"Of course, sir."

"Hey Greeley, when you light up, don't do it out in the open like that. You never know. "Well, sir…sorry. Figure we we're far off the line. Didn't have to worry."

"Can never be too sure. And yeah, I know, I am starting to get a little chickenshit," he quickly admitted, referring to all that little stuff that officers made enlisted personnel do just to keep them busy or punish them. Needing a haircut, too much cosmoline in your gun or not enough shine on the shoes were just some of the issues that *chickenshit* officers looked for during inspection. Getting caught one time enough for some officers, and it meant a little latrine time or kitchen patrol, otherwise known as "KP".

"But if you step inside, I might want one of those."

"Here you go, sir." Greeley quickly complied, handing him a Chesterfield.

Green smoked, in a way, though he tried to refrain. Before seeing combat in North Africa, he had never thought about it. But those shellings can affect the nerves. He figured after the war there would not be a need for Luckys, Chesterfields or any other cigarette. At least, he hoped that would be the case.

"Were you guys trying to light a fire or did you just put one out?"

Even in the dim light, Green could see them looking at each other for the best answer.

"I can smell the gasoline and the tarpaper. You're lucky I couldn't see the flash. For God's sakes, you can't stand a few minutes in the cold?"

Artillery shells came wrapped in treated cardboard. The men figured that they could use them to light low-grade fires for warmth without blowing themselves to smithereens. Just a little bit of gasoline on the cardboard with a match did the job. Of course, the Army did not condone such methods but most officers looked the other way because they had to do it too. So Green went through the customary, albeit faux, castigation of his men, knowing improvisation was a fact of life in the field.

"Suh," Davis began in his slow, wrenching Southern drawl, "it be cold and I need a smoke real bad. So I take the full responsibility for these heah actions. Some of those boys in there don't smoke. Can't be rude now, can we?"

"That's so big of you, Davis. And Greeley, you decided to smoke because you thought the corporal here would feel lonely?"

"Sort of, sir."

"Good to know you're always thinking of others."

Green began to finally smile, thankful they could not see him start.

The men of Green's battery were comfortable around him. They respected him, not only for his veteran status, but for his fairness. He was not 'one of the guys' per se, Green knew not to cross that line. Nor was he totally regular army. As a result, back in Indiana, they started coming to him with the most personal of problems: 'Sir, I got my girl pregnant,' or 'Lieutenant, I'm startin' to itch in a bad place, if you know what I mean.' It was only a small amount of guys who ran around, but they all seemed to be concentrated in one or two sections. After a while, he did feel like a nurse at a whorehouse, so he managed to get those guys assigned to the latest request for replacements.

As they entered the two-story stone house, he had noticed the men had really worked hard to make the place like home. The set-up was more than comfortable when compared with the infantry regiments. Some of the men had even found feather beds, which were on a first come, first serve basis. For warmth, most of the men sacked out together in the largest room located on the ground floor where there was a homemade stove left by the former tenants. So as he peeked into the darkened room, Green was impressed. The floors creaked, it was drafty and one could smell the dampness, but it beat a foxhole any day. The bathrooms were still working and some of the men were fascinated by them. The water chamber was mounted near the ceiling. After they finished their business, everyone had to pull the chain to flush. If the bathroom was not to their liking, they could always use the cowshed out back.

"Okay suh, um… suh? Can we ask you a personal question?" Davis began almost sheepishly. "Me and Greeley been tawkin' heah. We wonderin'."

"I'm game."

"Well suh, not that it any of ma bidnis or anythin', but what kinda name is Green?"

"It's German, sort of…" Green said turning around and answering rather hesitantly. "My father was Jewish, and my mom is Irish Catholic."

"Your Dad's a Jew? Like Biels. Ya don' lookit suh," Davis shot back, his high-pitched voice and accent beginning to wake everyone up. "How they…"

"What am I supposed to look like? You know, forget it Davis," Green had raised his hand, clearly uncomfortable now, "did you check the gun today, Davis?"

"Sure did, Lieutenant."

"Do it again first thing in the morning unless we get some fire missions tonight. Oh, and take your favorite Italian friend with you," Green shot back as he gave Corporal Darino a little kick in the shoulder to wake him from his always pleasant slumber.

"Arthur?"

"Hey," the corporal yelled as he was aroused, "what the… oh, sorry sir. It's you."

Davis' unlikely best friend was twenty-one year old Arthur Darino, one of Youngstown, Ohio's favorite sons. Darino fit every stereotype of the Italian kid who grew up in the depression: streetwise and tough. On top of that, he looked the part with his olive skin, jet black, curly hair and dark eyes. At 5' 5", he had the strength of a man twice his size, beating several in the Division's boxing championships in June '44. He became an excellent soldier and turned out to be mechanically gifted, fixing any of the GMC 6x6 trucks that served as prime movers before any of the mechanics were needed.

Completely opposite in looks, Davis was prematurely old. Although he was only twenty five, some of the guys thought he looked like he was in his thirties. His blond hair was now thinned to just one strip on top of his head. Wrinkles had already showed up on his freckled face, which had a sort of paunch to it. He blamed it on a life of outdoor living and 'good eatin'.

Davis promised Darino a tour of his favorite Georgia country spots and even managed to pick up one or two Italian words. "Mangia" being his favorite, which he pronounced 'man jay,' during every meal time.

Above all, they could operate their gun as well as any crew in the battalion. That's why Darino and Davis had the number one and two positions respectively in the section. Green called them his secret weapons. Without them, his job, to say nothing of Sergeant Prynne's, the section chief, would have been a lot harder.

"You guys better get some rest anyway, unless you're assigned a watch. I hear there is one more supply convoy on the way, this time with everything: shells, bandages, and yes, even ammo. By the way, who has the watch tonight?"

"Wallenbach, sir. The new kid. I told him to stay close and alert," Darino answered for the group. "Mullins is due next watch."

"I didn't see them and I was not challenged when I drove into the village. I'll check on them again. Are they at the outpost, with the .50 cal?"

"That was last night. Brown from fifth section and House are out there. But what's funny sir is that none of the guys who have manned that post since we got here, have ever fired a .50 cal. They say during the day they can see the Krauts eating and moving around right out in the open. At night, it's just scary. They can't see a thing and swear the Krauts go right past them."

"The guys did come and tell me about what they hear at night. I also know they are having problems with the telephone connection out there. It's so dark, I had to use the telephone line to find them last night. If Battalion gives the okay, maybe we can fire at that Krauts as they line up for chow. As for House, I'm working on getting him reassigned. He's a trained mechanic and had to mount those cab ring mounts on all the trucks at Le Havre by himself and he did so without complaint."

"Sir, what about supplies?"

"We've been promised a shipment tomorrow. Every unit gets the same unless there is a shortage. Unfortunately, we might be his last stop. I also want to know exactly what kind of shells we have. This next shipment should bring us up to a full complement of around six hundred and fifty rounds. I'll have you ammo guys go through the charges too. And remember, when you guys stack the shells, only four layers high. Try to keep the stacks more than ten yards apart. And don't forget the dunnage. I'll pass the word to the other sections. You must have boards in between the layers, especially on the bottom. Remember, the first load of ammo was laid right on the ground and it sunk right into the mud. And with this crappy weather, always remember to tarp it. Even though it comes in the crates, they'll still get damp. We have extra tarps somewhere. We're even getting some soda ash as well to keep our babies out there as clean as could be."

"More cleaning, sir?"

"Yes. And one more thing. I noticed this in the first shipment of shells. Make sure to look at the rotating bands. Crack open a couple of the boxes. If there are any burrs, powder gas will escape during firing and the rotation will be off. So be on the lookout."

The crispness and passion with which spoke, made the men hang on every word. Even in shadow, he was a commanding presence. Something as mundane as stacking boxes sounded vital coming from him. Because of that, they set out to perform their daily duties with an almost filial obedience to his orders.

"Does that mean the gun could blow up, sir?" Garcia, one of the newest of the men, got concerned.

"No. I'm not worried so much about a muzzle burst. But it can affect accuracy. The gas has to be contained to get the maximum blast. Those rings can bend. It might even be the weather."

"The cold is a bitch, sir," Darino continued, "the grease in the breech is already thicker than glue. I didn't think that stuff froze at all."

"Even after last night? With the firing and all. I thought it was a bit warmer out too."

"Yessir. But by morning it was the same old. I don't think the soda ash will do the trick."

"Did you try gasoline?"

"Not yet, sir. I will in the morning."

On the night of the 14th, the battery had fired over one hundred rounds at various targets. It was in part a response to the Germans' occasional practice of lobbing some 155mm shells over every other day. To the men, it had been like their training in Tennessee.

"Well, a little more firing will take care of that. But I'm sure we're probably a little short on cleaner and oil. So if you have to, soap and water will help as well. Grab some antifreeze from the trucks too."

"This supply crap is a crime, sir." Darino snapped. "Who do these supply guys think they are? There's a war on. Talk about rear echelon. Jesus Christ!"

"I tol' you not t' take the Lord's name in vain, you dumb Dago," Davis shot back, giving him a playful shove.

"Where did a lazy hillbilly like you learn the term *Dago*? Did Greeley just teach you that? Who told him that? You can add that to the list of shit never to call me," then Darino stopped and realized something. "Sorry, sir."

"Davis, you have anything to say for yourself?" Green asked with a smile.

He thought about it for a second, and then the cigarette dangling from his mouth began to move up and down slightly; three puffs of smoke slowly rose above him.

"Yessuh. Ain't e'ver gonna call the dumb dago a dumb dago e 'ver again. Suh."

"I am going to take more than your name in vain, hillbilly….."

"Okay, easy boys," Green interrupted smiling, as nervous laughter erupted around the room.

"Davis, if you have any other ethnic insights you want to share, see me first, okay? I'm sure the Army has an approved list of insults and regulations regarding their use. In the Army, all insults must be by the book."

All of the men were up now. Seeing their Executive officer banter back and forth with Davis was almost as good as a USO show.

"Now as I was saying, even Division is aware of the supply problems. Our Divarty, General McMahon, was not happy that it took some of the sections days to calibrate the guns. At least that is what I heard. He doesn't confer much with me, in case you were wondering. And I probably shouldn't be passing this on, but what the hell. I spoke with one of the engineers from the 81st who told me that when they asked for barbed wire, they got word from one of the supply clerks that they needed three days notice before they even requisitioned it."

A collective, exasperated breath was let out by almost everyone in the shelter.

"Well, I'll keep you busy tomorrow. The forward observer teams may need help laying wire. The weather is still making a mess of everything. The snow in some areas is too heavy for the wire. Also, I would like to get some of you trained to do other jobs on the gun. Maybe ride you guys up to the front line a couple of times too. You can have a look around. Down in Bleilaf, I hear some observers have a nice set up."

There was no response.

"Do I sense a *problem*? Where is your sense of adventure? Keeping warm through work is our only solution. Maybe a cannoneer's hop with Sergeant Prynne watching over you guys. Whaddya say?"

After a momentary silence, the men gave the automatic response that enlisted always had to give.

"Yes sir," was the less than enthusiastic reply from the group.

A cannoneer's hop, an exercise where the men of a gun section rotate and perform all the duties that exist to be done within the section, was a sort of test.

"Hey look, I can't provide wine, women or song, but senseless activity is my middle name. I am an officer, remember?" Green stated sarcastically.

"Okay, sir."

"Come on, at least we are somewhat dry. I realize how close we are to the front. But believe me, being even a couple of thousand yards back of the line is even better than just 100 or even 500 yards back. We could be on patrol every night and sleeping in a cold, wet foxhole with just a shelter half for cover. One machine gunner told me that when they go for chow up on the line, they have to pass through an open field which the Krauts have zeroed. So they occasionally will lob a shell or two at meal time. Second Division lost a couple of guys that way. At least we know, for the most part, that the guys directly in front of us are American."

"Sir, how long do you think we'll be out here?" inquired Greeley.

"You mean, how long till the end of the war?"

"Well, sir, you know, till we get some leave or relief."

"Greeley, we're in the artillery, we never get relief. Know why? Because the upper echelon never thinks of us as being *on the line*. Understand? We may be close, but not close enough. Even if the infantry outfit we are supporting gets moved off the line, there is always another to take its place. We eat the same chow, most of the time. Suffer with the cold and get shelled. But infantry guys think of us Red Legs as living a life of luxury compared to their existence."

There was a collective chuckle. Calling artillerymen 'Red Legs' went back to the Civil War when they wore red leggings to distinguish themselves. It had been replaced by red piping on an artilleryman's overseas and dress caps.

"Look, we've been lucky up till now with everything but the weather. So let's be thankful for that. Until spring, all we might have to worry about is keeping our feet dry and the occasional Kraut shell. Hey, if any of you want observer duty, let me know. I'm sure they would love to have you."

Pedro Del Valle, who the guys just called Pete, the unit's only Puerto Rican and the source of much curiosity because of it, asked from the back, "Sir, you ever fight in the cold?"

"Not really. Tunisia got chilly during night guard duty, stuff like that. Sicily was almost as hot as Africa. I was only there a few days before word came of my orders for OCS. Nights there were strangely beautiful. Etna glowed throughout the night, spewing stuff down the mountain. But this is my first time on the line in bitter cold."

"Lieutenant, are you telling us that you were not supposed to be in Sicily?"

"That's what I heard later on. Apparently, some division clerk never delivered the notice to my C.O. in Bizerte after I was released from the hospital and I was sent back to my old battery. My old lieutenant had convinced me that I had been hand-selected for a special program from experienced enlisted, which I think was a lot of bull. Off I went on another invasion and you know, I didn't mind. I always thought it was strange that I did not stay in Sicily until the end. Someone must have had their ass chewed out because they threw me on the next boat back to the States. My C.O. showed up with MPs and everything."

"So you really were in a lot of combat, sir, before OCS? Is that when you won the Silver Star, sir?" asked Del Valle.

"That's just a rumor," he replied with a wry smile. "I don't know where exactly how that got started. And right now, it doesn't matter. But I was an enlisted man for a while."

"C'mon sir, only some of the guys know about it."

"Some other, warmer day," Green quickly answered trying to deflect the conversation away.

Del Valle was still fairly new to the section, arriving in October. Guys like Darino and Davis, who had been with Green for a while, knew not to bother asking about his past experiences. It was sort of an unspoken rule. Occasionally Green would mention something that had happened in his past Army life, but only to make a very specific point. There was an occasional reference to his hometown of Yonkers, but that was it. Green became the master of deflection in more ways than one.

"How are you handling the cold? You grew up in Puerto Rico, right?"

"*Es* okay, sir. Lived on the island until I was thirteen, then moved to the Bronx. *Mucho frio,* but I'm used to it now, sir."

"Hey that reminds me, check your feet all the time. I am working on getting even more socks. Don't be lazy about it. Do it daily, twice a day. I know I sound like a nag, but the cases of trench foot in the 422nd are so bad already, the guys at Division are taking notice. I don't want that here. Understand? Captain Peters wanted me to spread that message all over the Battery."

Both Green and Peters were pleased with the overall health of the unit. Despite their inexperience in the field, the men had generally avoided the usual ailments that plague soldiers in winter. Although, it had been a rocky beginning. The trip from the docks of Le Harve had been brutal. Sitting in the back of the trucks with water sloshing around for all those miles, made many of the units come down with cold-ridden problems like frostbite and the beginnings of trench foot. Traffic accidents were numerous. The Battalion had already lost one man in a traffic accident, Warrant Officer Collins, the supply technician. He was hit by a truck while standing behind his jeep. It was a sudden and brutal reminder of how fragile their lives were becoming. The men responded well, chalking up to life in a war zone.

"What about overshoes or the shoepacks, sir? We keep hearing rumors about them." the bookish Ken Biels asked.

"Not going to happen. Rifle companies have priority. Even they are falling short in that regard. Word is that it will be another month, which in Army time probably means April, after the snow starts to melt. So keep that top buckle on your boot fastened. Even though they are not great, these boots are still better than the ones I had in Africa. The leather is certainly stronger. Get any water on those old boots and the leather just shriveled. And then they would tell us to wear those God awful leggings, which were useless and chaffed us something terrible."

"How come you officers don't get better boots, sir?"

"Are you upset about that, Davis?"

"No, suh. Just curious."

"Well, we only get better dress uniforms. You know, we get those nice gabardine pants for our pinks and greens. But that's about it."

Green squinted into the dull light, trying to see who else was present.

"Biels, what were you reading?"

"Yank, sir"

"Who's the pinup?"

"Gloria something, sir. Not sure. I'll make sure I find out."

"I have a copy of a new Raymond Chandler. Well, it might be a few months old, but it's new to us. I'll trade with you. Do you have a 'word of the day' Biels?"

Biels, the Ivy Leaguer who quit Columbia to join the Army, was strangely embarrassed by his education, even shunning officer candidate school. Green figured that's why he kept volunteering back at Atterbury for every duty imaginable: gun crew, ammo hauler, battery agent, radioman or driver. It didn't matter. But the men got a kick out of his extensive vocabulary and his almost reflex ability to use it. There were derisive comments in the beginning. First, it was his looks. Everything looked too big on stick-like frame, and with his helmet on, the only thing one could see was his glasses. Because of his innate ability to absorb everything he heard, Green used him as a sounding board for the men. There had been rumors of him being a 'snitch,' or even worse; he became 'Green's Jew' for a time. Gradually though, he earned their respect, never shying away from any task. If I guy like that was willing to get his hands dirty, it was okay with them.

"Well sir, I'll just say this. I refuse to be held captive by the solecism of my environment."

Another collective whistle rang out inside their little home.

"I admire that Biels. I don't know what you just said, but it sounded brave. Didn't it fellas?"

Another unenthusiastic 'Yes, sir,' was spoken.

"By the way, remember I have to check your letters that you send home, especially now that we are in a combat zone. So make it easy on me, okay? I'm too busy to be worried about you tipping off the Krauts. Just talk about how you love Europe and the Army. Don't mention where we are exactly or any other unit names, okay? It's absolutely gorgeous here and you are living in an alpine paradise. And put in a good word about your executive officer."

The men just rolled their eyes, but several of the men already had commented to their families about the lieutenant being 'their kind of officer.' When he had to read the letters, he blushed a lot, even going as far as to actually contemplate editing those portions out. He stopped short of that. Hell, he thought, everyone could use a compliment.

"Sir, any sight of the Krauts anywhere in your travels?" Greeley inquired.

"I heard there are some sightings by the forward observers and they have heard vehicles going back and forth. Tanks, possibly. There have even been reports of trains rolling into Brandscheid. The FOs I talked to have not seen much activity other than the occasional flash from their firing. This constant fog obscures a lot of things. Not exactly an observer's paradise. So a lot of the reports are just based on what they hear although sound ranging has been difficult as well. When I was at one of the observation posts the other day, I spotted a few Germans milling around a few hundred yards away. Heard a rumor about some Krauts being captured, possibly deserters."

"Sir, what about the fire we laid down yesterday, what was that all about?"

"Apparently, one of the observers saw a large group of Krauts in Brandscheid along with some mobile 88s. So I assume the threat was real, although there was no confirmation. Then I heard there were sightings of some trucks down in Sellerich."

"How many observers do we have out?"

"Not sure, there's a mix of observers from different units spread all over the valley. There's a OP on top of that railroad tunnel in Bleialf and another observation team from the 333rd inside Bleialf as well. They said not much is happening, except that they do hear lots of vehicles too."

"333rd? Aren't they the Colored outfit sir? Darino inquired.

"Yeah, they've been overseas since July. They seem pretty sharp."

"Sir, I hear you arc a brave man," Davis interjected.

"Why is that Corporal?" Green asked with some trepidation, knowing Davis was about to make one of his unique observations.

"You go and talk to the Coloreds all the time. I been hearin' 'bout it a lot."

"Well, they have been out here longer than we have and might be able to learn something. They're soldiers too."

"Is it true that we now have a lot of colored officers, sir?"

"Yes, I've met a few. Nice guys. What's the matter Davis, kind of surprised?"

"Well, sir. I don't doubt that they are not good men, sir. But things are changing in this Army."

"You bet they are and those troops might just save your whistlin' Dixie ass someday."

Snickers could be heard throughout the room and even Davis laughed when the joke was on him. The jovial Southerner often played into the stereotype that many of the men had of his kind, but Green saw through his act.

"Anyway, Division says the Germans are piping recorded sounds to spook us into thinking they have an entire army over there. I know I heard a low-flying plane the other day that did not sound like one of ours and the sound was not coming from a record player. So be alert."

"Sir," it was the ever curious Del Valle again, "Monahan says his radio is being jammed. At least that's what he thinks."

"Yeah, I know. For the past day or two, he said he starts picking up German music in the middle of talking. Then static and more music. The Krauts are probably playing games."

"What were those glows last night, sir? It looks like they were coming from our own positions," the always inquisitive Biels asked.

"It wasn't the Germans. It was our own infantry. It turns out that one of the battalion's field kitchens burned up. There is also word that one of the battalion CPs had a fire as well. Regiment was furious. But to everyone's surprise, there was no response from the Krauts, which might mean something or it might not."

"Sir, since we got here, you've traveled more miles than anyone else in the Division."

"It's too cold to stand still. And like I have heard one of you guys say, we officers stand still a lot," Green stated as he turned toward Greeley.

Greeley, a little embarrassed, tried to think of something to say.

"Sir, I didn't..."

At that, Green smiled again and put his hand up. The Seattle-born Greeley was sometime the third member of Davis and Darino's triad of trouble. Green referred to him as their 'getaway driver.' Oddly enough, they had all been in the same artillery replacement depot together near Ft. Bragg, North Carolina, but never met until they were assigned to section one, A Battery.

"Suh, you tawk with that Kraut family that live 'cross the road? Pretty sure they Krauts. Sounds like what they tawkin'."

"Well, the guys in the 2nd Division told me that the Army allowed them to stay because they have a farm that can supply us with milk and in a pinch, meat. Their cows don't look like much, but as long as they don't bother anyone, we should be fine."

The ever suspicious Darino did not like the set up.

"But how do we know that they are not, you know, sending the Krauts signals?"

"We don't. They'd be taking an awful chance doing that. If they were using lights, the guys at the outpost would see it."

"Could they have a radio?"

"We'd pick it up, I'm almost sure Monahan would catch it. I don't know how they would transmit gun positions. If you see the guy pull out a BC scope, I would go over and have a word with him ASAP. But I know Captain Peters has spoken to them through a translator, but nothing since. Biels, you speak a lot of languages, don't you?"

"I speak a couple. If you want sir, I could try my hand at talking to them. It's not exactly real German, it's some local dialect, but I'm willing to try, sir."

"Let's do that. I'll see you in the morning. We can take a couple of guys and search the place again. In the mean time, if you see them running towards the house or happen to disappear just before we get shelled, then you know we have a problem."

"Okay, get some rest. I'm going to check the other sections and the CP one last time. The Captain may want my hide for being gone so long. Oh, hey where's Prynne?"

"He's over here, sir," Biels waved, pointing down. Green could now make out the outline of the bulky sergeant in the next room laid out on his bed.

"He's been asleep the whole time?"

"We exhaust him, Lieutenant."

"You're right. Let the big guy rest. Good night, fellas."

As always, there was something else he had to cross off his list.

"Almost forgot, the Chaplain is coming by tomorrow. He wants to know who's Catholic, Protestant, Jewish, et cetera, et cetera. Darino, I know what you are. Del Valle, I assume you're Catholic?"

"*Si,* sir. You?"

"Yeah," Green replied and then could see the confusion form on Davis' face.

"Um, Davis, you have a question? You look like you want to say something."

"I thought ya said yer Dad was Jewish? I'm confused."

"That happens a lot. I'll explain another time. Anything else you would like to add?"

"Well sir, can that Priest of yores do a good Baptist? Can't find a good Baptist preacher since we left Indiana. Even then, I think he was really a Methodist who did Baptist on the side."

"Look, I am sure we can find one somewhere in the European Theater of Operations."

Darino, fighting to stave off laughter, finally spoke.

"You Rebs are always bitchin' about something."

"Listen, I'm tawkin' heah. You got that Pope of yours. He's Eye-talion, right?

"What of it?"

"Ain't they all?"

"Okay, Martin Luther," Green interrupted, grabbing Davis by the shoulder. "Simmer down. And don't forget to say your prayers to whomever. Let's hope for a quiet night this time. Pleasant dreams."

A collective 'good night' was heard as Green exited their quarters. A battalion runner caught him at the door.

"Are you Lt. Green?"

"I'm Green."

"Sir, meeting tomorrow, 0600."

"Both me and the captain?

"Yessir. Captain Peters has already been notified."

"Okay, thanks."

He was pleased to hear about the meeting, despite his general distaste for officers' meetings. If Colonel Lackey wanted the Captains and the Execs, maybe this could get interesting.

2

As GREEN CAME THROUGH THE former kitchen, which now acted as their radio room, and into the living room, he made out the form of his commander, Captain John J. Peters, sitting up in the darkness. Surprisingly, he smelled fresh cigarette smoke.

"Sir, you still up? Hope you weren't waiting up for me, sir."

"Don't worry. Your little excursions are okay with me. You're late and I don't particularly care for you roaming around in the dark so close to the line, but I know there's a reason. At least someone is getting to know the area. I need to start a little roaming around as well."

"Having a smoke, huh? First one I've seen you take since we got here."

"Yes I am," the Captain frustratingly replied, lighting a match for the lantern. "Guess it's too much time with our chimney-like radioman in there."

When they first met back in Tennessee, Green had his doubts about his new Captain. Peters had been an instructor since graduating from the University of Illinois. After numerous requests for transfer, he was given command of A Battery. He was a serious-minded, go by the book sort, who contrasted sharply with the 'rules be damned', but affable Green. Just one look at the two side by side made them an odd couple. The tall, immaculately-dressed Midwesterner with never a lock of his thick, black hair out of place, and his forever disheveled executive turned out to be the perfect match, though it took time.

Once Peters took command back in Tennessee, much of the freedom of action that Green enjoyed was taken away. Green's furtive manner, although unintentional most of the time, aroused the suspicion of his CO. There was jealousy from both men. Peters envied the loyalty that the men gave his executive officer. For Green, it was everything that Peters was: the college graduate, 'A' student, and the impeccable dress, no matter what the conditions. He never seemed to get flustered. Biels, ever the wordsmith, took to calling him the 'Imperturbable Mr. Peters,' a phrase that would take on a greater meaning in the days to come.

After a few weeks of clashes, the neophyte commander realized that he needed his executive officer more than Green needed him. With no ambition to rise above first lieutenant, there was nothing to hang over Green's head; the carrot and stick approach was a dead end. By the end of that winter they came to terms with their respective roles, gradually becoming good friends and in some cases, confidants. The austere bearing notwithstanding, Peters came to understand his lieutenant better than anyone, coming to see the inner torment that no one else could, without ever mentioning it.

"I was sacked out early but then figured I write some letters to give to my sister. She and the other Red Cross girls will be in St. Vith for about a week with their clubmobile. So I can send them down to her maybe tomorrow. She's still trying to work her way up here for a visit. Been chatting with our charges?"

"Yessir."

"Anything interesting?"

"Not really. Just want to keep them busy. We're not always going to have nights like last night."

"I talked to your buddy Jim Waters yesterday. He was heading back to Bleialf to meet up with his squad. Says the patrols have been strange."

"Noises again?"

"He says they hear trains constantly. Two of his men swore they heard tanks too. And he brought back rubber hoses found along the road outside of town with Kraut markings on them."

"Hoses? They must have to siphon gas. I believe him. I don't care what Division says. Jim's a West Pointer. He knows the difference between real tanks and a recording. I was just up to see Meck, he can't see much, but he also hears the Krauts shouting a lot and trucks going back and forth."

"Monahan told me that a Kraut patrol reached Skyline Drive last night and shot at the MP outpost near the junction, then ran off into that log road the Engineers built."

"The Cutoff? The MPs that I passed on the way back were jumpy. They flagged me down with guns drawn."

"Not surprised. Nobody saw the Krauts again. Patrols were sent out and everything. Guess nobody was hurt."

Skyline Drive, as it was affectionately known, was part of a road that ran from Auw in the north to the town of Bleialf. Along the way, it joined with the Bleialf - Schonberg road. The junction was a sharp turn along a small ridge which exposed drivers to German artillery. After a while it became known as 'Purple Heart Corner.' So the engineers cut a corduroy road made of logs through the forest north of there to avoid the exposed position.

"Too close for comfort. Think you can bring this up tomorrow at the meeting?"

"That's why I wanted you to come. We've both heard the same information. You make them uneasy, so they'll listen. So get some sleep. I may head over early to speak with Captain Fonda. Where's Grey? Upstairs?"

"Not sure. I didn't see him come in."

"How's he doing?"

There was an awkward silence for a moment or two. Green's thick brow furrowed and he stood perplexed.

"Coming along. With Meck on observer duty, he will need to take on a little more responsibility."

"I'm sure you'll knock that hesitancy right out him. You seemed to do it to everybody."

Grey and Mecklenberg had rounded out Able Battery's complement of officers. They were both artillery ROTC grads; Grey was from Yale and Mecklenberg, the more eager of the two, from Alabama Technical College. Green brought the intellectual Grey along slowly, trying to build up his confidence, attaching him to the gun line one day and the motor park the next. The officers in the battery become invisible, as Green often reminded his C.O. It was the section sergeants and gunner corporals who ran the show. Officially, Grey was listed as the firing officer. And he was quite proficient at aligning the guns with the aiming circle, among other duties. Being a former two-sport athlete at college, Mecklenberg's confidence was boundless. Green's only worry about him was a lack of discretion that might get him in trouble when the shooting started.

"How was Meck?"

"He says hello. The OP set up was not bad. Some Kraut bunker. There was a squad of dogfaces sharing the place. Cozy might be too strong a word. With this constant fog and clouds, targets are few and far between. Kingery and Underwood were still with him too. I drove Donatelli up there to replace Kingery, who went on sick call this morning. Russ Gunvalson is up there also. I need to rotate him out for a couple of days, but he refused to come back until the morning."

"That's a good group. Meck is gung ho, let's face it. Grey will have to get up there eventually."

"Alright Captain. Well, I'm going to have one more smoke before I sack out. Maybe take another walk through."

"Who's spelling Monahan on the radio tonight?"

"I have Bugner coming over. He's had some training. It should be quiet tonight."

"He could use the rest. Looks like Monahan's gonna fall off the chair in a minute."

Both could see their diligent communications man lying with his head leaning against the wall, still upright in a chair; a smoldering cigarette dangled from his mouth and the headphones were slung around his neck.

"And he's gonna burn us all down. Hold on, sir."

Green proceeded to carefully pull the cigarette out of Monahan's mouth, throw it on the floor and step on it. He never woke up.

"Well, sir, I'll see ya in the morning."

"Good night."

No matter how tired, the solitude that always came with sleep was a problem for him. It was almost torture to go to bed growing up and now it was now even worse in the Army. He let Peters take the only good bed and he decided to stick with an Army issue cot. Every night, a million thoughts ran through his head. He remembered that he forgot to talk to Peters about this or that gun crew. There were always reports to do. And what about writing home? When was the last time he wrote his folks? And how was his brother over in the Pacific?

It seemed he replayed every conversation he had over and over. Self-analysis had become his bane, especially since being lauded as the Division's 'hero.' Talking with his men did not help. He hated the personal questions, particularly when prodded for information on his previous service. But he was the veteran, the one they were counting on to get them through the war. Physically, he could not escape it. The long facial scar made his past visible to all. Retelling the harrowing escape he and his forward observation team made from Kasserine Pass is not something he ever wanted to do. Still, his men wanted to hear from the man himself how he destroyed a Kraut machine gun nest with a Thompson taken from a dead GI, saving everyone. Not all could be saved; his sergeant lay dying in the wadi as he stood on the hill waving his Thompson in triumph. Thanks to his lieutenant, a legend was born and it was off to officer candidate school. After that, he learned never make decisions from a hospital bed.

Being the only one in his OCS cadre without a college degree, left the former enlisted man with a fairly large chip on his shoulder. None of them could see the doubts that came to mind during the rare quiet moments, nor the self-hate that would inexplicably rise within him for no reason. He covered it all up in bravado, taking on the mantle of rebel within the unit.

What should have been the most rewarding day of his Army life was the most embarrassing. The sun was beating down on him during that sweltering afternoon at Atterbury, when he was ordered to Battalion headquarters by the Battalion S-1.

'Get over here on the double, Lieutenant," was the order.

"But sir, I…"

"I don't give a Goddamn about how busy you are, move it!"

What the hell did I do? Have I been too pushy with the brass? The old man is calling me on the carpet.

Green, in his drenched and dirty overalls, was even more confused when he drove up to see everyone in the office was dressed for a parade.

The devilish smiles on the faces of Peters and this other officer he could not recognize, just led to more nervousness. Their Battalion Commander, the stout Lieutenant Colonel Vaden Lackey, wearing his crisp khakis and shiny, silver oak leaves on each collar, came out of the office to greet him. Then Darino and Davis snuck out from behind one of the trucks. Nearing the office, he suddenly realized he knew the other officer as his former commander in Africa.

"Lieutenant Gustafson? Is that you?"

"Yes it is, Brendan. How the hell are ya?"

He rushed over and grabbed Green's hand, shaking it like a man back from the dead.

"Oh, sorry, it's now Captain. What are you doing here?"

"Came up from Fort Sill to see how you were 'doin, so the speak. I'm an instructor now. They sort of invited me up for this little get together."

"For what?"

Peters interrupted, clearing his throat.

"Green, the Colonel would like a word."

"Sir?"

His clerk handed him an official-looking letter.

"Lieutenant, I want to read the following:

Citation:
The President of the United States takes pleasure in presenting the Silver Star Medal to Brendan F. Green (39736112), Lieutenant, U.S. Army, for gallantry in action while serving with the 33rd Field Artillery Battalion, 1st Infantry Division, in action against the enemy in the vicinity of Kasserine, Tunisia, on 20 February, 1943. During a bitter engagement with the enemy, then Technician Fifth Grade Green boldly proceeded to an exposed position and destroyed an enemy machine gun team, which was directing harassing fire on his observation team who were attempting to extract themselves from enemy encirclement, saving the lives of many men. His dauntless courage and aggressive spirit, despite intense mortar and small-arms activity, were instrumental in saving many lives and helped lead them to safety. Headquarters, 106th Infantry Division, General Orders Number 19 (July 31, 1944) Home of Record: Yonkers, NY

Lackey then reached over and pinned the medal on his left breast. A mortified Green just stared straight ahead, never looking down at his medal, nor at any of the assembled group.

"Congratulations, Lieutenant," Colonel Lackey spoke with a smile, giving him a hearty handshake. "I'm very honored to have you in my battalion. Sorry this took so long to get done."

He was speechless for what seemed forever, holding the vacant stare far longer than he should have. The whole terrifying event which had lead to this ceremony flashed through his mind in just seconds. Peters saw Green's troubled expression and realizing his growing unease, spoke up.

"Well, Green, what do you have to say for yourself?"

Sweat stung his eyes as he finally peered down at the medal pinned to his left breast. All he could think about was how bad he must smell.

"I need a change of clothes," he responded, which broke all assembled into laughter.

In the proceeding days, guilt overtook him. His fellow officers held a party for him, but it did nothing to curb his unease. Against orders, the medal was sent home to his parents just before the Division went overseas. They could be the proud ones.

All he could remember of Kasserine was the desire to claw his way into the rock-strewn earth as shell after shell burst around him. If it had not been for his sergeant and Gustafson leading him out, he would have just been captured or killed like the others. His feeling of gratitude toward the lieutenant was the only reason he could think of as to why he had accepted the offer of officer candidate school. That and the chance to visit home, not that it helped any. His parents knew something had changed in him. Awkward moments of quiet pervaded their dinners together. All his mother could do was constantly touch his scar and try to figure out what was wrong. She kept murmuring in her thick Irish brogue, *'My boy, my boy.'*

Now he was responsible for almost a hundred men. He even felt responsible for Peters, but could never figure out why. Maybe there were other reasons he did not want to think about, reasons that now put him face to face with the Germans again.

Even in the midst of all his denials, a part of him wanted to be where he was. An obsession was raging inside of him. For the time being though, his rage would have to remain in repose.

As he began his slow walk around the perimeter of the CP ruminating about the battery's preparations, something rare caught his eye, thin strands of moonlight peeking through the dark clouds. The woods to his left were now bathed in a soft glow as its light burst through the storm clouds. He could see the gun barrels shine one after the other as they got caught in the glow. Hopefully it was a good omen for the coming days. As the light faded far too quickly, he reluctantly finished his cigarette, heading upstairs for another restless night.

3

Saturday, December 16, 1944, 0525 Hours, Forward Observation outpost for the 333rd Field Artillery Battalion

ON A DILAPIDATED FARM, JUST outside of Bleialf, Germany, it turned out to be another dark, cold morning at the tip of the American line. Sergeant Emmett T. Jackson, who had been on edge the past few days because of all the rumblings on the German side of the line, was setting up his transit and BC Scope early, despite the darkness. He was doing his buddy Due a favor. Due was late sleeper. If Battalion HQ called and they were not ready to go at the appointed hour, they would catch hell. So Jackson put on his boots, lifting his tall, lanky body out from under his blanket and Army issue wool overcoat, which he used as a second blanket. Stiff from the cold, he quietly got to his feet and headed to the small hayloft door, which was now used as a window from which the Germans could be watched . Its large opening faced east, a perfect spot for their tasks.

The transit held his BC Scope, which allowed the team to pinpoint fire on the enemy. The 'BC' stood for Battery Commander's and the scope contained a graduated reticule in its focal plane, similar to a crosshair, which helped them measure horizontal and vertical angles, making adjustments that much easier. Although it involved complicated calculations, adjustments and registering fire from the batteries, the crux of their job was finding the enemy anyway they could. Sometimes that meant just looking for a flash of enemy artillery or pinpointing a sound. The pointlessness of their task had been bothering them the past few days. Fog and heavy mist had shrouded all enemy movement. Their required message log that recorded every contact with the fire direction center was redundant and barely filled the last few days. *'No missions'* had been written in many times.

As forward observers, being in stationary position for a while, with a roof over their head, was the height of luxury. When traveling with the infantry, it was a very dangerous job. They lived in a foxhole waiting for the moment to come when someone screamed that they needed artillery support. Then, under pressure from enemy fire, the observer peered through his field glasses, called for one shot, adjusted and hope the next ones hit the mark. Other times they were running telephone wire across an open field back to battalion headquarters as bullets sniped at their heels.

Being black, they didn't mix with the white infantry units like other observers. Things did integrate a little out in the field, but never to the point of being comfortable. The men would line up for hot chow at a kitchen truck together occasionally, and then go back to their appointed groups. Small groups of white infantry, squads from the 106th Infantry division, had been occupying the lower half of the barn for the past week. One of their lieutenants had become friendly with Jackson and both welcomed the conversation. Shared discomfort brought men closer together and ever the optimist, Jackson hoped this was sign of change.

The battalion had landed in France in June and followed the Allied forces as they swept across France and into Belgium right up to the German border. They had been in the Ardennes region since October, initially supporting the 2nd Division. Its main weapon of the Battalion was the 155mm Howitzer. Like many black units, the 333rd was not assigned to any particular division, but was assigned to a particular Army corps, which doled out its assignments. In this case, it was VIII Corps.

Jackson was uneasy for the past few days. After several radio calls to his headquarters near Schonberg went unheeded, he figured it might just be his imagination. Trucks, tanks, and low-flying airplanes had all been heard with increasing frequency since last weekend. Trains rumbled by every night for the past week, with their steam engine hisses echoing in the valley. But this morning, his nervousness was more pronounced with a pounding in his chest and a constant tapping of his pencil against the scope. And now as he checked his watch, 0525 hours, the sounds of German activity were increasing dramatically. Multiple truck tailgates were heard slamming down and then the sounds of boots scampering over gravel. Still, he could see nothing in the blackness of the field that lay below. It was over two hours till first light, not that it would help. Finally, he could take it no longer and had to share his unease. He decided to take action, first trying to wake the slumbering Turner, who just grumbled; then he looked downstairs to stir up his fellow GIs.

He saw Lieutenant Waters in the corner of the barn trying to heat up coffee with ration tablets.

"Lieutenant! I hear the Krauts right outside. They sound awful close. Heard more tailgates, sir.

"Shit, I thought I was hearing things. At least I'm not crazy. Did you call your HQ?"

"Last night, sir. What do you think they told me?"

"I know. They think we're nuts. Okay, stay up there for a little bit and let me know if you can see anything in this pea soup. Keep your ears open. They could easily jump us in this barn. It won't be light for a while. Check your weapons."

The lieutenant was right. They might have only seconds to decide what was happening. Jackson looked around for his carbine, checked the clips and put it next to the scope.

"Alright fellas, get up!" Waters began shouting as he went around tapping everyone's legs, waking most of the up from their slumber.

Two men were found lighting up in the back of the building. After one last drag, they immediately grabbed their Garands and formed up near the door. The sleepy men moaned and complained until they realized it was the Lieutenant who awakened them and the adrenaline of fear made them jump. An early morning patrol was as bad as going out late at night. Suddenly there was the sound of the men popping their 8-shot clips into the M-1 Garands in unison.

"Coleman, get on the radio. Who's got the watch?"

"Think it's Fullmer and Dansereau, sir. Not sure."

As Coleman answered, Waters was barely listening as he surveyed his squad.

"Healy, look at you. You're lying over there and your BAR is twenty feet away. Get with it. Grab all your bandoleers. Get yer ass in gear!"

The men, a squad of the 423rd Infantry Regiment of the 106th, were still adjusting to life on the line; it took much longer than a week. They were due to be relieved later in the morning. In and around the town, was a mixed bag of forces, which included men from the anti-tank platoons and the 423rd cannon company as well.

As Waters began to speak, one of his men who had been on watch came running down the dirt lane leading to the house, his Garand waving in the air. The lane was now mostly puddles of melted snow. It led right out into a wooded path that took one deep into the woods. He was heard long before he could be seen, making Waters zero his weapon into the blackness. Jackson heard the shouting too and strained to listen from above. The panicked soldier's splashes and mud-sucking steps made everyone jump.

"Lieutenant!" he shouted.

Waters, who had been stressing the need for stealth while on the line, was annoyed.

Jesus, this guy needs to learn to be quiet.

Waters let out a deep breath and lowered his rifle.

"Hold on Fullmer," he ordered after grabbing the man. "What's the problem?"

The young soldier was soaking wet from head to toe.

"I hear Krauts everywhere. They're shoutin' at me and everything. They seem to know where I am, but I can't see 'em. All over the woods, sir. I heard this funny sounding machine gun they have. Didn't hear nuttin' like that in training."

"Where's Dansereau?"

"Oh shit. He said he was right behind me, sir."

The fear on Fullmer's face was clear even in the bad light of the farmhouse, his huge, unblinking eyes casting an empty stare. Two shots suddenly rang out from an M-1 Garand, followed by a quick burst of that strange gun Fullmer had mentioned. Waters tried to scan the tree line in front of them looking for a flash, to no avail.

"Hear that, sir? That's it."

"Stay here with us. Form up with Private Bicknicki over there."

Waters pointed to a small group of men now nervously checking their weapons and Healy finally putting a fresh twenty-round clip in his BAR.

"Leavitt! Set up your gun facing down the lane. Listen for Dansereau. He's out there somewhere. Probably lost. But if you see Germans, don't hesitate."

"On it, sir."

"Taylor!"

"Yessir!"

"Use my jeep and get over to that girls' school they're using as a CP in town. You know where it is, right?"

Taylor, wide-eyed and eager, shook his head affirmatively. "Yessir."

"Okay. Stop there and see Captain Manning of Cannon Company. Let 'em know what's going on down here. Tell him Lieutenant Waters is attempting to set up a line of defense against what we think might be a raid or reconnaissance in force. He knows where we are, so he'll know what to do. Got it?"

"Yes…sir."

"Then head to 590th HQ. On the way back stop at A Battery too, if you can find it. See Lieutenant Green or Captain Peters. Do you remember where they are?"

"We went through there the other day, so yeah. The HQ is in Radscheid and A Battery is just down the road from there."

"Good. Hightail it to Regiment after that and get in touch with the wire section. If anyone asks what's going on, tell them that the Krauts are making a raid on the town. Maybe that will shake everybody up. Got it?"

"Yessir."

"Okay, get going. Be careful on the way back. I don't know where we'll be…"

"I got it, sir."

With that the young private, rifle in hand, ran to the jeep, spun the tires a little, and took off down the dirt path leading to the village. The last part about a raid seemed presumptuous, maybe even dramatic, to Waters, but something was imminent. Tired of the constant snickering from Division intelligence, he was desperate to have someone believe him. And it would be a good excuse to get the phones fixed a little faster anyway.

Jackson listened from the window as the young lieutenant calmly positioned his men, setting up a machine gun just off the lane and having two men set up their mortars behind the barn. If tanks roll up on us, he thought, we're still goners.

He liked what he heard from Waters. Unlike many of the white soldiers he had encountered since joining up in '42, most of the latest group of fresh divisions and individual replacements did not make the kind of ugly comments at them that so many had in the States. There had not been many stares either. In fact, the men had almost been friendly, asking a lot about their experiences of the past five months, and showing them respect. They did not have to ask for respect anymore, they had earned it. There was always a wall between them, albeit unspoken. The wall had ramparts as big as any ancient castle.

In the United States Army, skin color was a fixed fortification. Jackson knew that for most of these guys, it was the first time these new men had been under the same roof as black folks. He felt that the last week or so, he and his group had been accepted as part of the landscape, which is about all a black man could wish for in the Army. Even a soldier from Georgia had offered him some hot chocolate made from those bitter D ration bars He prayed they would have at least a few more days to actually get to know some of these men.

As Jackson strained to listen for anything, he checked his watch, 0531 hours. Suddenly, there were several flashes from far off in the distance. Flares then lit up the sky with their pop and sizzle crackling just above them. Then came their ominous hissing. Red, white and yellows tore up the darkness, bathing the landscape an eerie hue as they filtered down. Spotlights then appeared, bouncing off the clouds, creating an artificial dawn. Small artillery booms echoed in the distance with their distinctive *crump,crump*. There was nothing too close. He peered through his scope to spot the artillery flashes. The spotlights and flares against the gray mist created a kaleidoscope effect before his eyes. It was useless. Quick flashes of machine gun fire lit up the forest. Then German shouts of 'Heil Hitler' and the faint staccato of the German burp guns.

"Due, you up yet? It's morning, man. Get up! "

"Yeah I am. Nother mo'nin wit you. I takin' mah time. What the hell was that?" the radio operator growled as he heard the whoosh of a shell fly over. "What all the yellin' 'bout?"

"Get your gear and load your rifle. We got trouble. I think we're gonna have to move out to a better spot. Get on the phone or the radio before you pack it up. Try the FDC or HQ. Hell, try both. Try and get a hold of Lieutenant King. Gibson is probably still at HQ."

Sergeant Turner was not the kind of man who took kindly to orders from people he thought were barely his equal.

Bossy motherfucker.

"You got any mo' orders fo' me, *Staff Sergeant*?"

"Look, just do it. Those damn Krauts are everywhere."

"*Yez Suh*!" Turner mockingly saluted. "It's like Camp Claiborne all over again. Goddamn sonovabitch."

There was more bad feeling behind the joking than even Jackson wanted to think about. Due was older and light-skinned, his prematurely salt and pepper hair as well as his slight paunch gave him a distinguished air. At a height of only 5'5, he contrasted sharply with the tall, lanky and very dark-skinned Jackson, whose urbane manner put off many of the men in the Battalion. Turner had lived almost his entire life in rural Georgia and the lines on his face showed it. Jackson understood his bitterness and in the first few months that they were together had let the 'Uncle Tom' comments slide. Eventually, Turner grew to respect the younger Jackson and kept his taunts strictly to 'college boy.'

Instructors marveled at Due's innate ability to take care of the radios back in the states. How did a negro sharecropper from the South know anything? Technical abilities were not supposed to be the purview of the Negro. Nobody told Turner that, although he felt the burden of the doubters much more acutely than Jackson or the other men. Young Due had fixed everything on the farm growing up, even for the white land owner. When one of the white farmers discarded a tractor that he regarded as a total loss, Mr. Turner brought it home as a project for him and his son. The shock of their landlord seeing that tractor moving would always be a source of pride for Due. But the embarrassed farmer's shock turned to anger as he charged them with stealing the tractor. Due and his family fled the county, never to return.

Despite his groggy state, Turner reached for the canvas pouch that held the black EE8 field phone, wound it up and listened for a connection.

He first tried to call his Battalion CP in Schonberg. Nothing. He did not even get shocked from the winding of the telephone. Then he grabbed the radio and in a very deliberate manner, trying to suppress his rural Georgian tongue, began calling his fire direction center just north of Schonberg.

"Castle Red, this is Castle Charlie 1. Castle Red, this is Castle Charlie 1. Can you read over?"

After three times, there was still nothing but static and a low hum.

Then he tried the other Observation post with Lieutenant King and his team, located on the other side of town. All he could get was sharp whistling and some static. Everything was out.

"Damn diaphragm prob'ly frozen stiff. I thought I had kept it warm enough."

"Alright, enough of that," Jackson quickly replied. "Let's get the hell outta here."

Machine gun rounds were now piercing the sides of the barn. Then a mortar round fell short, hot metal shards showering the building.

Jackson took apart his transit, carefully laying his scope down. A stunned and shivering Turner jumped to his feet, laced up his boots and threw on his overcoat. He took a peek out the window and then checked his watch.

"Emmett man, what the hell time is it anyway? All that light frum flares?"

"I have no idea. Just move it, man."

"Jackson! Get your buddy and get the hell out of there!"

It was Waters yelling up a last warning.

"Lieutenant, what is going on?"

"Germans, everywhere. Coming across that field. It's like Goddamn Fourth of July out here with all the light. Too late to try and get fire on them. Set up outside of town and call in a strike or something. Radio any artillery guys you can find, tell 'em to lay everything they got on our map coordinates.

"Way ahead of you, sir."

"Can you use your radio?"

"Not yet. We'll try when we get out of town, sir."

"I'll try and get a runner over to your other OP. Think the Germans are now in between your guys and us. Good luck!"

Jackson took a last look at the window and finally was able to make out the forms of Germans making their way over the rolling hills and glimpsed them from small openings in the foggy mist. Some were just ominous, dark figures silhouetted against the eerily lit horizon. They were walking rather slowly for an attack, almost nonchalantly.

There was only one rickety ladder to climb down from the loft. So they threw their gear as gently as they could to the floor below, although Jackson lowered the BC Scope to Due once he got down. He slid down the ladder like it was a pole. Small arms fire was ricocheting around inside of the barn.

Swarms of Germans began hitting Bleialf from three sides. Flares were still going up and actually made many of the Germans easy targets. The inky blackness had been torn open like a curtain, revealing onrushing Germans dressed in dark, green camouflage, while others wore white snowsuits. But the size and suddenness of the attack kept the men back on their heels. The flashes from their multitude of different weapons burst everywhere. Some fired at whatever shadow or flash they saw. The Americans posted up the road began firing wildly but that was quickly drowned out by the German fire.

Another GI came running from the opposite side of the path yelling that the Germans were coming right through the rail tunnel and were already in town. The heavy patch of woods that ran astride the farmhouse concealed the tunnel and most of the tracks. A scout car from the 18th Cavalry unit was heard opening up with its 37mm gun mounted on top from somewhere north of town.

All kinds of rifle fire rang out from the center of the town, as German mobile assault guns, began rumbling over the frozen fields from all sides. The vehicles looked very similar to tanks, and spread as much fear. Shouts of *'tanks!'* rose up everywhere. A blast of its 75mm gun could be heard crashing into the trees. The GIs were firing in all directions. The Krauts began shouting at them with their own version of the rebel yell, wildly screeching as they got closer.

Jackson's hopes were raised again when he heard Garands returning fire intermittently in the woods. But then the rapid return fire of a MG42 German machine gun quickly ended that. Mortar fire became intense, showering the walls of the barn. Shouts from increasingly desperate GIs filled the air. The Germans had machine gun positions set up on a rise overlooking the village and bullets now whizzed over the heads of Waters and his men. Frightened GIs came running down the lane, past the house and heading through town. One of them was Dansereau, minus his helmet and soaking wet, too stunned to even talk. He was unable to catch his breath to explain how he had escaped from certain death. He could only mouth the word *'Krauts.'* Waters grabbed him, trying to find out what he saw. After a few mumbles, he passed out. The lieutenant grabbed his Garand and dragged him to the house, yelling for the medic.

Jackson and Turner found their three-quarter ton observation car next to the lane and threw everything they could in it. The sergeant took one last look for Waters, who was now clearly visible in the artificial dawn. He was directing a mortar crew to begin firing at the onslaught and still trying to get his young troops to settle down.

"Let's go, Due."

"Where the hell to?"

"Just outside town," Jackson frustratingly answered as he pulled out his message log. There is an abandoned house on a small rise. We can see the valley from there. Get some fire support for these guys."

"But it dark 'til round eight."

"Well, we'll try and call Battalion on the radio to find out what to do. There are Krauts everywhere and Lieutenant King and our guys are still in that town somewhere."

Jackson was indignant as he took out his log book.

"Are you writin' in the log agi'n. There ain't nuthin' t'report. How many times can ya write, *'No fire missions?'* You ridiculous sometime. Mah God. If this was a Black Man's army, you'd be a general by now fo' sure. Of all the black folk in this worl', I git you."

"Will you just drive or are we going to take a round because of your frustration with me?"

Suddenly, bullets pinged against the back of the car.

"Shit! I'm gittin'. I'm gittin! B'quiet an' lemme drive."

After spinning the wheels for a couple of seconds, they took off back towards town. It would be slow going. A crown of mud an inch thick now covered their running boards. Maneuvering through town, and up a narrow, winding road, the Church came into full view. Father Hartzel, the village Priest, could be seen standing in front of the Church's two, huge wooden doors, looking up at the sky with apprehension, mesmerized by the strange lights. Jackson waved, but Father Hartzel did not notice. Fear had taken hold of everyone.

They were cut off several times by other jeeps trying to get around town and had to stop as some of the men from the 106th were running forward to set up gun positions As they cleared the last street and made their way out of town, a couple of inches of freshly fallen snow still lay on top of the usual muddy roads. As once they had fishtailed on the cobblestone street from going too fast, they now ground to a crawl. Jackson noticed a strange sign emerging out of the morning mist and ghostly light. It had been put up by the U.S. Army, but now lay propped up against the base of a tree. It was in German.

He strained to see, leaning sideways, but couldn't understand it.

'Wir Kommen Nicht Als Sieger, Sondern Als Befreier'

Turner looked over in disgust.

"What you doin? Dammit, you still tryin' to learn whiles you in the Army, Mister Language. You think them Krauts gonna throw books at you."

"Just drive, Corporal Turner. Just drive."

Germans mortars now fell to their right; hot metal and mounds of dirt rained down on top of them. GIs waking from their slumbers were popping up trying to grab their gear. Some just stared at the sky, confusion was reigning as the artificial luminescence held them spellbound.

They followed the road out of town and ran into another observation team that had the same idea as they did. An armored car from the 18th Cavalry was making its way in the opposite direction forcing them off the road. Old attitudes were hard to die as Jackson heard one of the men holler.

"Get outta the way, Boy! There's a war on!"

"Keep going Due. We have to catch up to those white boys."

"Why? They gonna take our positions. Y'know that."

"Strength in numbers, Due. The more the merrier."

"You crazy. Can't believe you went t'Howard. Crazy college boy. They ain't gonna wanna share a house wit us. Some of deeze Crackers as bad as the ones at Camp Claiborne. Maybe all of 'em."

"Will you just drive? Or do I have to pull rank?"

"Mah car. I'll drive. Sonavobitch! Sometime Emmett, I think you worse than the white man, sometime. Livin' up there in Chicago. You think you're the Negro Al Capone or sumpin'. Maybe Gibson should give you his lootenant's bars."

Jackson just laughed that off as heard the tires spin again. The mud was beginning to swell as the once-frozen road melted from the traffic. Numerous jeeps were now coming up behind them. Some of the men in a business-like fashion and others, telling from their shouts, were on the edge of panic. The illumination of the spotlights was starting to die down, so seeing was getting more difficult in the early morning darkness. But the lingering odor of battle began hitting the senses. Clouds of smoke, reeking with cordite, penetrated the air. The firing behind them seemed to increase. Ahead of them tracers from anti-aircraft batteries could be seen firing aimlessly into the sky; its staccato thumping was a strangely comforting sound. The occasional lone shot from a carbine or Garand could be heard. What they were shooting at, nobody knew. The Germans just appeared to be everywhere.

They finally reached the house after what should have been a five minute ride took a half hour. There was a patchwork of men from different units. It was almost 0630. Many GIs were already there milling around with stunned looks on their faces. Jackson told Due to wait as he ran inside. He saw a white officer from the 590th field artillery observation team who he had befriended earlier. The man recognized him immediately and put down the receiver.

"You're Jackson, right? You're with the 333rd?"

"That's right, Lieutenant. You need some help?"

"I just tried to use the phone that they had set up here. The lines are down. Even the radios garbled. All I'm picking up is that Goddamn German music. We are going to have to get fire on that town. My team is northeast of town dug in with some infantry guys. I got here ten minutes ago. This is something big."

"I left one of your fellow lieutenants down there. He was setting up some sort of defense. And there's another 333rd OP crew inside the village.

"Yeah, we just heard them calling for fire before everything went out again. At least on my end."

"But that town might be overrun if they don't get help soon. Place is being ringed by MG 42 fire and the Krauts hit us with mortars. They're swarming the town. Somebody yelled about tanks too. I could hear 'em, but didn't see them."

"Well, it looks like they might be on their own. But I ordered these guys from the anti-tank company out here not to go anywhere until another lieutenant showed up. So far they are listening and seem pretty eager to get in the fight. Look, do me a favor. You know what you are doing with a radio, right?"

"Sure do. My buddy out there is even more of an expert. One of the best."

"Great. Get moving toward Schonberg. Aren't the rest of your guys up that way?"

"Our HQ is on the road to Andler."

"Well, get back there for your own safety but do me this favor. Can you try and find my unit? I'm actually from A Battery, 590th. At this point, any of the batteries will do. Battalion HQ is in Radscheid, but my battery is in Oberlascheid. So we're down the main road a little bit. If anyone asks, tell them that Lieutenant Mecklenberg is trying to contact them. I've tried Battalion and it's useless."

"We have a Captain Horn who's supposed to be up at your HQ, Lieutenant."

"Even better. Take this piece of paper and get it to whatever battery is ready to fire. It's got targeting information for points east of Bleialf."

"We got our maps too, sir."

"Great. We need to get a mass concentration on the road leading into the village. I'd send a runner but I'll need every man I can get at this point. Looks like I'll be fighting as infantry and I need to get back to my guys. I just came back here to try to make some calls. If you can get your radio calibrated, let me know. I might still be here. My call sign is Dogwood Able 1, okay?"

"Dogwood Able 1. Got it, sir."

"Thanks Sergeant. What is your first name?"

"Emmett."

"Okay, Emmett. Good luck. Maybe I'll see ya around."

"Stay well, sir."

"There's no chance of that."

As Jackson left the building, he felt some stares.

'Where did these Negros come from?'

Due was now standing next to the jeep having a smoke with a young white soldier who just couldn't stop shivering.

"Time to go, Due."

Turner dropped his cigarette in the snow.

"Take it easy man. What was your name?"

"Archer, Gerald J."

"Okay Gerald, it was nice talkin' t'ya. Stay warm."

"Let's go, Due."

"That might be one of the longest conversations I e'ver had wit a white boy. That po' soul is eager, but scared shitless. Y'know what? I don't blame him either. We he're almost sis months and that guy barely a week. Now he gonna fight off them Krauts. Tole me he jus graduated high school in June."

"Damn."

"He'll pass out 'fore he fire a shot. Man, it gonna be a long day."

As they drove on though, it became amazingly quiet, except for the flashes in the sky and the waning echo of small arms fire. Jackson could even hear the heavy mist hitting his jacket. The wind blew into his eyes, adding a stinging insult to an already chaotic morning. Despite the artificial light, nothing seemed to penetrate the darkness of the forest canopy, so he felt the urge to grip his carbine tighter. If someone were to pop out of the woods, it would be difficult telling friend from foe. Turner brazenly put his headlights on for protection against friendly fire. After another half-mile, some GIs waved them down from a clearing in the woods.

"What the hell is going on down there?"

"Germans hit the town. We're heading to Schonberg to try and contact some of the artillery units."

"You guys in supply or something?"

"Supply? We are artillery observers from the 333rd." Jackson replied with a smile, and pointed his thumb to the gear in the back of the truck.

A look of surprise registered on the faces of the young privates. It was a mistake that both Jackson and Turner were used to, but they ignored it. The precise technical abilities required for artillery observation teams were considered by some beyond the realm of 'Coloreds'. After some uncomfortable seconds of quiet, Jackson spoke again.

"Well, if I were you, I'd check my weapons and get ready to move out. Where's your lieutenant or sergeant for that matter?"

"The lieutenant went forward to make contact with the rest of the company and see what was going on. Our sarge is rounding up ammo. Told us to leave our guns where they were for now. We're not sure what to do."

"Same as everybody. You guys an anti-tank unit or something?"

"Yeah. 2nd anti-tank."

"Alright, I have to go and try to get you guys artillery fire. Those fellas need a hand down there. I'd get your guns, wherever you're hiding them, and set them up along here somewhere. Get your trucks and jeeps warmed up. Lots of Krauts may be coming this way. Good luck. Stay alert."

A collective hard swallow could almost be heard from the five privates who stood by the side of the road after that comment. Then the observation car bucked, and lurched forward, until finally catching a piece of the road, sending them on their way.

4

Dec 16,1944, 0530 Hours, A Battery Command Post, 590th FAB

As HE HAD ASKED, THE sentry came and woke Green at his usual time. Any formal officers meeting usually required a shave. It was his one concession to Peters, no stubble. As he filled his water bowl, a brightness seemed to be emanating from behind the black curtain on the window. Rays of light were now coming from underneath the back door. He could hear some of the men starting to stir. Then the ominous *crump, crump* of artillery falling somewhere. As he stepped out of the house, water dripping from his face and still shivering, with the pop and sizzle of flares transfixing him, the sentries came running to ask what was happening.

"Sir, are we attacking someplace?"

"No, I think we might be the ones being hit. Get back to your …"

As they spoke, they were interrupted by the *whoosh* of shells headed for their target. It was as though they were skimming the trees. Green ducked and the sentries dove into a slit trench nearby.

They were followed by two concussive booms as they impacted, thankfully not too close, but the sounds of tree limbs shattering and the mounds of earth being tossed up was nerve wracking enough.

The *88s* could be 'calling cards', rounds the Germans just shot off to remind the new arrivals of the 106th that this is the front. But those searchlights were something else and this firing was coordinated. Try as he might to convince himself otherwise, he knew better. Green put down his razor and picked up the field phone. He tried to call Battalion, nothing. Then Division, nothing. The phone was dead.

"Corporal, wake up." Green hollered as he shook Monahan, the battery's indefatigable communications man. Despite having someone for relief, he slept in the communications room anyway. He really was a technician grade five, the equivalent of a corporal. So Green, like everyone else in the Army, thinking 'technician' sounded a little haughty, just called him corporal. Monahan didn't care what you called him, as long as it was not lazy.

"Have any outfits up front tried to call during the night? What about Battalion?"

"We haven't heard a thing, sir," replied the groggy Monahan, who although it never appeared like he slept, had been sleeping like a baby before coming back on duty.

"Try to get in touch with the other batteries and central switching in Schonberg. The phones are dead. Keep working on it. But in the mean time, use the radios and call one of the units up front to find out what's happening," Green barked as he grabbed his gloves and Thompson submachine gun.

"Yes, sir, Lieutenant," the corporal dutifully, now back to his fully awake.

"Hey, where's the Captain?"

"He rose early, sir. Gonna have chow with Captain Fonda. Said he would see you at the Battalion meeting."

"Think I'm going to skip that meeting. I'll bring ya some coffee. Keep at it."

Again, the sounds were getting closer and then shells began whistling overhead. Distant explosions echoed off the hills with an eerie frequency, their flashes adding to the artificial illumination.

Private Krause came splashing up the road, completely illuminated by the artificial lights.

"Sir!"

"What the hell is going on down there, Krause? Couldn't you call?"

"No, sir. Every…Everything is out."

"Any signs of Krauts out there?"

"That's why I'm here sir. A dud…," the young private was now bent over from the hard run, holding his stomach.

"Okay, catch your breath. What happen?"

"A dud… looks like a 155mm, hit in front of the bunker sir. Thought we were goners."

"Any more rounds hit near you? I didn't see any flashes out that way."

"No, sir. But House and Campagna are back there. Should we pull back to the Kraut farmhouse, sir?"

"No. Stay in your position. Listen. Go back and prepare for an attack. I'll send down another MG crew and send breakfast down too. Okay?"

"Thank you, sir."

Now, the rest of the battery was stirring and peering up at the sky. The conversation with Krause had reminded him that there were civilians among them, German locals. Peering around the cluster of houses, he spotted the man he needed.

"Biels!"

"Yessir!"

"Go over to the Kraut family and find out what they know. If anything. We may have to move them on our own."

"On the way, sir."

He sprinted across the sloppy road and down towards the house. The upstairs was taken by the communications section, what was left of them, but the rest of the place belonged to the Klaus family.

The door was ajar, and pitch black inside. The smell of cigarette smoke lingered even after all the GIs had run out. Biels rummaged through the house first and found nothing. With the electricity out, all he could was open up the blackout drapes. The German spotlights provided enough illumination to see the main rooms clearly. Pots and pans were gone. No smell of food. All coats and shoes were cleared out. So he ran outside to the cellar door after he was unable to find an entrance inside. The tiny cellar would be the most logical place for the family.

"Herr Klaus? Sind Sie dort?"

The sinking feeling in the pit of Biels' stomach told him all he needed to know. They were gone, and knew about this ahead of time.

Sprinting back to the CP through the now frenzied activity of the gun crews and drivers, he bumped into those transfixed by the lights. He finally spotted his lieutenant as he implored Monahan to get a line before he headed towards the guns.

"Sir?"
"What's up, Biels?"
"They're gone, sir."

"Who?"

"The family."

"The Krauts are gone?"

"Yessir."

"Shit."

Both men knew what that meant. If the Krauts were getting word to the locals, they were in big trouble.

"How did we not see them leave? Goddamn it. Alright, thanks and get back to your crew. Keep your ears open, I may need a runner."

As he turned to go inside, a jeep came bouncing down the road from the direction of Radscheid. Headlights were blazing. It was carrying a lone GI and Green waved him down.

"What is going on down there?"

The excited soldier was only too eager to share his experiences.

"Lieutenant, there's searchlights everywhere. Flares and everything! Been flashing in the sky since around 0530, sir. Then shells started going over our heads. And some of the men thought they saw some Krauts charging up the roads on our flanks and coming out of the woods. Some of the Krauts were even yelling something. They heard tanks too, but no confirmation sir. Mortar rounds landed just short of our line."

"Where you headed?"

"Back down to Buchet. Regimental, sir. But my lieutenant couldn't contact HQ or anyone else."

"Who's your lieutenant?"

"Lieutenant Waters, sir. Are you Lieutenant Green? Is this A Battery? Think I drove right passed Radscheid by accident. He wanted me to stop at your outfit and let you guys know what's happening."

"You're in the right place. You came from Bleialf?"

"Yessir."

"I'll keep trying to make contact with Lieutenant Waters. Get going but switch over to your blackout lights."

As the excited soldier drove off, Green could only hope that the commotion was not having the same effect on all the men.

"Monahan! What's up on the radio?"

"Nobody responding on the radio sir. Don't know why. It's all garbled."

"Keep at it. See if you can call Lieutenant Mecklenberg or one of the other observation teams, get them to lay some wire fast. Try Bleialf too. I heard they're going to need fire ASAP. Sergeant Pryne!"

"Here Lieutenant!" the husky Prynne shouted as he bounded towards the CP.

"Make sure everyone else is up, including your fellow section chiefs. Ready your guns. We could be moving out too. I'm waiting on Captain Peters. I do not have targeting yet."

"Yes sir," the quiet but very efficient veteran answered. Prynne began barking orders as soon as he turned around and men started scurrying.

The prematurely gray Prynne was a hulk of a man, leftover from the pre-war Army. He was old by the Army standards of 1944, having just turned thirty. As senior section chief, the other sergeants looked to him more than the officers for direction. His height, well over six feet, and broad shoulders, gave him instant respect. The salt and pepper of his once dark hair occasionally got him called 'the ol' man.' But never to his face. There was never a lot of bombast from him, but the few words he did speak could be caustic. A raised eyebrow, flared nostril or sometimes just a stare from those cold, dark eyes was usually enough to make a man move just that much faster.

After the crews prepared the guns, the most urgent need was the motor park. The narrow roads of the Ardennes were not made for the heavy traffic of a modern army; although the Germans seemed to think so and had been successful at it in the past. On roads and fields that were heavily traveled, mud was a problem, even with all the frost. Heavy travel melted the snow but just created a sloppy mess. After a couple of hours of no traffic, they would freeze again. Vehicles either slide off the road or just get stuck in it. It was vital to get the trucks warmed up, but the drivers had to be careful not to allow them to sink into the sticky mud that would form around them. Hooking up the guns made matters worse of course. Attaching an almost 5,000 pound howitzer to its tail did not lend itself to quick maneuvers. While driving them, if the prime movers turned one way, sometimes the guns went another, that's if they turned at all.

Darino and Davis were often sent over to help the motor sergeant coordinate the movement of the trucks, and make sure the drivers were ready to go. If there were any mechanical problems, or vehicles stuck in the mud, they would solve it the way Green wanted it done. Movement of the two and a half ton trucks, the ammunition carriers and jeeps all had to be choreographed. When the men in that area saw Darino and Davis, they started moving faster. Vernon Mixon, the motor sergeant, and expert mechanic himself, was not exactly thrilled, but he learned that they spoke for the boss.

With no exact firing orders as of yet, all the men could do is prepare the guns for firing by making sure everything was in decent working order, move the shells closer to the crews and make sure everyone was at their position. This was all while trying to ignore the ominous sounds of thunder and confusing lights flashing across the sky. There was no panic, just a nervous excitement. Green wondered what was going through their minds. The GIs kept anxiously pushing down their helmets, checking their boot laces, buttoning their overcoats or zipping up their jackets. Gloves were pulled even tighter on the hands. Men rubbed the weariness from their eyes and jumped around to stay warm. Many lit their first cigarette of the day while others ran to the latrine. There was a sea of olive drab beginning to form atop the patchwork of earth and snow.

Grey was finally awakened by all the excitement and came running out of the house still buttoning his pants. Green then had an inspiration. He waved the young lieutenant over.

"You alright, Dick?"

Green was worried about his confused look.

"Ah, yes. I'm good…Lieutenant."

"Look, Dick, I want you to get a driver and head into Schonberg. Tell them who you're with and find out what is going on. Something big is happening and we're going to need more eyes out there. Stop at the switching station to confirm our lack of communication once you get in town. Then on the way back run over to the 589th HQ after first light. At HQ, try talk to Lieutenant Clausen, the Survey officer. Lieutenant Wood at A Battery will also give you the straight poop. Use some of the firebreaks to cut through the woods. This fake light should help guide the way. Talk to anyone you can. I want to get a clear picture of what the hell the Krauts are doing. Questions?"

"No problem, sir. I'll take one of the new guys?"

"Take Mullins. I don't really have a job for him yet. He's new, but a good driver. I took him with me a couple of times. Keep your weapons ready. Get yourself a sidearm as well. Map, compass, and whatever else you think you might need, like a radio. Be prepared to be gone for a while. We may displace while you're out. Be alert. It might be dangerous out there."

Grey's jittery exterior had changed to a look of determination; it was an encouraging sign to Green. Probably just adrenaline, but he'd take it at this point.

5

As THE MEN READIED THEIR guns for firing, Captain Peters arrived back at the CP ready to go.

"Brendan, what's up so far?"

"Couple of wayward shells,

0.. sir. And one dud hit our machine gun post. Still awaiting firing orders."

"I hear communications are down, regiment or battalion will have to relay by radio or runner. None of the F.O. teams came by?"

"No, sir."

"Have any of the observers been heard from? Meck or anybody?"

"None that I know of, sir. Also Captain, the Kraut family took a runout powder. Left with everything."

"They're gone. All of them?"

"Yessir. Biels checked the entire house and cellar. None of our guys even heard them leave. Must have been packing up and moving stuff out for a while.

"Sonuvabitch. First the German army, and now the locals helping them out. It's gonna be a goddamn interesting day."

Not prone to swearing, Peters surprised his executive and anyone else within earshot with his less than gentlemanly phrase.

"Yessir, it is. Did you see or hear anything on the way back, Captain?"

"Nobody knew anything. I was at the Battalion mess with Captain Fonda when the shelling started. C Battery got hit. Two cooks wounded. We ran to the CP and apparently some observers from the 333rd were trying to radio in a mission. The reception was bad, kept getting garbled. But I didn't stay long enough to find out the details. After hearing the artillery, I left to get back here. Apparently, all the wire crews are being sent out as soon as possible."

Peters decided to take a run through the battery. This was going to be his big moment. Sustained counter-battery fire under adverse conditions was a big test. For the first time, his actions might have a direct effect on a battle. The months of being an instructor would now pay dividends, he hoped.

The feverishly working Monahan, cigarette dangling with an old ration can full of butts next to him, struggled with the telephones and SCR-610 radio for over an hour until finally getting some good news. He joyously interrupted his officers and began shouting from the doorway. They arrived back simultaneously.

"Sirs! I think I heard someone on the other end of the telephone. I will confirm."

A battalion runner finally arrived by jeep .

"Captain Peters?"

"Yes?"

"The orders are to stand-by, phone lines should be up soon. If firing is needed, we will use the radios."

"Is regiment in touch with Battalion?"

"Yes, sir, by radio only right now. The Krauts are hitting their flanks. Targeting is imminent."

"Thanks, corporal. Where you are headed?"

"Back up to Battalion, sir, you were the last battery to contact. No offense, sir."

"I understand. Please tell them that A battery is standing by."

"Yes, sir," the corporal replied with a salute and left.

"Green, go..."

"Sir, I'll run by every section and let them know to stand-by."

Peters nodded, having gotten very used to Green's interrupting mid-sentence and anticipating his every move. So he turned to the other men at the CP.

"Pritchard."

"Yes,sir," the lanky fire direction technician answered smartly.

"Do you have the targeting information from the other day?"

"Yessir."

"Read them off," he ordered while grabbing the overlays.

"Concentrations 329 through 335."

"Alright. Confirm and standby. I'm not sure if that's where we're firing, but you never know. I think we should cover all the approaches."

Pritchard's job was enormous. Very few guys neither could, nor wanted to, handle his position. They called him 'Abe' because his long, dour face resembled the President's. But they respected him as much as anybody in the battery. Every detail of the fire missions had to be logged: deflection, elevation, type of shells, type of fuse, and number of powder bags used. He was the accountant of the battery. Now in the frenzy of battle, it was going to be even tougher.

As the section chiefs received the latest news from Green, the shells were loaded, angles of fire adjusted and the number one cannoneers anxiously stood to the right of the breech blocks, ready to give the lanyards a strong pull. The sections' gunner corporals, on the left side of the breech behind the steel safety plate, would constantly peer through their quadrants, ready to make any adjustments. The cold metal of the guns could be felt despite their wool gloves and sweaty palms; the gunners gripped the traverse and elevating wheels so tight, their hands ached. The 105mm could be moved sideways using the traverse wheel, which lay directly below the quadrant. They knew that the proper direction had been reached when the hairline in the scope covered the aiming stakes, located ten yards in front of the guns. Once the elevation number was received and set, the gunners would spin the elevation handle until the water bubble in the telescopic sight became level. This ensured the exact trajectory to the target.

As Green arrived back to the CP, to his surprise he found the Captain just hanging up the phone.

"Phones are back?"

Peters, facing the wall maps, gave an affirmative nod.

"Brendan, looks like Regiment is sending down another anti-tank company and other service units to back up the guys at Blelaif. They have two companies headed there already, but there are getting hit pretty hard. Cannon company is scattered around the town. Sounds like house to house fighting with the Krauts. There were observation teams around there somewhere but nothing has been heard from them. I'll contact Captain Horn from the 333rd at our HQ. They're his FOs and we'd better be prepared to deal with them directly."

"Sir, what are the red markings on the overlay?"

"Well, I kind of went a little crazy with the grease pencil. Anyway, from the parsed information we have, I've taken it and tried to piece together where I believe the attack is going. This road network is picture-perfect for a flanking maneuver, look at it, almost a perfect triangle. If they move fast enough, the Krauts could be behind us in a matter of hours. We're going to displace eventually, probably west of the Our. Should have been done before we got here."

The sudden ringing of their EE-8 phone, broke the tension. It seemed as though it would ring itself right out of its brown leather case.

Green grabbed the phone this time. It crackled and came to life. The distinctive voice of the Battalion communications man was heard.

"Dogwood Able, Dogwood Able. This is Dogwood Red. Can you read over?"

All movement stopped at the CP. Peters even looked up from his map.

"This is Dogwood Able, over. Go ahead, Dogwood Red."

Then heard the sequence of orders begin with a term he had heard so many times before, 'Fire Mission, Enemy Infantry.' After he had jotted down the orders, he hung up and immediately rang the sections. As he read them, he realized how close the target was.

"First section! Battery adjust, shell HE, fuse quick, base deflection right… 200 mils, elevation 1050; one round to adjust…number one gun only."

Then the reply came back from Prynne.

"Ready, sir."

Green relayed 'Ready' back to the Battalion FDC.

The reply was instantaneous.

"Fire!"

Prynne repeated the order and Davis pulled the lanyard. The shell was on its way.

Green answered back to the FDC, "On the way."

They waited anxiously at the HQ for another transmission from the Battalion FDC as outside the crews tried to keep warm. Battalion had to wait to hear from the observer.

Normally, one section would fire in order to register the gun on the assigned target with guidance being given by the observer. Another shot was usually called for from the observer. Once accuracy was confirmed, and the targeted bracketed, the other sections joined the firing. But with the observers scattered, the orders from the Battalion fire direction center were probably just calls from desperate infantry units. Mass concentration missions would come later. In some cases, the observers could call any battery that would answer. The process was astonishingly fast. Although to Green, it was an agonizing few minutes.

Battalion relayed a slight adjustment to the mils and off went another shell, fired by Section one. Despite not having to fire, the other sections adjusted as well. Shells had already been loaded in all the guns. Finally, after what seemed like an eternity, Battalion rang again. The final adjustments were recorded and relayed. The target had been bracketed. The phones at all the sections rang. Green barked out the new orders as he looked over at the line of guns to see the section chiefs with their arms raised. Almost out of instinct, he gave a final glance at Peters, who nodded. The moment they had been waiting for finally had come. Green checked his watch. They had beaten the five minute mark.

"Battery three rounds. Fire for effect!"

"Fire!" was relayed to all the crews and the section chiefs' arms finally sliced the air. The battle had been joined. A cacophony of booms hit the air almost simultaneously and the howitzers rocked from the concussion. The dark of the early morning had been light up as the guns belched fire. Shell after shell was grabbed, loaded and fired. With each opening of the breech, an acrid, yellow smoke cloaked the cannoneers. The gunner corporals, now with tired eyes, kept a constant check on range and deflection between shots. Hordes of men stooped around their guns picking up shells to load. Behind them, other men armed the shells with the powder bags, aligned the rotating bands, and then put them back in the casings. The clang of the empty brass shell casings piling up behind the sections was beginning to echo around the battery along with the continuous sucking sounds of boots trying to maneuver in the morass of mud that now swamped their positions.

Green waited for confirmation of the effectiveness of their fire and that it was not falling on the wrong soldiers. With the front line situation unclear, and no word from any of the observers, fire would have to be adjusted by someone. Three rounds per section was the normal mission for an entire battery. But right after the twelve rounds had been fired, Battalion ordered another fire mission with minimal adjustment.

After five minutes, orders came to cease fire. Peters, worried about the lack of ammunition, ordered sections three and four to stand down until further notice.

"Brendan, sections one and two will handle any more fire missions that come in. I want to find out what the other batteries are doing. If we're staying, those damn supply trucks better arrive tonight. We may have to move out soon and getting our guns out of the their pits is going to be tough.

"Just sighting them in another direction would be difficult."

"And good luck registering on a new base point."

Because of the Battalion's proximity to the ridges of the Schnee Eifel, the gun pits were dug deep enough to provide high angle fire. This was to closely support the infantry that was manning the ridgeline.

"If communications can hold, we'll be fine. But I knew that set up they had from the switching station was going to be a problem."

"What do you mean, sir?"

"All the lines, you know, between regiment and division or regiment to the battalions, were laid into one cable to make it easier for installation. So if one cable went down, it might cause a real problem. Well, Colonel Killman was not pleased. But we're not the ones who set this up, are we?"

"Was not aware of that, Captain."

"Finally, there is something you didn't know about," Peters joked. "I feel honored."

"Gimme time, sir."

Green checked his watch. It was almost 0800. Thankfully, the eerie spotlights and multi-colored flares the Germans were using had subsided as dawn approached. Sounds of German artillery, mortars and small arms could still be heard all around them. Brilliant flashes still lit up the sky, bouncing off the low hanging cloud. Throughout the morning, the battery kept a brisk pace, but no panic. Battalion's orders had sounded just like training, no emotion in their voices, almost matter of fact. Monahan was monitoring all frequencies and he was hearing a different story. Within the last thirty minutes, panicked calls had come from all over. One desperate forward observer with the aptly titled call sign of 'Hotshot,' called the battery and ordered a fire mission on his own position. They never heard from him again.

The diligent Monahan very stealthily let Green know what was happening as he tried to listen on other units' communications. It was good to know what the big picture was, but it gave him one more worry: where was Mecklenburg and the other men?

6

THE ROAD SOFTENED AS THEY drove on and a worried Turner increased his speed, turning right on almost two wheels and then a quick left to straighten out. They were now on the road to Auw, racing to beat the early morning thaw, before it brought forth its inescapable muck. If the rubber met the road for too long, they'd be stranded.

"Slow it down here, Due. I think those other artillery units are around here. Bear right toward that sign that says Radscheid. Then just keep bearing right and we'll run right into their positions."

The artillery positions of the 590th came into dim view as they accidentally drove past the village of Radscheid. In the distance, one gun was adjusting fire, its sudden flash temporarily lighting the way. Seeing the men scrambling around was encouraging. Jackson and Turner were one of the few in the Ardennes who knew how serious this attack was.

"Make the next right and pull up to the group over there, where their trucks are."

In between the gun flashes and the German spotlights, the batteries could be seen in a flurry of activity. They were trying to get their ammo trucks lined up to the guns. Tarps were being loosed and men were on their knees checking the shells and cutting powder bags. He tried finding someone who looked like they were in charge and finally saw an angry driver who had been shouting down from one of the trucks.

"Hey Corporal. Corporal!"

"What do you want?" he asked with a strong sense of annoyance, not realizing he was talking to a sergeant in the dim light. He just saw an unknown black face.

"You guys hear anything from Bleialf or on the radio?"

"Not a thing, Mack. Radios are dead. Phone lines down. Check in Schonberg."

"I spoke with a Lieutenant Mecklenberg, an observer down there."

"He's A Battery. Can't he use the radio?"

"No, everything is out or garbled. I need to get to A Battery?"

"Down the road, buddy!"

"And your HQ?"

The corporal, becoming increasingly annoyed at all the questions, began to nervously put the truck in gear again as he spoke.

"They're right in Radscheid. You probably drove by it."

"Thanks!" Jackson could barely be heard over the engines but he felt his teeth chattering. Standing still for more than a minute made one freeze.

"Let's move on."

"You ain't gonna getta straight answer. They here somewheres, but nobody know what the hell goin' on. Les find our own guys an' move back wit 'em."

"You're right, but let's stop at the switching station and see if we can help those fellas out in Bleialf. Then we'll hit our own HQ."

After turning around and reaching the Bleialf-Schonberg road again via the cutoff, they came to the crest of the small rise just above the village of Schonberg, its rust-colored roofs emerging from the valley. The road was filled with guys running every which way. Wire crews passed Jackson and Turner on their way to find the breaks in the lines that were causing so many problems. Getting to the switching station was impossible. So they turned right and headed north towards Andler, where just up the road their HQ and C Battery were located.

Being a *'Colored'* outfit, they didn't get the best HQ. Even the unit's designation in the official Army roster had *'Cld'* attached to it. But they made the most of it. Holes in the walls and roof were patched up and the furniture repaired as well. The aroma of coffee, cigarettes and body odor filled the air. The Battalion's FDC was abuzz with activity and concerned faces. The officers stood staring at maps, holding handfuls of overlays.

He finally got the attention of one of the lieutenants who he knew well.

"Sir, Due and I just got back from Bleialf. It's being overrun. Those men need fire now."

"We're working on it. Couldn't you call us?"

"No, sir. Everything was down. One of the lieutenants from the 106th asked us to try and get some fire down on the town as soon as possible. It's pretty crazy down there."

"Hey, where's Lieutenant Gibson?"

"I thought he was still here."

"No, he charged out of here as soon as those strange lights started, saying he needed to get back to Bleialf. You didn't see him on the way up?"

"No, sir. But we coulda missed him. Maybe if we contact Lieutenant King's OP, he could be there."

Due could never miss an opportunity to share his opinion.

"If he lucky," he said out of the corner of his mouth, not loud enough for the lieutenant to hear.

"Did you guys try to get to Lieutenant King's OP?"

"We couldn't, sir," Jackson quickly responded, realizing the lieutenant's tone was rather accusatory. "The Krauts sort of rushed the town, cutting us off. That's when the infantry lieutenant told us to move back immediately, and set up outside of town. When we stopped at a cabin, we found an observer from the 590th trying to get in touch with any unit he could find. He asked us to stop by his HQ, but in all the confusion we thought it best to get back here."

To Jackson's immense relief, the lieutenant, seemingly satisfied with their efforts, nodded in the affirmative.

"Well, right now we're waiting on orders. I'll try and contact Captain Horn at the 590th HQ. Let 'em know that one of their observers is out there. Looks like we might set up on the other side of the Our. But we're spread out as well. A and B batteries might be on the move. At least one was told to stand down for right now and might get a march order. There's another artillery battalion supposed to be withdrawing through here soon. For now, just spell the guys working the radio. Standby, we might send you out again or use you as runners. Captain McCloud may need help up at C Battery. Colonel Kelsey will want a report on what you saw as well, so stay close."

As they sat down, one of the radios crackled to life and the ominous words brought home the reality.

"Enemy advancing on town! Hold on! Enemy now in Bleialf! Repeat. Enemy just passed my position," the voice now had gone down to a whisper before the radio went static.

The look on the operators' faces told the story for Jackson. This was not going well. It was only 0830 hours. The operators were picking desperate calls from everywhere. The situation up north seemed the worst, as one worried CO called for help:

"Enemy is in Kobscheid and Troop A, 18th Cav is now cutoff and unable to withdraw. Situation critical and deteriorating."

Jackson had resisted a position at the FDC. He did not want to have officers constantly looking over his shoulder. But now, on a day like this, it was an exciting and scary place to listen to the war unfold. Men ran back and forth with messages to the officers scattered around the room. Maps covered every inch of the wall space. There were enlisted men using slide rules to make calculations which confirmed the data that the forward observers radioed. The room was cramped, loud and dimly lit. Plumes of cigarette smoke hovered everywhere. The floor palpably creaked from the strain of so many scampering around. There was a row of three tables set up towards the middle of the room. Each table had a map laid out on it with a technical sergeant pouring over grid coordinates, while simultaneously scanning the artillery tables that held precomputed values. At the opposite end of the table sat his assistant, a T/5, recording data. All this while their officers hovered close by, waiting to confirm the calculations. It was as though there were a hundred conversations going on at once as the telephones rang and radios hummed. The officers discussed every topic that mattered: intelligence, weather, supplies, gun maintenance, and most of all they tried to ascertain the 'big picture'. Jackson was almost in awe, and thought if only the folks back home could see their own, black soldiers, in the newsreels performing such complicated and important tasks.

The operators' voices could be heard repeating the same thing as they tried every unit or observer in the vicinity. Responses were lacking.

"This is Castle Fire Direction, can you read me over?" the first operator went on and on to anyone out there. Then he finally switched to their own units, using proper procedure.

"Castle Charlie, can you read over?

"Castle Charlie 2, can you read me over?"

This went on for hours. Jackson felt like he heard every call sign in the book: 'Dagwood Red,' 'Decoy Blue', and there was even an 'Ivanhoe,' 'Hardtack' and 'Potshot.' But 'Charlie 2' was more personal for him. That was Lieutenant King's observation team in Bleialf. The longer they went without an answer, the harder it was to remain his usual optimistic self.

There was the occasional success with a tidbit of information. It was even difficult to get in touch with C Battery, situated just up the road from HQ on the road to Andler. Runners were continually sent out. Jackson knew it would be his turn soon.

Due finally stepped out for a cigarette and Jackson followed with some coffee. There was slight break in the clouds, and the wind had picked up, blowing snow into their cups.

"It's gonna be a long day," Jackson matter of factly stated.

Due just laughed to himself, then pounced.

"Mr. Obvious o'er here. Day? It gonna be a lon' winter."

7

1130 Hours, A Battery, 590th Field Artillery Battalion, Village of Oberlascheid

As THE MORNING WORE ON, there were down times, enough time to grab a meal or straighten up from the relentless physical exertion and cold. The men fusing the shells were covered in mud. Their hands ached as they tried to get the fuses a little tighter each time. For many it would be hours before they realized how cut up their hands really were. Adrenalin had taken over. The silk bags of powder were tied together with a thick string and that string had to be cut; the men's hands often slipped. Those bags were then loaded into the brass casings and the shell screwed on tight. Another man would then set the fuse to the proper position with his wrench.

From all around their positions, artillery fire of all calibers could be heard. Targets had become ubiquitous as the morning progressed. For Able Battery, fire missions were still coming, but some required only three shots, others, only two. The observers had to keep moving. So they'd get a shot off, maybe two, then hightail it out of their positions.

Green ran up and down the battery line checking on the men, supplies and performance.

As he approached section two, he saw Wallenbach having trouble with one of the metal bands.

"Wallenbach!"

Green yelled over the noise to no avail. Finally, he squeezed his way in the crowd of men and tapped him on the shoulder. The new kid, the end of his overcoat dripping wet and his face smeared in mud, looked up to see Green motioning him aside. He grabbed the wrench from the young cannoneer and began a quick lesson.

"We need to set the fuses for superquick. So you have to turn the setting sleeve so that the slot is parallel, not perpendicular, to the axis of the shell. Got it?"

"Yessir, sorry."

"It's okay, watch the other guys. Don't be afraid to ask. We have to get this right."

Green scampered off to another section, taking turns instructing the men on how to do things better or just jumping in to help until he was wanted back at the CP.

Monahan and Pritchard were feverishly barking out information at the command post. As Green entered the CP, he noticed that Peters had stripped down to his sweater and was foregoing his helmet.

"Brendan, the north end of Skyline Drive has been cut. Krauts have apparently taken Auw."

He was stunned by the news that Auw had been taken so quickly.

"So the approaches between us and Regimental are going to come under increased pressure from German artillery."

Trying to not show any emotion over the ominous report was difficult, but he quickly composed himself, sounding more like Sgt. Prynne, then the executive officer.

"I figured as much, sir. Everyone can hear it," Green mentioned ruefully, referring to the occasional shells lobbed by the Germans that now were becoming more frequent.

"Fire control is getting orders to pour down fire on the Bleialf-Sellerich road. Regiment reports that there has been no let up in enemy movement towards the village. In fact, Bleialf might already be in German hands or at the very least surrounded."

"Any word form Meck?"

"Sorry Brendan, nothing. I would have called you over if I had, you know that."

"Will we be moving, sir, taking up new positions anywhere?"

"I don't know yet. My sense is that we still might fall back toward Schonberg, on the other side of the river. The way things are sounding, that should have been done already. But we also might need to concentrate fire further east and get in tight with the 423rd. This might mean moving toward Halenfeld. I am assuming of course, that the men still up on the Schnee will be digging in and need reinforcements while they await a full scale counterattack. I don't think they will have time or the firepower to regroup *en masse*. This all depends on where the Germans appear to be in the next hour or so. There was word that the 422nd was going to try and retake Auw but they were called back to defend their own perimeter. Our last transmission from Battalion said the 423rd HQ may be shifting as well."

"Have you looked at the data sheets lately, sir?"

"Every other minute I seem to be checking them. I'm driving poor Pritchard crazy."

"Will you want to see the chiefs' notebooks too?"

According to Army standards, section chiefs for each gun were required to keep their own notebooks to record shell usage, changes in targeting info and gun maintenance issues.

"At this point, if they are doing it, great. It shows that they are keeping their heads about them. But if they are not, and the sections seem okay, don't worry about it. Battalion won't care. Just keep checking on the ammo. If we get a request for a mass concentration, we might be done. The next few hours are critical."

"Alright, sir."

To his immense relief, Peters was using his own common sense and adapting to the situation. The grim news had finally sunk in for both men and there was a moment of uncomfortable quiet, until Peters remembered another missing officer.

"Hey, where's Grey and how is he doing?"

"I sent him up to Schonberg to talk to the guys at the switching station, and find out a little info on what might be happening. I figure an officer would get more out of them, sir. Then I told him to head over to the 589th to see how they making out. Maybe scout new positions as well. He's got a driver and a radio. Hope you don't mind."

Green was looking from some validation as he became increasingly doubtful about his decision.

"No, of course not. He's a smart kid. He does know the password, right?"

"I went over it with him before he left."

"By the way, what is the password?"

Green smiled, knowing Peters had a lot on his mind.

"It' 'Armored' and the reply is 'Knight', sir."

After a quick but totally unnecessary salute, Green decided to do a check of the roads and motor park. As he stepped out of the CP, a battalion ¾ ton wire truck was passing through, its telltale large spool of black cable attached to the back. He whistled as loud as he could to get their attention.

"Hey, hold it up there!"

He ran towards them.

"Sir?"

"Where did you guys just come from?"

Both men looked confused as to what they should answer. The driver, a sergeant, finally spoke.

"Well, sir. We've been all over."

"Have you had any contact with our forward observers?"

"Yessir. Uh, we ran inna one about two hours ago. Probably somewhere between the 423rd CP and Bleialf, sir. "

Green knew that there had to be more to the story than that, but enjoyed hearing the sergeant's New York accent fade in and out.

"Could you show me on a map?"

"I think so. Maybe sir."

Green pulled his sector map from the inside pocket of his jacket and unfolded it on the hood of the truck.

"Alright, come here."

Both the sergeant and his much shorter assistant got out. Their heavy eyes betrayed their exhaustion. The diminutive young private was now shivering, his pants soaked and stuck to his legs. Caked mud fell from the Sergeant's jacket. Both men's wind burned faces were about two shades darker than they should be. Their gloves were in tatters, a testament to the dexterous nature of their work.

"Here's our CP," Green started marking with his pencil. "And here's the road you just came on. There's Bleialf. And the 423rd HQ is still in Buchet, right?"

"Yessir," the sergeant said pointing to the area north,

"Anyway, where did you see the observer team?"

"A little northwest of there, sir," the sergeant sternly stated, pointing to an area just outside of Bleialf. "Battalion told us to drive around looking for any groups of either observers or infantry that needed a phone line. Easy for them to say. We're supposed to have a bunch of our guys around there. Then we tried the radio and got nuttin'. We didn't see nobody at all. Just a lot of guys from Cannon Company filtering back and there was some shootin' going on somewhere, didn't sound like ours. There was so much smoke around, we could barely take a breath. Felt like there was a Kraut behind every damn tree."

"Can you describe their position?"

There was small dirt road off the main road, and we hit it on the way back just in case. He flagged us down at the edge of a bunch of trees which sort of sat up on this little hill. They were well hidden. We weren't even too sure he was an American after he jumped out of the trees, because of all the rumors. And he thought we might be Krauts. But he had on the officer's short coat that you guys wear, sir and his carbine at the ready. It kinda convinced us. Said a Kraut patrol had marched right up the road about a half hour before we came down. Those were the ones that probably fired on us later on. It scared the you know what out of us."

"Well, what did he say?"

"He yelled for the tech sergeant, who came down with the phone. Asked us to run these lines up toward any battery of the 590th we could find ASAP. Then a bunch of guys came down to ask us if we knew what was going on. Saw a couple of their wounded too. Minor stuff but in this cold, ya know? So the lieutenant asked if we could go back to the 423rd aid station with a couple of the squad's men. He knew a shortcut. And at that point sir, I was glad to have anyone with a rifle."

"Did you get a *name* of the officer?" Green now clearly exasperated

"Oh, yessir. Sounded like a Kraut name. Meglen.. something."

The private then piped up through his chattering teeth.

"Meck-len-berg, sir," he stated real slowly, trying to convince himself of the pronunciation. Then he was certain and proud of himself for remembering.

"Lieutenant Mecklenberg. Know him, sir?"

"Yeah. He was one of my officers."

"So you must be Lieutenant Green. I think he mentioned your name. Said if we saw ya to let ya know that he's okay."

"Was he hurt?"

"No, sir. Other than freezin'. They were wet and jumpy. He thought they were cut off. I really wanted them to come along with us. The whole bunch of 'em. Ya know, safety in numbers. They had two jeeps stashed off the road covered in pine branches. But he said no and so did the dogface sergeant. Figgahed they'd be more of us coming down soon and waitin' for orders. Personally sir, I think they were nuts. They were kind of surprised there were only two of us. All they'd seen for the past couple of hours was Krauts. I don't know how we even made it back."

"Did you get any other names, maybe a Gunvalson, Donatelli or Underwood?"

"The phone guy was probably one of yours. And there was another guy with a carbine, probably not an infantryman, sir. Those dogfaces hate the carbines, so that's what I figgah. He was a big, tough guy, built like Red Grange or something. He probably coulda carried the wounded himself."

"That's Donatelli."

"What was going on at the aid station?"

"Pretty busy, sir. Lots of the guys coming and going. Starting to fill up though, sir. The doc mentioned they might be withdrawing real soon."

"Have you tried any of the connections?"

"Yessir. We tapped in a couple of times along the way. But nothing so far. Took us forever to find the break. Couldn't stop for too long, we kept hearing machine gun fire. Scary out there, sir. A lot of the poles are down. Some of those snow drifts are pretty deep."

"But they had a radio too?"

"Yes, sir. Two of them."

"What happened when you left?"

"After we left the aid station, we went back and picked up the phone line again from your lieutenant. Then we thought it safer to stay off the main road and conceal the cable better too. There was another path just inside the woods which your buddy recommended. So we headed through there. I know we were headed almost due west for the first few minutes, and then turned north towards Halenfeld again. At least we think."

"I know the path you're talking about. Did you see the Krauts?

"Just for a split second, sir. We heard them shoutin' and everythin'. Bullets wizzin' by. Ya know that *Pop..Pop..Pop.* First time under fire for me, sir. Helluva sound. They get right by your ears, you can feel the air just cut in half. Strange sounding guns too, sir. Nothing like they let us hear in training. Maybe a new machine gun or something. Cocky bastards. Yelling Yankee and Amis, and crap like that. I just hit the gas and managed to keep the wire intact. It's crazy out there."

"Where's your Line route map?"

"That was useless, sir. It won't help ya at all. We found wire strewn everywhere. It took us two hours just to find a cut. We did a ladder tie and tag across one of the roads. Then we bumped into some old railroad tracks that had some cut cable. So we did a splice as well as another tie and tag under the tracks. Threw some branches and snow on top. These Goddamn Krauts seemed to have known where all the wire was, sir. It's like they been out in these woods for months waiting to attack."

"They have been out here for years. We're inside Germany. The Germans invaded through here while we were in high school."

As Green spoke, he noticed the hands of the shivering young private. One hand was gloveless while the other one's glove was practically torn in half. Two fingers on his left hand were swelling. The thumb's skin was darkening, almost black under the thumb. The rest of his long, bony hand was calloused and cracked. Already underweight, he had the look of a beggar. His sunken cheekbones and bulging gray eyes displayed desperation.

The stocky sergeant's hands were not much better, just a lot meatier, almost like a bear's paw. How he could splice cable and do the other intricate work required of the wire men, nobody could know. The squish of water inside their soaked boots was clearly audible as they shifted from foot to foot to keep warm. Green wondered how he could have missed knowing these two because they made such an interesting looking pair.

"By the way, both of you have signs of frostbite, particularly you private. What's your name?"

The private looked down at his hands before answering. His shivering getting worse.

"C..C…Condon, Dominic J…*sss*ir. Through the chattering teeth, there was a hint of the south.

"Where you from?"

"Mississippi, sir."

The sergeant patted him on the back and laughed.

"These Southern guys ain't used to cold like we are, sir, huh? He's also the only Dominic I've met from the South."

"Sergeant, you sounded like you were from my part of the world."

" Queens, sir. And believe it or not, my parents were born less than thirty miles from here. Came to the States right after the last war."

"Is this the first time you've been sent out for down wires?"

"Well, sir. This was our second trip since yesterday. Battalion got a report last night of some down wires. Got back around 2100. It was so black last night I'm surprised we made it. I bet those Krauts were watching us the whole time. They had already started screwin' with the damn lines."

"Sergeant, what's your name?

"Stein, sir. Armin W."

"Alright Stein, and this goes for you too, Condon. Take care of those hands and feet immediately. In fact, go see one of my medics right now. He pointed toward the ramshackle house that was being used as an aid station. Leave your shit here except for your carbines. I'll move your truck to where our CP is. We got dry socks too. Chow wagon is still open. Right behind that house to your left. Hop to it before they shut down. Find a place to warm up. Get going."

An order from an officer to, in GI parlance, to 'knock off' and go see to your own well-being, was a new development to the men. In unison, they both thought of the only possible answer.

"Yessir!"

The sergeant even attempted a salute and then felt ridiculous.

"Thanks, sir. I'll nurse this kid back to health."

Green's accent was even audible now. As he jumped in their truck, he saw the puddle of water on the floor board. The seat was the only semi-dry part. The sergeant's backside had apparently soaked up all the water.

8

Buoyed by the news that Meck was still alive and fighting, Green charged over to the CP.

"Monahan, the wire guys just saw Lieutenant Mecklenberg and he might have a phone line. Stay with it."

He finally located Peters, who was in the bathroom. Undeterred, he just started knocking on the door.

"Sir, I have news about Meck and the others."

"Okay, on the way out."

"Sorry, sir."

"Sorry to keep you waiting. Too much coffee. Shoot. What's happening?"

"The two wire men saw him outside of Bleialf. They were with a squad of infantry that had been cut off. At least they thought they were cut off. All refused to come out with the wire guys. The position was well off the main road. There's a logging road that turns slightly to the east as you proceed north out of town. Think he's about a mile northeast of Bleialf. So he's close to Regimental, but for some reason he has not attempted to get there."

Green then took out his own map as Peters began checking his.

"Right here," Green fingered the probable position, "there's a large bank of trees that curves along a small hill. The top of that hill apparently faces due east, then slopes down and gives a good view of the valley down between Buchet and Weidinger. Maybe that's why he's there."

"That's not where he was supposed to be."

"No, sir. Should have been further east. They probably saw the whole attack as it happened. If all they've seen are Krauts crossing the roads on their flanks, that means the 423rd CP is under a lot of pressure. Meck probably figures we're already surrounded or about to be. But the wire party made it back after running into a German patrol. Said it was clear after they went about a mile up the firebreak and then turned onto the main road toward our position. So they could get out."

Peters stood up and took a deep breath.

"I know what you are going to say. And no, you cannot have permission to form a search party."

It came out half-mockingly, but that was not the intention. Peters suspected Green was formulating a plan.

"Sir, I know under circumstances you wouldn't let me go but if I could get the wire sergeant I spoke to and a couple of other guys together…"

Peters put his left hand up like a traffic cop. The other men in the CP started to notice and knew what was coming.

"No. Meck may call again. But for all we know, he's been overrun. It'd be crazy to try and get down there. Besides, we're likely to get orders any minute for more fire missions or a march order. Our infantry is falling back. Those signalmen were just lucky to get back here. It's my decision. I'm sorry, Brendan. But keep trying to get in touch using the radio or give the 423rd a call. See if they've heard from anyone."

"It was worth a shot, sir."

"Look, with Grey missing, you are to stay put. Got me? Don't leave the perimeter. I'm sorry to have to sound like a school marm but…"

"Sir, I'm not leaving."

"And neither is anyone else, got me?" Peter said with more than a little sternness.

"Of course, sir,"Green replied, feigning meekness.

"The most important thing is to let the 423rd know that there is still an observer team out there. And that the Krauts are only a mile away, although they should have figured that out by now. "Yes, sir."

"Well, keep trying get in touch."

"You got it, Captain."

"Also Brendan, let's increase our perimeter a little bit. Do we have another .50 cal laying around?"

"Yes we do. The guys in fifth section scrounged up another one but I'm awaiting your orders."

"You're awaiting my orders?" Peters smirked as he said it, knowing that Green was being falsely deferential again. Whether it was out of a sense of being a nice guy or being sarcastic, he could never tell. "I think you know where to set that up."

Green smiled. "You got it, sir."

"But let's take a couple of men and get them patrolling the woods east and south of here. Not too far. The Krauts could roll up on us real quick now."

"Since section three is shut down, I'll have Sergeant Crawford take them out."

"Good. I know he's a hell of a shot."

A sudden bang from the kitchen area startled both men. Monahan's tin can ashtray had been knocked to the floor along with his chair.

"Sir! Lieutenant Green!," Monahan was shouting and gesturing Green over to the radio set. He was holding on to his headset with both hands.

"What's up, we got a mission?"

"Sir, one of the forward observers is trying to contact us. But it keeps breaking up. The phones are down again… sorry sir, you already know that. Someone is coming through the static and the voice sounds familiar."

Green stood behind Monahan, waiting for the static to clear. But instead the phone unexpectedly rang.

" They weren't kidding about getting those damn things working again."

"Sir, I think it's the same observer somewhere. I'm confirming."

"Not battalion? You're talking directly to the field? Got a name?"

"Yes. Hold on. Okay, here we go."

Monahan's face then lit up.

"It's Lieutenant Mecklenberg, sir. At least it's his call sign. Lotta noise too."

Green picked up, and what he heard confirmed it was Mecklenberg.

"Dogwood Able. Dogwood Able. This is Dogwood Able 1. Can you read me over?"

"This is Dogwood Able. Go ahead Able 1. Meck?"

"Brendan?"

"Meck! Go ahead!" Green was now shouting.

"Fire Mission, enemy infantry. Listen..."

His voice was trailing off as he tried to maintain visual contact with the onrushing enemy.

Green knew what he wanted to say: *'It's gonna be okay. Stay on the air.'* Hearing a friendly voice helps calm the nerves. But Peters made his displeasure about using first names over the air known by just his look; the men knew it as *the stare*. Maintain a military decorum, he always warned.

Green could picture Meck trying to relay orders over the line while raising his head just enough to peer out at the Germans swarming toward him, ripping up the ground around him with machine gun fire.

He listened intently, writing the whole time, then relaying it to the fire team. Peters studied the overlays while Pritchard checked the firing tables and inspected the chart.

"Brendan confirm it and that goes for everybody! Monahan call Battalion fire direction if you can and let 'em know we're in touch with an observer. Give them the position. Remember, the Krauts may have the line tapped and are working our phones. Make sure of who you are talking to. Check your fire direction carefully."

"It's the Lieutenant's voice for sure, sir."

"I'll do the relay." Green stepped out of the CP, pulling the telephone line out as far as he could, so he could look down once again on the line of guns.

For the first time all day, he had a pain in the pit of his stomach knowing the situation his friend was facing. After a deep breath, it was back to business.

The first call was for section one.

"Able Battery, Adjust!"

"Shell HE!"

"Charge Three"

"Fuse Quick!"

"Base Deflection…right……two fifty."

"Number one, one round, at my command."

"Elevation, Twelve Hundred!"

Darino, thumb and index finger on the quadrant knob, turning it ever so slightly, squinted through the lens. Davis opened the breech and grabbed for the firing pin. Del Valle pushed in the shell. Greeley cradled another, kneeling on one knee to steady the weight. Davis connected the firing pin, cleared the area behind the gun and grabbed the lanyard.

Within seconds, Prynne reported back, "Number One ready!"

Then came the order, "Fire!" and Prynne's arm sliced the air.

After an initial adjustment of a paltry few degrees in deflection, the target was then bracketed and a full volley of fire from section one was unleashed. After five rounds, the order came to cease fire. The other sections all stood at their guns, holding their energy like a rubber band ready to snap.

Green stayed on the line during the barrage. The sounds were deafening, having to pull the receiver away. The line went dead but then he put a call through hoping against hope that the wire had held. After twenty windings, there was a connection. As Meck picked up he could hear the attack continuing on Meck's position.

"Meck! Where are you?"

Peters glared at Green, but allowed him this breach of protocol. In the confusion, things would have to be double confirmed. All the men at the CP stopped what they were doing.

"Dogwood Able! Brendan?" Mecklenberg shouted, "Can you hear me, over?"

"Go ahead. I can hear you, over!"

The German pressure had increased despite the barrage. Machine guns continued to rattle and mortars began to hit close. A shower of shrapnel could be heard tearing into the trees and the rush of air crackled over the line.

"Hold on, sir!"

Green waited.

Then the desperate observer began shouting over the increasing staccato of strange machine gun fire.

"Okay, listen! Correction, Drop a hundred. Fire for effect!"

"Meck! I'll give you twenty seconds to get the hell out!"

"No! Fire for Effect! Do it now!"

Green shouted the orders out to the men in the HQ. Monahan picked up the phone to the sections.

"Wait!" It was the Captain who raised his hand.

Peters, upon hearing this became concerned at the strange order.

"Brendan, confirm those orders! This is crazy. We'll have to give him to time run outta there. I don't want to be responsible for killing him. Pritchard, check those figures and get me some coordinates."

Before Green could speak, Mecklenburg began shouting again but with all the interference, his words were fragmented.

"…drop one zero zero…! Fire for effect! Can you read, over?" Mecklenburg was now screaming into the phone. A final click and the phone then went dead for the last time.

Green turned the handle a dozen times, but got nothing, not even a shock. He slammed it down while Monahan grabbed from under his reach.

"Monahan, get that radio working and try to reach the lieutenant now."

"Already workin' on it!"

Green, shaking with anger as he grabbed the phone to the sections, turned to an increasingly concerned Peters.

"Sir, we have to fire those rounds!" he retorted angrily.

A nervous Pritchard finally spoke up.

"Sir, I confirmed the position as southeast of Halenfeld. Go to grid square…"

Peters raised his hand to cut him off, as he now faced his angry executive officer.

"That firing we hear outside echoing in the distance is probably him under attack,"

Both men locked eyes. The silence in the CP was deafening. There was just a slight *zzzzz* from Monahan's radio. Pritchard had stopped recording. Even Biels stood in the doorway, afraid to make a move. What seemed like an hour, lasted only seconds. Peters began tapping his grease pencil.

He finally nodded, "Make the correction. Fire five rounds, one section, that's all," and then went back to his charts.

A very audible, collective breath was let out by all. The frenzy that is a battery HQ began anew. Green nodded, and relayed the orders, shouting over the phone, "Battery Adjust!" to begin the series of orders all over again that would start the new fire mission.

As he finished, he became chilled at the sudden realization that Peters was right. He may have just given the order that would end up killing one of his own men. The fire mission continued until the section had completed five rounds. The sound of each round being fired was like a bell tolling. Green knew that Peters had given up on Mecklenberg. He could not be angry with him. A commanding officer had to think long-term, always worrying about the 'big picture.' Wasting valuable shells on a man that was probably dead at this point was dangerous. His CO could be cold at times, but Brendan knew he was right, although admitting that was impossible. As usual, his frustrations would manifest themselves by lashing out, which is how he coped. It might not happen right away. Maybe in a few hours or the next day, but eventually flood gates of emotion would burst.

Peters sought a normalcy that could only be gained by issuing orders.

"Monahan, stay on it. Keep listening."

The radioman nodded, knowing he was already doing it.

"Brendan, call the Fire Direction Center again if you can get through. See if they have confirmations on any of the observer parties by now."

"Yessir," he replied in an almost mocking tone that Peters struggled to ignore.

"I'm going to try and pinpoint again where he called from based on his orders. After Monahan gets done, have him call the 423rd and tell them what we heard. There might not be anyone between them and their HQ. Maybe they could send out a patrol. Give them Meck's last position."

Before Green could answer in the affirmative, Monahan piped up.

"Doing it now, sir!"

"Brendan, do you know any of the officers at their HQ?"

"I've met their S-2 sir, Major Johnson and I know a couple of their other staff guys. Plus, Charlie Meyer said they are getting ready for another push on Bleialf."

"I don't want to send anybody out right now, especially with Grey out there somewhere as well. Let's keep pressing them for information so we can coordinate with them for the attack."

"I'll keep at it, sir."

By any measure, Green had challenged his commander during a combat situation. The bridge of respect that had built up between them could have been blown. But the seemingly unemotional captain knew better. Green's indignation was not a threat. In the adrenaline of combat, emotions would run high. Being the impassive one of the pair, he anticipated that. His exec may have been a '90 Day Wonder,' as the OCS graduates were derisively called, but he also had a hundred days in a previous combat zone. A little latitude went a long way.

Peters then moved closer to Green, lowering his voice.

"Who was with Meck? I know you told me already, sorry."

Remembering it was more than just one of his men out there, he took a second to compose himself before answering.

"Kingery, Underwood and Donatelli."

The dejection on Green's face was palpable to Peters. All energy had elapsed from his body. The effervescent lieutenant that Peters had come to rely on was showing pain that he had not truly shown since that steamy day at Atterbury. Green turned away, not wanting Peters to see his face. He just walked out of the CP without a word. The Captain said nothing. The click of Green's lighter was heard. It was finally time for a cigarette.

9

By late afternoon, the air was still, and an eerie aura of smoke settled over the firing positions, unable to be penetrated by a leaden mist that began to fall. The oncoming darkness was stopped occasionally by flashes of firing, which gave the 105s a dragon-like presence, emitting fire with every breath. The low rumblings of distant artillery still reverberated throughout the hills.

The gun crews' movements were machine-like: fuse the shell, open the breech, load it, lock the breech, position the firing pin, and pull the lanyard. But things had slowed down considerably in the past hour as the freezing rain had turned to sleet. The cooks had even come out in the early afternoon to help fuse shells. Anti-aircraft crews were still firing at unseen targets, much to everyone's annoyance. Their distinctive hammering echoing in the hills was causing more unease for the Americans than for the Germans. Desperate calls for fire missions had subsided and Battalion had only called for fire twice since early afternoon. Two of the sections decided to wash down their guns. They had gotten so hot, that smoke still billowed out of the breech. Bore cleaning was not an urgent task right now, but the fact that the section chiefs decided to do it kept the men busy. Green suddenly missed the excitement of the past hours. Not the pain of desperate men calling for help, but the rush of constant battle. It gave one the ability to focus on the present. The clunk of the breech was a reassuring sound in itself. It meant there was another shell. He knew the gun crews would welcome the split-second flashes; anything that penetrated the claustrophobic darkness of the Ardennes was a relief.

With the stillness, came concern. Everyone watched with a wary eye as their once fully restocked ammunition supply dwindled. Shell casings continued to pile up in pyramids behind the gun crews, so many that the men were now tripping over them. Continued pleading had only brought more promises from Battalion headquarters. They all could hear the other batteries firing, knowing their stocks were also diminishing with every shot.

Green, searching for something to do to get his mind back on track, called Biels over and asked him to check with all sections on their ammo. As unobtrusive as the private could be, he was always there within a second of being summoned. He figured if there was any other information he needed, somebody in those sections would pass it on to Biels anyway, who was sort of the batteries' scribe. Information being his specialty. There was a sense of urgency for everyone, for they now realized that no matter what your job was: clerk, band member, cook, quartermaster, or Executive Officer, they'd all be firing at the enemy before this battle was over. Runners were still going from battery to battery for their various commanders to assess what was going on around them.

Slogging his way back through the ocean of melted snow, Biels reported back on the situation. All the sections were well below a fifty rounds left. No wounds or bad injuries to speak of, except cuts and bruises. All the guns appeared to be operating fine.

Green stopped by section three and spoke with their chief, Sgt. Crawford or 'Crayfish,' as he was known. His New Orleans accent was very heavy, and sometimes almost unrecognizable.

"How y'all doin' suh?"

"Well, that's what I'm here to ask you. I saw House slice his hand open earlier. How is he?"

"He okay. I sent him to da doc. Couple of stitches. Gave him extra glove. But he wonna get back to work, suh."

"Alright. Look, I guess by now you know that we might move out at any time. When your crew finishes cleaning the gun, start packing up. I'm keeping Prynne and Galt in position until just before we leave. We have to make this process as orderly as possible. I'm having some men extend our perimeter, so I might grab some of your guys once you're done. Of course, I want you out there with them."

"Yessuh. Does Mancini know suh?"

"I'll tell him."

"Ah, suh?"

"Yeah?"

"What town we goin' to?"

"My guess is probably to a forward position, maybe between Halenfeld and Buchet.. Try to get fire on some of the Kraut supply columns coming from Sellerich and that area. Close up with the 423rd."

"Where dat?"

"To the southeast near the regimental CP."

"Okay. Sorry for the all da questions. Jus' want some good news, suh."

"So do I. Keep at it."

As Green walked away he heard a jeep bouncing down the lane behind the guns.

Lieutenant Charles Meyer, from Battalion S-3, had come down and was doing his own recon of the Batteries for Battalion HQ. He also had news of his own to pass on to his best friend.

After being told by Colonel Lackey to get an honest assessment of the situation, he went to A Battery first. Green always gave him the straightest answer. But he already knew what was going on. Telephone communications had been reestablished earlier and now the sections were getting orders to cease fire. So for Meyer, this was just a break from the stifling stress of Battalion HQ and a yearning for action.

"Brendan, be ready to move out. I don't know exactly where but we'll need to grab everything and go fast as soon as the march order comes down," Meyer said in a low voice."

"Peters is already planning it. He mentioned Halenfeld. Do you have confirmation?"

He cut the engine. With the noise lessened, he lowered his voice even more to continue, checking to see who was close.

"I hear Division is contemplating some sort of counterattack. Not sure where. There might even be a pullout to across the river. The pressure on the infantry is too much, so we'll have to tie in with them in order to give them support as they pull back. Peters could be right. We'll know soon. I have a couple of things to check and have to get back."

"What's happening with the 422nd?"

"So far, very little in terms of a direct attack. I guess you heard about the Auw situation. The 589th is providing some fire support, but they are getting hit on their flanks as well and it looks like Kelly is going to pull out soon. Kelly's survey section is already looking for a new CP. The 424th has been hit hard, but they're holding. The 592nd is supposed to be moving out tonight from what I heard."

"Shoulda be done when we got here. The 155s don't need to be that close. They better get moving because if the Krauts are moving on Andler and driving up from Bleialf, their options are going to be limited."

"Weber's their CO. If anybody can get them out, he can."

"Charlie, this is going to be a crazy request..."

"Supplies?"

Green nodded.

"Don't ask. We don't even know where our own guys are right now, no less the enemy. Last I heard, there was a supply convoy in St. Vith. But they stopped and did not go any further because of all the crazy reports. Be tight with everything. We're waiting on Cavender, who is probably waiting on Division. Lackey drove off with Colonel Kelly to speak with him now."

"Is Cavender still in Buchet?"

"Not for much longer is my guess."

"What kind of reports are we talking about? We're not only the sector getting hit but how big is this thing?"

"Looks like it is going to be quite the fight. We do have reports of heavy fighting up north. That's all I know. But the road to Schonberg has been clogged with Krauts at different times trying to rush the village. So the side roads are crowded with our own guys and I know Lackey is worried about telling everyone to move out at once."

"Shit. You ought to be wearing more than a sidearm. You know that?"

"I'll be fine."

"Also, Grey is missing. I sent him out this morning to Schonberg and he's not returned. I'm hoping he's just lost. So if you spot a jeep with my markings and two guys in it, pull him over."

"He's not been to HQ, I can tell ya that. I'll keep you posted. Hey look, you had no idea the scope of this thing when you sent him out. Don't feel bad, there's a lot of guys probably lost in these woods."

Meyer knew Green's almost paternal view of his position and tried to find the words to make Green feel less guilty; he could not find a more impossible task.

"Hey, where's your rifle anyway?"

"It's in the back. I have to stay mobile. I have the sidearm and I'm a fast draw."

"You can't hit the side of a barn with those damn things."

"It looks good. Makes me feel like a cowboy or something," Meyer hollered as they spun away.

Uncle Sam's army of citizen soldiers had brought together large amounts of men from different backgrounds. The friendship between Green and Meyer was no different.

Meyer's upbringing had been one of privilege, culminating in his acceptance to Yale where he became a member of the artillery ROTC. Upon graduation and advance training, he was assigned to the 590th just in time for the winter maneuvers in Tennessee. Although well educated and trained, his skinny frame, baby face, red hair and freckles to match, belied the 22 year old's abilities.

He spent the winter acting as a liaison officer for the Battalion S-3. It was a temporary assignment, but one which would allow him to get to know the entire outfit and learn a variety of jobs. It was assumed with his polished demeanor that he would quickly rise up the battalion staff. But before got a chance to meet Green, he began to hear about him, mostly in reverent tones.

"If you have a problem getting anything, see Green in A battery," was the constant refrain from almost everyone.

When they finally met on that snowy day, it was almost underwhelming. As he approached what he figured were the vehicles of A battery, he was expecting a combination of Generals Patton and Custer.

"Hey, any of you guys seen Lieutenant Green?"

"Yessir," came the group reply and salutes, then their eyes glanced downward.

"Hold on one second," came another friendly voice out from under the prime mover stuck by the side of the road. "I'm here."

From underneath the rear axle of the truck, popped Green, wearing only his overalls and GI sweater for warmth. Covered in mud and grease, he looked like a typical GI from the motor pool. He offered his greasy hand to Meyer.

"What's your name, lieutenant?"

"Oh, I'm sorry. Charlie Meyer, with the S-3."

"Operations man, huh? Sorry about my hands."

Green turned away and signaled to his men with a clenched fist and pumping arm. The tow truck began pulling on the stuck mover and helped liberate from its muddy grave.

"Sorry Meyer. What's the news?" Green shouted over the noise.

"Well, I just wanted to introduce myself and let you know that you have a new CO, a Captain Peters waiting at HQ."

"Great. Well, when you see him, give him my best and tell him to find me as soon as he can."

"Where's your CP?"

"Right now, you're looking at it. It's in one of those trucks. These damn roads are pathetic. Had no idea Tennessee had terrible winters. I am going to lose men from accidents even before we go overseas."

Meyer just smiled, trying not to laugh at the casualness of Green's manner.

"Tough day, Lieutenant?"

"I'm dirty and cold, but we're moving again. Thank God. What is it you do Meyer? Are you new?"

"For right now I am sort of a liaison officer for the S-3. Probably receive a new assignment as soon as they find one."

"Where you from?"

"Near Bethlehem, PA. You?"

"Yonkers, New York. Born and raised. Well, I'd love to stay and chat Charlie but my guys are freezing. All kidding aside, if you see this Captain, tell him to sit at Battalion. I'll send a runner as soon as I can but we are nowhere yet. Oh, and by the way, just call me Brendan. You'll be a first lieutenant soon anyway. I can tell."

"Thanks." Meyer gave a quick salute anyway.

"Let's move!" Green shouted.

Green then jumped behind the wheel of the prime mover, waving his left arm forward, continuing to shout orders. Meyers got back in his jeep.

"Does he always drive himself and do his own maintenance?" Meyer asked his driver, a man who had been around Green a lot."

"Sir, it might be habit. He was an enlisted man before. You heard the rumors?"

"Rumors? What about?"

"He supposedly did something crazy and ended up gettin' promoted because of it."

"Really?"

"I would love to get assigned to him sir, if I didn't hate the cold so much."

Meyer now figured that there was a man from which he could learn a lot. A friendship had been born. But there had to be a more complex side to Green. Maybe the stories were right. Meeting him had just raised his curiosity. He managed to get temporarily assigned to A Battery for the rest of the Spring of '44 until called back to Battalion. It was long enough for both men to become best friends and many at Battalion HQ noticed the new moxy that Meyer displayed in doing his duties. Whenever Meyer spoke his mind at an officer's meeting, his superiors regretted the day they let him work with Green. He was often chided for "going Green" on them.

As he watched Meyer drive off, Green turned back to his immediate problems.

"Pryne!"

"Sir?"

"Keep your section ready to fire, but I am getting at least two sections ready to move out. I'm grabbing Darino, move Davis, Del Valle or whoever you think up to his place."

"Yessir."

"Biels!"

"Right here!" he shouted as he came running back.

"Go let Sergeants Mancini and Galt know that the move will probably have to wait till morning. Tell Mancini to pack up, but have Galt standby. I don't have an exact timetable yet."

As he spoke, he noticed Biels' calloused hands and a small trickle of blood coming from his right arm. In between assignments from his Exec, Biels had been fusing ammo nonstop. After an even closer look, he really looked like hell. Green was speechless for a second as he watched water drip from the rim of his helmet while trying to straighten out his crooked glasses.

"Go take care of yourself or else, got it? Especially that arm. I won't bother you for a while." he stated as roughly as he could. Then he saluted back.

"But I'm not bothered, sir. I mean…"

"That's an order."

"Yes, sir."

10

As Green spoke to the section chiefs, small arms fire erupted on the other side of the road behind the mess hall. Shouts from all over the perimeter began to rise. Flashes from the firing lit up the woods. The men at the guns became frozen in position, some wisely grabbed their carbines. Then more machine gun fire and more shouts. Green left his ever ubiquitous Thompson at the CP and he was sorry he had. Darino came up behind him.

"Sir?"

He noticed a look of concern on the lieutenant's face as he turned around.

"What was the firing sir?"

"I don't know." As he answered, Green pulled out his *.45*. Despite his own distaste for it, at least it was a weapon, something he could put his hands on. Shouts in English were emanating from out in the woods. A concerned Green ran down the gun line.

"Hold your fire!"

After several seconds of silence, out of the dim forest came two GIs, one in his field jacket and other in an overcoat, looking haggard, and wild-eyed. They were obviously not from the battalion; the M-1 Garand gave that away. Both groups were surprised to see each other. Green finally broke the silence and waved them over and they were eager to talk.

"Sir, a bunch of Krauts in white suits just came up on our flanks through the woods. Lots of MGs sir."

"How many exactly?"

"A whole lot," the taller exclaimed

"What happened to them?

"They ran off as soon as we poured fire on them. Scouts sir?"

"Probably. Who are you guys?"

"I'm from the 423rd, sir," the GI in the field jacket stated as he caught his breath.. "They told us to watch your perimeter for the time being. I'm corporal Bicknicki and this is Private Archer, from cannon company.

"423rd also, sir." Archer interjected.

"But we have guys from the 18th Cav out there too. Some engineers as well, sir." Bicknicki continued.

"Are we that scattered?"

"At least we are, sir."

"How many Krauts do you think you saw?"

"Who knows, sir. Around Bleialf, two companies maybe. Took over a couple of the buildings. There were some tanks or mobile artillery. Not sure what they were. They poured through the railroad tunnel. We fell back from our outpost into town, and then we started taking heavy fire from the houses near the station. Then we got trapped on the wrong side of the road leading out of Bleialf. The Germans had swung around us, and our artillery started pounding them. But that fire was falling on us too. So we headed due north, then into the woods and got onto the path leading here. Got a little lost. Had to go cross-country for a little bit until we got back in the woods. That's when we met an officer from B Battery, and told us to stay close until we got orders. Right after that we bumped into that Kraut patrol."

"Are you guys all enlisted?"

"Yessir. Only a couple of guys left from my squad. Healy, my BAR man and my sergeant are still back there. The sarge wanted to follow the Krauts for a little bit and then report back. My lieutenant was killed."

"Who was your lieutenant?" Green quickly asked the sergeant, dreading the reply.

"Waters, sir."

Immediately Bicknicki saw Green's expression change from curiosity to pain.

"Did you know him, sir?"

All Green could do was look away, let out a deep breath and keep from letting his emotions take over.

"Yeah, I knew him."

"Sorry, sir. He put up a hell of a fight around the house we were staying in. Told me to get back to the village with as many of the guys as I could grab. Covered us the whole way. One of the guys later told me he was caught by somebody's artillery."

"What else went on down there?"

"My Captain was killed too sir," Archer added.

"Who was that?"

"Manning, sir. Captain Manning. Some Kraut shot him from the upstairs of the dairy right in town there."

His shock had turned to frustration and now anger.

"I guess I should feel lucky. Is that the first group of Germans you ran into since you left Bleialf?"

"No, sir. They were just the closest. There seems to be small groups of Krauts all over. My squad has been falling back since all morning, picking up stragglers like Archer along the way. We thought we could meet up with a unit moving down toward Bleialf, but we never saw them. Instead, we got hit by these German snowmen and sort of cut off again."

"Are you still waiting on orders?"

"Yes, sir."

"Well, welcome to the 590th Field Artillery Battalion, corporal. We have some .50 cals I think you'd like."

"Thank you, sir…I guess?"

"Alright, I'll tell my Captain. You guys head back and tell your sergeant to see myself or Captain Peters when he can. Stay in touch. Do your best to keep that Kraut patrol from getting any closer. We may be moving out as well. We'll pass the word to the rest of the battalion. Oh, I'm Lt. Green."

"Yessir. We know. Thanks."

"Hey, any artillery observers from the 106th with you down there?"

"Not with us, sir. Our squad was in some farmhouse near the edge of town. We had Coloreds with us too. Nice guys. They were FOs from one of those Colored Artillery outfits or something."

"Do you know what happened them?"

"Sorry, sir. Not really. I know that Lieutenant Waters told them to reposition somewhere and try to get us some fire support. I don't know if they even made it out of town sir."

"Sir," Archer now perked up, his memory jogged. "I think I shared a smoke with one of the Colored troops at that cabin. This guy Turner told me he was part of the 333rd. "

"What about this cabin?"

"We headed there when the strange lights started, trying to get in touch with somebody at our HQ. That's when we met up with an observer. I think he said he was with the 590th."

"Was he alone?"

"Yessir. He said his crew was still at their OP somewhere east of there."

"What was he doing there?"

"Trying to get in touch with you guys, I think. He spoke to the Negro sergeant but I don't know about what exactly, sir. The guy I had a smoke with said they were headed back to their own CP."

"What time was this and when did you last see this guy from our outfit?" Green was now asking in a desperate tone.

"Maybe 0700, thereabouts, sir. He was still there when we started down towards the village around 0800."

"Okay. Thanks fellas. Our chow truck is still functioning. You're welcome to it."

With that, both men nodded and the two staggered back towards the woods.

"Alright Darino, get the vehicles ready again. Tell Mixon not to break up the entire motor park, just keep 'em all warm. But make sure every man has ammo for his carbine. Got me?"

"Yessir"

"I'm not waiting until we're surrounded. At this rate, we'll be overrun within hours."

"Goddamn, sir."

"Keep that to yourself. And be careful, guys are running all over and the Krauts are close now too. Get a truck and line it up for your section, but don't load up yet. We might be providing fire support through the night right here. And it might be direct fire too. How would like to see your targets, Arthur."

"That could get a little dangerous, sir."

"It could. Also, send someone down to the outpost. We can't get them on the phone again. Tell them to check in with us through the night. Find out exactly whose there. And I'll keep working on the phone line."

"Consider it done, sir."

Before Darino could run off, he grabbed him by the arm, lowering his voice.

"Hey, just in case, nothing of use should be left behind, understand? Even the personal stuff. I don't want to tell everyone that right away. But you understand?"

Darino just nodded.

"Okay, dismissed."

He struggled not to make these moves seem like they were running away or give the slightest hint of trouble. As far as he knew, they were taking the offensive. That's what he would portray to his men. Every command post in the area should have been informed that German armor was already charging up toward Schonberg. He had half his officers out there in the middle of an enemy onslaught. Green was seething. Good men were dying and no one seemed to know what the hell was happening.

11

As Green neared the CP, Captain Peters was on the newly established phone line to regiment, but straining to hear what was going on.

"Damn it, it's dead again. Don't we have any one-ten wire left, Monahan?" Peters shouted, but before he could answer, he moved on to another issue. "Green, by now you've heard we're definitely moving out?"

"I assumed so, sir. I have Darino passing the word but told him we're gonna keep a section or two in place for the night. Sir, did you hear the infantry guys ran into some Krauts in the woods to our right?"

"We heard the firing and saw some flashes. Even Monahan here grabbed his carbine for the first time. He's gonna go down with his radio."

As both men looked over at their favorite radioman, he acted as though he had not even heard them, lighting up another cigarette.

"Anyway, what happened?"

"Apparently a bunch of Krauts in white camouflage worked their way up to our perimeter. Once they got close, they hit them with everything they had and ran off."

"Which means they are close."

"Captain, Charlie Meyer also told me that there are Krauts running up toward Schonberg on the main road already."

"I know. Meadows just called and said they've had heavy German patrol activity on the main road."

"Charlie says it's heavy armor or self-propelled artillery. The whole show, sir."

Peters just shook his head in disgust.

"What units were these guys with?"

"A mix. I spoke to a guy from Cannon Company and an infantry corporal."

"Were they forced out of there?"

"Yeah, but they had even worse news sir."

Green now lowered his voice again.

"Jim Waters is dead, so is Manning from Cannon."

Peters was clearly stunned. He momentarily stared at Green, as a look of perplexed anxiety came over him.

"Jesus Christ, what the hell is going on down there?"

Green remained quiet for a second, knowing he was seeing something rare in his captain, a show of emotion. With typical style, Peters quickly regained his sense of duty.

"I'm sorry, Brendan. I know you and Jim were friends."

Unable to respond, taking a cue from Peters, he moved on to the living.

"And this guy from cannon company also told me he saw Meck at some cabin, at least he says it was an observer from the Battalion. It had to be him though, sir. The location is closer to Bleialf, but he was alone at that time. Guess he was trying to get in touch with us."

"Well, that's typical of him."

"I think I know where the place is, sir"

"Not now, Brendan. Stay put. If he can, he'll get in touch with us."

Frustrated, he struggled not to sound surly in his response.

"Well then, sir, have you heard anything new?"

"Hold on a second. Monahan, get me Battalion or Regiment again. Whoever you can find. In fact, call Major Tietze directly. He's assumed command of the Battalion for the next couple of hours. Have Hartman scrounge up some wire, will ya?"

"Sir, Hartman got run over by a jeep. Broke his foot. I'm having Biels take over Fifth section for now, maybe he could do it. Temporary promotion, so to speak."

"Now it's car accidents. Okay. Keep me posted on him. But find some wire guys and see what you can do. Okay, where was I? Oh, Lackey and Meadows are heading over for a meeting with Cavender."

Peters, still staring at his map, continued.

"Brendan, covering the withdrawal is going to be a real concern. I assume we are still going northwest. Nobody seems to know exactly. We might be firing on Bleialf all night. Apparently this Kraut attack is also hitting the other sectors hard as well. Sounds like we need to get observers along the road to Schonberg."

He paused for a moment, stepping away from his overlays.

"This is what happens when an outfit gets too spread out. Twenty damn miles. Ridiculous. For God's sakes, the Krauts have probably had their old bunkers zeroed since they were forced back in the fall. Should have asked an artilleryman. Well, so much for those noises we heard being 'recorded'. It doesn't take a military genius to see that. Better keep that Thompson of yours close by."

"Try to, sir."

Green nodded and gave a weak smile, thinking about what Waters had told him. "I guess intelligence sort of let us down sir."

"I second that motion, Green. But you know, we'll have to keep the second guessing to a minimum for now. Okay?"

Green nodded. Peters, although he didn't always show it, seemed to appreciate Green saying some things that young officers weren't suppose to say.

"I'm not looking forward to displacing in this weather. We'll have to use paths through the woods and some of the men will have to go on foot."

"I have Sergeant Pryne keeping the first section in tact until the others are ready to move out. And I have some of the men extending the perimeter, sir. At least that'll give us a few extra minutes in case more Kraut snowmen approach."

"Just a few. Now that the Germans have gotten close, they probably can relay where we are. I still think the Germans will hit us *88s* or their own *105s* at any time. Their counter battery fire as you can hear, has been sporadic so far. That's probably by design. Eventually they'll get us bracketed and walk their fire right on top of us. They have just been opening pathways for their infantry up till now."

"It sounds like that job has been done."

"What about ammo?"

"Getting low. Couple of hundred rounds, maybe. That's with smoke. Luckily, the ammo pits have remained untouched by enemy fire."

"I'll call Captain Fonda. See what he's got."

Both men suddenly stopped and glanced skyward at the whistle of a lone shell flying over and landing harmlessly back in the woods.

"*88*s?"

"No, *105*s. The *88*s don't whistle. It just sounds like they're tearing papers or something. First of many, I assume. They have a flat trajectory. Anyway, they say if you can hear the whistle, you are probably okay."

"I've heard them both several times today, Brendan, but I still don't want to take any chances. There's always a first time."

"I understand, sir. I never got used to it."

"Alright, I will let the other battery commanders know what is going on. Maybe we can divvy supplies up amongst ourselves. I also don't know how we can all get on the road at the same time without being sitting ducks. Spread the trucks out and all the other vehicles for that matter. We don't want to lose everything in one shelling. But let's get one section hooked up just in case. We're low on ammo anyway."

"I have the men doing it right now.

"Any word on Grey?"

Despite knowing that the question was coming, it still hurt when he heard it.

"No, sir. I talked to Charlie Meyer and asked him to keep an eye out."

"Look, I know your kicking yourself about Grey and Mecklenberg."

"I'm okay, sir. Really…"

"I don't think you are. But listen, our only responsibility now is to the men right here. I may be talking out of line here, and you being a veteran and all…"

Green knew where the conversation was headed, and seized the opportunity to interrupt.

"Captain, I got ya. Don't worry."

After a long, hard stare, Peters finally decided to end the conversation.

"Alright, it's almost 1600 hours. Let's hope we know something in an hour."

12

GREEN STOOD OUTSIDE THE CP still struggling with his emotions. Lighting up his fifth cigarette of the day was proof positive of that. He had not had this many smokes in one day since Sicily. Peters was right. He knew it.

As he walked down the gun line, he could see the first of the guns being hooked up. The men struggled to maintain their footing while lifting up the trailer spades from the mire, the squish and sucking sound of their boots as well as their collective groans, a testimony to their struggle. The men's' pants were darkened and stuck to their legs from the soaking they were taking. Helmets fell off and the back of many a jacket was coated in a thick morass. The motor section guys were still moving the trucks to keep them from seeping into the mire. The shouts to Davis and Greeley to get their 'dumb hick asses' out of the way were strangely comforting to all who heard them.

As if on cue, the whistle of more shells could be heard overhead, but this time, they seemed a lot closer. All the men stopped to look up. Then the explosions began right amongst them. Amid the shouts of 'incoming' and 'hit the dirt,' Green dove for a pit near the first section to find Biels and Greeley already there. Others just hit the ground and hoped for the best. One shell landed so close it deafened Green and his trench companions momentarily. Tree bursts and shrapnel rained down on them. The shelling appeared to have stopped until another volley tore open through the sky with a *whoosh*, followed by the inevitable *crump!*

The ground felt as though it would split beneath them. Greeley screamed in pain. As Green stuck his head up, he could taste the dirt and feel the heat of the explosions. The sickening smell of cordite and sulphur pierced his nostrils. His lungs filled with smoke. There had been a hit on an ammunition pile. A towering flame was sent high into the sky, searing heat burned all around them. Subsequent explosions occurred in seconds as it ignited a chain reaction among the shells, sending hot metal shards whirring down the gun line. Men grimaced in pain and grabbed their heads; the blast had broken some eardrums.

As the smoke cleared, the CP finally came into view, a pile of rubble lay where one of its walls had been. Monahan lay upright on the ground right beside the pile clutching his arm and, yelling for help. With the ringing in his ears and the coughing, Green could hardly hear him. His right ear in particular was giving off a piercing ache. A huge splinter had cut into his jacket, right down to the skin. After yanking it out, instinct took over and Green jumped up to help. Shouts of medic were heard everywhere. Greeley was kneeling on the edge of the trench, holding his head. Blood ran from his right ear.

"Hold on Greeley," he shouted and tapped him on the shoulder. He grabbed Pryne and told him to take care of his young charge.

Garcia came running over.

"Sir, over by the mess hall. It's the Captain! He's been hit and Pritchard too!" he shouted, not knowing if Green could hear yet. His ear pain subsiding, he took off running across the road to the mess hall.

Captain Peters was lying face down in the dirt, his legs under a pile of plaster and wood. Everyone yelled for medics. Green knelt down to see if Peters was still alive. The captain had a faint pulse but was not moving. Green threw the debris off his legs and rolled him over. There were obvious wounds to his cheek. Trickles of blood ran from beneath the caked mud on his face. His helmet had been blown off, but there was no sign of a head wound. Bleeding was sparse. No response came from Peters. The medics arrived and went into action, carefully lifting him on a litter and laying him on the back of a jeep.

"I can't even find where he has been hit."

"He's alive sir, but barely. The concussion alone can kill sir. There might be a bunch of small wounds too. He might have a broken neck, sir."

The medic ripped open the Captain's shirt to reveal three small holes. Hot metal had just ripped into him, tearing up the insides but no exit wound. He was bleeding internally. Green saw the medic point out the wounds and remembered having seen it all before.

"Where is the new aid station going to be?" Green asked the medic in charge.

"I don't know sir. We're moving out, but I guess we will have to bring him over to the Battalion aid in Radscheid, sir."

A stunned Green realized now that whether Peters survived or not, he would not be back. His thoughts turned to Pritchard.

"Pritchard! Hey Biels! Take a look around for Pritchard. I can't find him."

From the woods behind the building, shouts of 'medic' arose. One of the other men found the mangled body of the clerk lying just along the tree line. The blast had thrown him almost fifty feet. The medics wouldn't do him any good except for taking care of the body. His lanky body lay grotesquely twisted around the base of tree, legs turned almost behind his back. The arms were stretched out as though begging the tree to protect him to no avail. Pritchard's jacket and pants had been shredded in the blast and his black hair singed. Green knelt down to confirm he was dead. The medics arrived and peeled him away from the base of the tree. As they turned him over, the men could see that his left eye was missing and blood was pouring out of the socket. A crowd had gathered around and when Green saw this he snapped up.

"Get back to your positions until I tell you otherwise! Move it."

It pained him to snap like that, albeit by design. The men cared and wanted to help. But he was now in charge, however reluctantly, and keeping their heads about them was the biggest concern right now.

Biels instinctively stayed behind. The two bodies were the first combat casualties Biels and most of the men had seen. But the private remained composed, ready to assist his lieutenant. Green stared mournfully at the medics as they lifted Pritchard onto a stretcher. Most of the trees around them had been laid bare by the blasts and their bark had been ripped up. Even in the dim light, white marks could be seen on the trunks where they had been torn by shrapnel.

"Biels, find out where he bunked and get his gear together," he told him in a very low voice. "Do it quickly and quietly. When you're done, bring it to me. I'll take care of the Captain's stuff too. I don't now when the supply guys will arrive. At least we'll have it ready. Talk to the medics when you have a minute. I want a casualty tally as soon as possible."

Biels nodded and was on his way.

Green stood and watched the medic's jeep haul Pritchard's body and the barely alive Peters away. Pritchard was just another one of those smart young kids who seemed to inhabit artillery command posts and did their job without much notice. His weapon had been the pen.

"Sir, I need your help!"

It was one of the medics waving him over. Monahan was still on sitting against the debris of the CP. Green arrived to see his radioman waving at the aid men to leave him alone. From the looks of things, he needed help. His face had some cuts and bruises, and streaks of blood were still fresh. His left eye was all puffy from getting hit by flying debris. The only real serious wound was a chunk that was slashed out of his upper left arm, but still hanging on by a piece of skin. He was holding a blood-soaked bandage to it.

"Monahan, let the medics help you." Green barked.

"Sir, I will be fine. I was outside of the building and far enough away when the shell hit. You're in charge now and you need a good radio man. Besides sir, you been hit as well."

'It's just a splinter."

Green stood there, took a deep breath and waved the medical personnel off for a second. He then reached in his jacket for two cigarettes and lit them both, shoving the other one in Monahan's mouth.

"Listen, you dumb Irishman, at least let them finish wrapping your head properly and arm, okay? Then you can get back to your post."

There were a few seconds of silence, almost a lifetime for Monahan, as he inhaled deeply. A realization seemed to finally hit him as he looked at his executive officer.

"Okay, Lieutenant. As long as there's no goin' to the aid station. Go ahead guys, do your thing," he mumbled through the cigarette, smoke exiting his nostrils.

With that, they descended on him with gauze, sulphur and iodine swabs.

There were still men running around, straightening out since the shelling. But word would spread fast about their Captain being gone. The realization of the task ahead began to sink in and Green thought about what his first order would be. Darino's familiar voice snapped him out of any deep thoughts.

"Lieutenant, sir, is it true about the Captain?"

"Yes it is. I'll have to check with Battalion now and see if the move is still on. Maybe we can wait until first light."

"We have almost have two sections packed. Waiting on the fourth. I guess you are the new commander now, sir?"

"Just think of it as temporary, Corporal. I have no news yet. Must find a radio. First section must remain in tact until further orders. We may have to conduct counter battery if this keeps up. I hate to tell you this, but the whole battery might have to drop trails again right here. Get going. Find me as soon as you're done."

"Yessir," Darino smartly replied, snapped a quick, but unusual salute, and was gone.

He decided quickly that his main task as the de facto commander of the battery would be to get the hell out of this mess, orders be damned. The Army knew it as a 'strategic withdrawal,' their technical term for it. Getting away from a trap was what concerned Green. He knew his claustrophobic nightmares would return. Already his throat felt like it had two hands around it. The horror of being buried alive in a shelling had stayed on his mind. It took every ounce of his energy to keep from shaking sometimes. But the ring was tightening and he to do something.

"Garcia!"

"Sir?"

"Get over to B battery. Take my jeep. Let them know that our communications are down again along with our CP. Also, ask around about Lieutenant Grey. Make sure you let them know about the Captain and the possibility of Kraut observers in the vicinity. Take somebody with you. Grab Del Valle."

He saluted and jumped in the closest jeep.

What's with all their salutes? I better put a stop to that.

As the jeep finally peeled away, another one came barreling down the narrow lane. The speed of the jeep always seemed to be a measure of the importance of its passengers. It pulled right up to Green as he was siphoning through what was left of the CP.

"Green!"

He turned around and there was Major Meadows, the Battalion S-3.

"Sir," Green gave an automatic crisp salute.

"Is Peters dead?"

"No, sir. He's in bad shape. I lost one man from the CP and there a couple more wounded. They should be fine."

Green always hesitated using the men's names even back in the States. He worried that that would be making it too personal for the upper echelon. Maybe they cared and maybe they didn't, but he would play it safe. Short and sweet was the motto when in conversation with anyone above Captain.

"I'll send Charlie Meyer back down. Where are your other officers?"

"Lieutenant Mecklenberg was on observer duty, sir. We last heard from him early this afternoon. And I sent Grey to Schonberg this morning. He's not been heard from since, sir."

The gravity of A Battery's predicament clearly registered on Meadows' face. His raised eyebrows and tired eyes betrayed his outward sternness.

"Alright. I'll be back when I can. We haven't talked to Division HQ in over two hours. Be ready to move out at a moment's notice. Watch your perimeter tonight."

"Sir, are we moving back toward Schonberg?"

"Not yet. We still have men up on those hills."

"But sir…"

Meadows knew what was coming and wanted no part of it, quickly tapping his driver on the shoulder.

"Take care, Lieutenant. I will keep you posted on Peters."

"Yes, sir. Thank you."

With that, the Major hopped back in the jeep and commanded his driver to head for B Battery.

That last promise would be hard to keep, he knew. Peters was now one of many wounded men sitting at a Battalion aid station. And Meadows had an entire Battalion to check on. But strangely, he appreciated the words.

13

December 17, 0600 Hours, HQ 333rd FAB, Schonberg-Andler Road, Belgium

FINALLY, AFTER A LONG DAY and night of trying to keep busy and then get some sleep at the HQ, Jackson and Turner got orders.

"Jackson," Captain Roberts, S-2 adjutant grumbled, "go with the wire crew. They are heading down toward those positions held by the 106th. Getting into Bleialf is probably still a no go. We're going to try and establish new lines from 423rd and 422nd, so as their artillery displaces, they'll be able to contact us for support. But while you're down there, see if you can get info on Lieutenants Gibson and King. It's been a while since we've heard anything from them. Take Turner with you and a working radio. Stay in regular contact. Check your weapons too. We have reports of Krauts everywhere. But Division wants to keep our C battery east of the river. I've heard that some elements of the 589th are displacing west of the river as we speak. But we're not sure where they are right now. We might be moving out as well. Just be prepared to be gone a long time. I can't stress enough to maintain frequent radio contact with us."

"Yes sir, that's why I got Turner," was his enthusiastic reply and ran over to Due, who was just lighting up near the mess truck.

"Due! Let's go. We're heading' out."

"Goddamn it. I jus' got mah damn clothes dry. 'Nother cold ass mo'nin wit you."

"You know, if you weren't such a great radioman, I'd..."

Turner cut him off.

"I know college boy, I know."

To add insult to injury, it was another hour before they got going. Their jeep would not start. But they found their old three-quarter ton truck. Finally around 0700, they hit the road.

The small band consisted of seven men. Jackson and Turner were in their observation truck and a wire truck followed. A new replacement, Private Quarrles, joined them. Jackson had his carbine pointed to his right as he sat in the front. Quarrels was ordered to keep an eye out for the Germans, especially after they turned left onto the road towards Bleialf. The wind had picked up and snow flurries began swirling around them. It was turning into a slow, very bumpy ride.

Rumors of Krauts jumping from the woods had everyone on edge. For right now though, it was just a flood of vehicles moving back toward St. Vith that was beginning to clog the roads. Random American troops could be seen filtering past. Most in some semblance of order. There was the occasional panicked driver in a rush to get over the stone bridge that cut Schonberg in half. Fear and shock registered on many of the men's faces. Jackson tried to study them, a dangerous thing for any black man to do, but he could not fight the urge. He thought he made eye contact with some; for the most part, they just stared straight ahead.

He saw a colonel from the 81st Engineers, a roughhewn and red-faced man, calmly shouting orders in the middle of a traffic circle and getting his men organized while standing on the hood of a jeep. The man was soaking wet, and obviously had not slept in a while, but still made an imposing sight. No helmet, no gloves. All he wore was his Army issue five-button sweater and wool cap. As he drove by, Jackson saluted sharply on instinct. There was a man who deserved our respect, he thought.

"Glad to see somebody going in the right direction. Let 'em through!"

The colonel just smiled, and returned the salute.

Jackson tried to focus on something else than the danger that awaited them, taking in the natural beauty around him. No matter the weather or how many times he had driven on these roads, nothing dampened the view for him. The echoing sounds of battle in the distance erased any thoughts of a nice Sunday drive though. It was almost eight o'clock. Sounds of machine gun fire and mortars began echoing down from the Andler area.

"We should check in with HQ as soon as possible."

"Why?"

"You hear that noise. That sounds like it's comin' frum up near C Battery. We gotta know what's going on."

"Ain't nuthin' we can do right now. I'll check when we reach whir we goin'."

With that said, he tried anything to cure his unease.

"Quarrles, where you frum? How come I don't know you already?"

"I just arrived at the battalion three days ago as a replacement volunteer, Sergeant. I'm from Detroit."

Due rolled his eyes at the word 'volunteer.'

"What did you do in Detroit?"

"I worked at my dad's dry cleaning business. It was pretty busy. I was trying to save up money for college."

Due let out an exasperated breath.

"Not another one. Volunteer? What fo'? I'm surprised they didn't make you a houseboy fo' some cracka officer when dey found you was a dry cleaner. Ya know, like 'Here Boy, fold this shirt for me,' ya know, shit like that. Mo' starch in my shirts, boy.'"

"Well, I volunteered for this. My dad and I played some with radios growin' up, so I thought this might be interesting. Beat driving a truck I guess. In Detroit, police were arrestin' every Negro they could find since the riots last summer. So it was jail or the Army. Glad I'm not there."

"Radio expert too." Turner was even more indignant now. "We got ourself an expert here Sergeant Jackson. And you happy you not home?"

"Easy Due."

"You boys up north always be riotin' or sumpin'. You know, like you gonna get somewhere with that. They ain't given us nothin'."

"You best be quiet. I could make him drive."

"Ain't no college boy gonna drive me 'round. Hum."

"Hey Quarrles, who else is back there in the truck? I don't recognize them."

"The only one I know is Corporal Stokes."

Due's eyes light up and spun his body around.

"Stoke! You back there. Sneaky. How I miss 'im?"

Turner became animated, a rare occurrence, stopping the car.

"Hey Stoke! Happenin' Man, where mah winnins'?"

Stokes, who was close to thirty, and looked twice that old, just waved back with a smile.

"No wonder you not talkin'!"

"Excuse me, Corporal Turner, we need to keep it moving."

"Mmm. I tell you Emmett, still wondah 'bout you."

The road finally began to clear and the small rise that led away from town came into view. A convoy of vehicles was coming down. They were waving frantically at the Jackson and his men. The convoy stopped as an angry and very husky lieutenant came running out.

"Get these things turned around Sergeant. We got orders to set up west of the Our in Schonberg. There might be Krauts right behind us. Pull it over to the side of the road."

"We got orders, sir. Some of our men are still in Bleialf."

"Look Sergeant, I don't care what your goddamn orders are. There is no way in hell you'll get wire hooked up out there. The Krauts will get you before you make one connection. Now pull over and get behind our convoy. I got artillery to get over the river. Then you could work with us. We'll be glad to have you."

"You heard the man, Emmett," Turner whispered. "He right, 'cept 'bout that '*bein' glad to have you shit*."

A mournful look came over Emmett. He knew this hard-charging lieutenant was right. Reluctantly, he abandoned his mission.

"Alright. Do it."

The two vehicles obediently pulled over and watched as the two and a half ton trucks struggled on, weighted down both by the men inside and their 105mm howitzers towed in the back. As he stood by the side of the road, Emmett looked uphill and saw a gun sitting at a right angle by the side of the road. It was obviously stuck in the mud. The driver had swung too wide. The crew was struggling to get some chains on it and pull it out. He also noticed the markings on their trucks, 'A/589'.

"Hey Due, we got some room along the shoulder here. Pull it over some more. Let's go help them boys out. At least it will keep us warm."

"Mah Chesterfield is keepin' me warm right here."

"I know. It's my college boy ways. Let's go."

"We prob'ly gonna git stuck here jus' like dem. Got t'keep movin', Emmett. You heard that Lieutenant."

Jackson, ignoring his friend's warnings, signaled to the men in the other truck what was happening. They made their way through the mud, struggling to keep from sliding back down the hill.

"Hey you guys need a hand?"

There was silence for a few seconds. The surprised men, clearly wet and exhausted, just raised their eyebrows until their lieutenant spoke up.

The silence spoke volumes. Emmett had seen the looks before. This was not a time to make new friends. Some had probably never spoken to a black man before. Then the silence was finally broken by a more decisive presence.

"Why not. Jump in. Make room fellas! I'm Lieutenant Wood, 589th Field Artillery. I should have introduced myself earlier."

Wood reached out to shake hands, much to Jackson's surprise.

"Over there is one of my section chiefs, Sergeant Scannapico and our driver, Ken Knoll."

Both men showed the strain of the past two days, but still looked up to wave hello and crack a warm smile.

Jackson was more than pleased.

"Alright, you heard the man. Let's go."

With their help, they finally dug enough room around the wheels of the gun, and hooked it up to the back of the truck. It took almost an hour. The air was still cold but the wind died down. It suddenly fell very quiet until some of the men heard the clanking of tank treads somewhere. Then just as their sense of accomplishment sunk in, *wrack*! Shells began falling amongst them, some smashed into the trees. The men jumped in the nearest ditch. Jackson ran back to try and grab their radio. Another shell exploded just down the road. As showers of hot steel filled the air, Emmett continued to try and secure his equipment.

"Dammit Emmett. Fuck the radio! You never learn nuthin', man. Les go!"

Another close shell drove Jackson away and next to Turner, right by the edge of the trees.

There was a thunderous explosion as one of the 589th's trucks was hit and then the observation truck was completely blown up into the air, landing in two pieces and on fire right in the middle of the road.

Wood began shouting at the men to 'Load up!'.

""Hey, you men," Wood shouted as ran down the line, "load up now! Get in that last truck! That was a Panzer, not artillery!"

The truck was pulling away as Jackson was trying to get his feet up. Quarrles and Turner were the last two, but it looked like they weren't going to make it. In the distance, a German self-propelled artillery piece came out of a large firebreak to turn onto the road behind them. Emmett screamed for the truck to stop. Finally, one of the men banged on the cab, yelling for the driver to hold up.

"What the fuck for? Are you nuts?" shouted the angry driver.

It was enough time to get Due and Quarrles up. Due had leapt onto the barrel of the howitzer in order to get away. But the young private had a bad wound to his leg from a machine gun opening up on them. He was dragged in bleeding but okay.

They had now fallen behind the rest of the convoy. It was just the two trucks left trying to make it down the hill into Schonberg and over the Our.

"Hey, where's the lieutenant?"

"He's in the lead truck, holding onto the driver's side mirror until we get past town. Looks like he's almost at the bridge now."

Jackson turned around in the open truck to see Wood waving frantically to the driver as he hung on with one arm to the truck's side mirror. As they crossed the stone bridge, it appeared that the way was clear. Then the long barrel of a tank turned the corner. The trucks slowed. Lieutenant Wood was shouting that it was okay, it was a Sherman. His vehicle started across the span.

The driver was unconvinced and slowed. As the tank made the turn, it was clear he had been right. They had a split second to duck after the flash of the gun appeared. A shell landed right along side the first truck. The driver pulled over and looked back for his lieutenant. Wood immediately began shouting orders as he ran to the back towards the trucks, pulling everyone out that he could. He then took off back to the front of the column across the bridge. Jackson realized they were trapped on the wrong side of the river.

"Get out! Grab that bazooka we have in the back and form up across the road," came orders from the sergeant who was driving. We gotta get across that bridge!"

Due and Emmett watched in stunned silence. They looked back but the other tank had not caught up with them. A horde of German infantry was now pouring out of Schonberg and coming up the rise. Their route was completely blocked. His driver turned off the road, grabbed his carbine and jumped out. There were a couple of infantryman in the truck that no one had noticed. The hard clicking sound of their eight-shot cartridges being loaded into their Garands made the artillerymen envious. There was a large field off to their left with an irrigation ditch cutting it in half. Most of the men dove into there. Small arms fire began ripping into the men still in the truck. One of the infantrymen got hit and fell dead onto the road, blood pouring from his mouth. Jackson checked the body, picked up his rifle, and ran in the opposite direction. He made it to a truck that had slammed into a large tree. More and more bullets ripped into the dirt around him as he began climbing up a small rise, desperately trying to reach the trees. The mud just sucked him down and he slid right back to where the truck lay.

Jackson yelled for Turner, but he was helping Quarrles and the other men get down into the field. All Jackson could do was lay on his stomach watching the action from beneath the truck. He peered back down the road, knowing another tank was on its way. Shells blasted craters amongst those trapped in the field and tracers ripped the air right over their heads. Several of them could not get to their feet before they were cut down. He wanted to scream as he watched Due, standing ramrod straight, until ripped to shreds by the tank's machine gun. The men left alive began waving their arms; some removed their helmets to signal that they were giving up. Panic set in for Jackson; he felt helpless. He began crawling up the hill.

It was quiet for a few seconds until he heard the German shouts of '*Halt*!' and machine gun fire tore the silence. Bullets began kicking up the dirt around him. Finally he reached the crest. The Germans had stopped shooting. Even on his stomach, Jackson could see the streets of Schonberg and beyond. Just past the last houses, he could make out one lone American soldier, carbine still in hand, running for the trees north of town while machine gun fire tore the ground around him. He managed to make it to the woods and freedom, at least for now.

Jackson gripped the Garand tighter, desperate for an escape route. There was only one choice, through the woods behind him. The Germans could not see him. Thick black smoke billowed all around. As he made his way up the small rise deeper into the trees, Jackson waited for the inevitable shots to ring out. Nothing happened. With all the prisoners to round up, they must have gotten distracted. Suddenly the whir of a shell ripped the air. There was only a split second before a shell blasted into the trees to his right. Something hit him between the shoulders, knocking him down the other side of the knoll. Everything went black.

14

Monday, December 17, 1944. 0700 hours, Battery A Command Post, Village of Oberlascheid

AFTER A RESTLESS, CONFUSED NIGHT, orders came for a close-in concentration on Sellerich. The 423rd needed all the fire that the Battalion had at its disposal. Green had stuck to Peters' plans leaving only sections one and two on call for fire missions. Another twelve rounds were used, taking their supply of shells well below a hundred and fifty. Green put a call through to Battalion, and to his surprise, actually spoke to Major Meadows himself. Although Meadows listened respectfully to his pleas, Green could tell the Major was trying to placate him until the supply picture became clearer.

Sporadic firing had occurred during the night while Bugner relieved Monahan for a spell on the radio and phone. The activity kept everyone's mind off the Battery's first losses. As soon as the cease fire order had been given, there was an extended lull in activity. Much of their gear had been loaded. Some men grabbed some sleep when and where they could, although that was in short supply too. It looked like another day of living off adrenaline and D ration bars.

As the cold, misty dawn took hold, a few rounds from a carbine could be heard. Then shouts. Green rushed out from the CP to hear someone yelling 'Armored' without a reply. Then a weak 'Knight' was heard. It was Grey's voice. Green rushed across the road. The young lieutenant was emerging from the woods on the verge of collapse, hunched over and clutching his shoulder.

"What happened Ernie? Where's Mullins?"

"He's dead," Grey replied weakly, letting out a deep breath and struggling to stay on his feet. His crimson face was a testament to the icy wind of the previous night. A small trickle of blood ran from the right corner of his mouth. There was a deep gash in his right cheek and his right eye was almost swollen shut.

Green shouted for some blankets. One of the mess cooks rushed over with some coffee and Biels came over with blankets.

"I'm sorry, Brendan. Been walking all night. Can't believe I found you guys."

"Take your time, Dick. Can you grab the cup? It'll warm your hands. Medic!"

"On the way back from Schonberg, we came around the first turn and there was a German patrol. Mullins couldn't stop in time. I shouted to get off the road. He made a right turn and we slammed into some trees. Then the Krauts opened up on us. Mullins took the brunt of the hits. He fell right into my lap."

"Catch your breath," Green cautioned as he looked down at Grey's blood-stained pants and jacket. The blood was pooling at his left shoulder.

"I leapt to the ground and then got up to run. I got hit…," he was struggling to talk, grimacing with every breath. "It's my shoulder. But I lost my helmet when I took off. Sorry, Brendan."

Grey was now gasping loudly. The warm blood was still oozing out. His shivering became more violent.

"Medic!"

"We'll get you to the aid station. You should be fine."

"I'm sorry… about Mullins."

"It's not your fault. Be quiet, that's an order."

"Medic!"

In frustration at the lack of response, he decided to drive to the aid station himself, when Biels drove up in a jeep.

"I got him, sir."

Green looked at Biels with a blank stare. He appeared to be lost in thought.

"I got him, sir." Biels had to repeat again, this time gently grabbing his Lieutenant by the arm.

Mullins held up his right arm trying to get Green's attention.

"Brendan," he labored to say.

"Relax Grey, what is it?"

Green placed him in the back of the jeep, before letting him speak.

"I ran into another bunch of Krauts in an American jeep parked along one of the firebreaks. Think it was four of them. Wearing white. At least two of them had GI helmets on. I was about to approach them down when…I realized they were talking in German. Near the Auw road."

"Okay Dick, we got it. Don't worry."

Green tapped the back of the jeep.

"Get moving Biels, and then back here as soon as you can. Be careful. And stop by HQ and let them know about the Lieutenant."

Green was now out of officers and time. He looked up to the hills surrounding him and now realized they were probably full of Germans, in many different uniforms, even American. Out of the corner of his eye, he noticed someone staring. When he turned, it was Wallenbach, who had obviously overheard the whole encounter with Grey. Mullins getting killed was probably shaking him up more than anyone else. But all Green could do is turn away, realizing he did not know either of their first names. Before turning back, he decided that he should get to know his young replacement.

"Hey Wallenbach," he hollered, waving him over.

He didn't move right away, looking almost fearful to come over. Finally he took his steps.

"Sir?"

"What's your first name?"

"Miles, sir."

"Miles? I'm sorry I couldn't remember. You're new, and that's my very weak excuse."

"It's okay, sir."

"Where you from?"

"Buffalo, sir. Really Tonawanda, but I just tell the guys it's Buffalo. Lot easier."

As he spoke he shuffled his feet to keep them warm. He was shivering and just kept staring straight ahead at the woods. Although he wanted to make eye contact, Green refrained, opting to just keep talking.

"Oh, so we are sort of fellow New Yorkers. Sort of."

"It's a little different up there."

Both men then continued to stare in silence into the woods until Green thought of something else to say.

"What did you do before you joined this outfit?"

"I was in the Air Corps, an armorer with a B-17 squadron back in the States. Mullins was too."

"Air Corps? That's a pretty good gig. How did you end up a Golden Lion?"

"They came around two months ago and asked for volunteers for the ground forces. My buddy went, so I decided it was the brave thing to do. Neither of us qualified for flight duty. Our squadrons showed no sign of going overseas anytime soon, so we wanted to be in the war. After our training, I thought we would both end up as dogfaces somewhere together. But my pal got sent to Italy and I ended up at a Repple Depple in England. Figured since I got assigned to the artillery, I thought I would be okay. At least that's what I told my mother."

His voice was starting to crack.

"I forgot you didn't join us until we got overseas. Yeah, the Army is sort of strange that way, Private. Plans always get screwed up and you end up learning on the job. Story of my life."

Over the past twenty four hours, Green had been reminded constantly of the things they did not teach you at OCS. One of them was dealing with death. That was a skill strictly learned on the job. Finally, Green turned to the young man, his voice a little sterner that it had been in the past.

"Well, why don't you get back to whatever you were doing. What is it you were doing?"

"We're still supposed to be cleaning the guns, sir, and they told me to go get some anti-freeze to put in the water."

"Best idea I've heard all morning. Get going."

As he watched the lanky Wallenbach quickly walk away, he remembered the old adage to never volunteer.

15

AROUND 1100 HOURS, WORD FINALLY came from Charlie Meyer that they were to move out. A sense of excitement rose among the men when they heard they would be heading west, but it would take a while. Division wanted to avoid a logjam on the roads. The Battalion would be following on the heels of the 589th, which had started its move early this morning. Before they could make it through Schonberg, A Battery was ordered to drop trails on the other side of the Auw road, near Hill 575, in order to support Lieutenant Colonel Puett's 2nd Battalion of the 423rd as they helped guard the 589th's rear. Once that mission was accomplished, they were to drive down to the Engineer's cutoff, and head to Schonberg. Within a short time of their arrival at the hill, word began trickling down about the 589th running into trouble at the Our crossing. By mid-afternoon, anxiety began to reign among the ranks again as the reality of the situation took hold. As Green expected, and much to his chagrin, the batteries got word to move southeast towards the high ground in close consultation with the 423rd. Although he knew that was coming, it still made him livid. Despite his deep affection for the infantry, Green felt that he really could not do much to help them, unless they issued all his men M-1 Garands and machine guns.

They were to set up positions near Halenfeld in order to eliminate any counter-battery fire and cover the withdrawal of the infantry entrenched up on the Schnee. This would allow Colonel Cavender to consolidate his forces. Orders were supposed to come down about an eventual counterattack, so everyone guessed with some confirmation from Charlie Meyer, that this move was very temporary.

The rest of the day and night on the 17th, it was stop and start. The trucks were moved up close to the guns just before a fire mission. Then as soon as the mission was over, they hooked up and moved, even if just a half a mile or so. The Germans seemed to have them zeroed. Almost every time they dropped trails, there was incoming.

As another dull, gray day dawned on the 18th, German fire increased. The 590th and elements of other units were ordered back toward Schonberg, as expected. The village was now in German hands. The pincer movement had sealed the roads to St. Vith shut. The artillery would now be firing to the north and west for their own survival. By attacking Schonberg, a desperate Division HQ hoped to relieve some of the pressure now building on St. Vith. Some of the men began to feel like sacrificial lambs.

It was another day of fire and move, leapfrogging with the infantry throughout the afternoon. The battery even ended up in their old position at Oberlascheid for a time. Finally orders came to move out towards Schonberg again. As the move got under way just before dark, the other batteries and part of his own inadvertently fell behind. It was easy to get lost using the side roads, which were more like paths.

Traveling back, the chaos of fighting a war in the throes of winter became abundantly clear. The excitement that had accompanied the opening of battle had given way to a dull lassitude among the men who now huddled in the back of those trucks. Some continued to thrive on the chaos, while others just recoiled at the thought of a third day of futility. The infantry guys walking along the road were wild eyed, telling stories about the hordes of Germans that had been sighted along with some tanks. Many of the men had not even seen a German but had heard the firing and listened intently to the reports that were being circulated among them. Morale seemed to be holding steady, but doubts were creeping into their minds. The feeling was that one strong thrust up towards the village could cause a breakthrough. Whether the commanders shared this confidence, no one was exactly sure. The aid stations for both infantry regiments, located near the constantly moving regimental command posts, were beginning to fill up.

The trip was supposed to be only a few miles, but soon Green's convoy was alone, slogging through an old logging road, still trying to go cross country, thereby avoiding the threat of attack by roving bands of snow suited Germans. He assumed many of the infantrymen had taken the same routes. But to keep up, they had to cross the Auw-Bleialf road, where the convoy could be broadsided if caught in the open.

The night, that had begun cold and clear, was turning ugly as a freezing rain began to fall. Within a short time, this would turn to snow. Coming to another narrow turn, two jeeps were stopped at a bend, with one of the men waving his arms. Green knew right away it was Charlie Meyer.

"What's a matter Charlie, need directions?"

"No, just checking on my favorite battery's movements. Can we tag along? I'll get behind the last trucks or whatever."

"Sure, glad to have you." Green replied, as he jumped out his own jeep to stretch his legs.

"Any more news that you can confirm?"

Meyer thought for a minute, and carefully chose his words.

"It looks like there is now heavy pressure west of Schonberg. We have reports of the 592nd opening on the St. Vith road around Hueum."

"When was that? So they made it out?"

"Around 0900 this morning. Weber made the decision to pull back across the river late Saturday night and McMahon concurred."

"That long ago? What the hell is going on up there?"

"I haven't heard anything in a while. Division apparently got word from some colonel who was on the road when the Krauts were pouring through.

"St. Vith is already under attack? So the Krauts have the bridges."

"Setz is also gone. There was an engineer outpost there."

"Who was the Colonel and what happened to him?"

"Not sure. I know the 81st is up there. So maybe it was Colonel Riggs. By the way, how are you fixed for ammo?"

"Ten, maybe fifteen rounds. A lot of those probably smoke."

"Well, from what I hear the whole battalion has less 200 rounds left. So make them count."

"I always try."

"There is also word that the Krauts may have another armored roadblock southeast of Schonberg. So there won't be any clear path into the village. We'll have to stay off the main road altogether and set up positions on those hills. So keep your eyes open for the rest of the outfit."

"Shit. What about up north?"

"Nothing confirmed. Radio traffic is scattered. Supposedly, the 99th got hit pretty hard too. The 14th Cav is still scattered. Some of them have ended up with us. The Krauts have been seen all over the Losheim Gap area."

"We've been pinched haven't we?"

Although it was obvious, Meyer wanted to avoid admitting to their precarious position.

"But they're talking about airdrops for all of us and a counterattack."

"Airdrops? By who, Santa? Not in this weather. Have any of the 589th passed through here?"

"None that I've seen. A bunch tried to punch through Schonberg earlier, but there has been no further word on them. Colonel Kelly has been trying to get an accurate report on where everybody is since he showed up at our HQ, but one of his batteries has not been heard from in some since early yesterday. There are reports that before they displaced, Wood's battery may have taken out a tank with direct fire."

"Well, that's some good news. Have any outfits tried to come down from St. Vith?"

"I really don't know, Brendan," Meyer finally snapped. "I'm in Operations, not the S-2, remember? Hey, let's keep to the task at hand. I'm cold, standing in almost ankle deep mud. Do you where we are heading?"

"Okay, okay. Feel like I've been cooped up in the forest for too long. Well, I know the vicinity we are supposed to be going but not where we might drop trails exactly. Figured I would start running into more of our guys. Looks like we fell behind."

"Yeah, a bunch of the 590th passed me but it was a while ago. I knew there were more of you and wanted to make sure you madc it out."

"Are things that bad that you thought we were cut off?"

"I was not sure if you guys were GIs or Krauts until you got closer. Can't see much with this sleet hitting you in the face. But whatever you do, don't linger on the Auw road. Get across it as fast you can."

"Thanks Charlie. Alright, mount up!."

With a wave of his right arm, they began the long crawl through the night once again.

16

0130 Hours, December 19, 1944

"It's pitch black, sir. These lights are useless in this blizzard," Sergeant House exclaimed, while trying to keep the truck from sliding off the road.

Allowing someone else to drive his jeep was unusual for Green, but he needed to keep an eye out for the destination. Besides, a little time to think was never a bad thing. Vernon Mixon claimed Pete House was the best driver in the battery. Darino thought otherwise.

The weather had gone from blizzard, to sleet, to rain and back to sleet, eventually to blizzard-like conditions again. With the darkness, all it took was just a minor snowfall to give the impression of whiteout conditions.

"I know Sergeant, it's black and cold. You must be getting used to this by now."

"Sir, I'm from Jacksonville, Florida, so I'm not exactly used to driving in this stuff. I did learn some in Tennessee, sir. But it's been a while. These roads are shit. If you could even call this thing a road. More like a big path. I'm sorry for the language, sir."

"Nothing to be sorry about. They are shit. It's like driving in pudding. Where the hell are our guys? I don't even see any signs of our army anywhere. No vehicles along the road. The Krauts could be watching us go by. By the way, how's the hand?"

"Not bad, sir. Doesn't hurt to grip the wheel. So I should be okay. Don't look like there'll be any more powder bags to cut anyway."

"I hope you're wrong. But first we need to find our new home, so to speak. I may have to get out and see what's doing."

They were barely moving at five miles an hour in the blowing sleet. Even then, as House hit the brakes, the jeep kept sliding for another ten feet. Green's biggest fear remained the same, getting stuck in the mud. He could shoot at the Germans, but mud was just indifferent.

"Just say the word and I'll pull it over."

"Well, be careful. I'm more worried about the truck behind us.

As they led the convoy into a curve and slowed down, tracers lit up the sky ahead of them. Then the sudden boom and flash of an artillery strike illuminated the road again for just seconds. It was far enough away not to be an immediate danger, but close enough to fray nerves. Green strained to catch a glimpse of anything when the flashes occurred. Staving off disorientation was next to impossible. All he could see were trees; they so close to the jeep, he could reach out and grab them.

"Turn on our headlights, the hell with it. If we get to a roadblock and start to slowdown, let's be sure that they are GIs before we approach. In this weather, knowing who's who, is hard. If we see guys wearing white snowsuits, I'll let you know what to do. Let's pull it over here."

Green proceeded to jump out and run along the column warning the men to stay sharp, carbines at the ready. Keeping the men alert, and not put them in a state of panic was an art form that could not be taught. So as he shouted the order, he had to make it sound routine, regardless of how precarious the situation was getting. Dashing back to the jeep, he was glad he could not see the men's faces.

"Let's go, Pete." Green, out of habit, stuck his right arm out, waving the column forward. With everyone else using their blackout lights, he could barely be seen.

As they reached the next curve, the trail widened and two lights, one red, one green, flashed on and off just to their right.

"This could be our guys, sir."

"Let's hope. But what's up with the different color flashlights?"

It was an MP outpost. Two jeeps with six men were standing about, all wearing the MP markings on their arms and helmets. A couple even wore white sheets as ponchos. One of them, a burly man with a large scar on his right cheek and a bright white bandage just above the left eye, waved the jeep to stop. Green tightened his grip on the Thompson, and then relaxed.

"Hello sir, who you with?" the MP asked after a salute.

"I'm Lieutenant Green with the 590th Field Artillery. I'm supposed to be moving past Radscheid to keep up with the 423rd. Did we cross the Auw Road already?"

"Not yet, sir. Real close."

"So you guys are from our MP platoon?"

"Yessir. We knew they'd be more of you. A bunch of trucks passed through here a while ago."

"So we're getting real close, I hope?"

"Yes, sir, just stay on this path. Another mile, maybe. Be careful sir, Krauts might be anywhere."

"I know. Sergeant, what is your name?"

"Wexford sir, sergeant first class."

"Were you one of the guys I used to see at Purple Heart Corner? You know, your old grouchy sergeant was there a lot too."

"*Ah*...no, sir. We have been forward most of the time since we got here. Up and down the roads."

"Been standing here long?"

"Maybe a couple of hours, sir. Not too long, but in this weather, sir, you lose track of time. Been waiting for everyone to pass by. Wouldn't happen to have any smokes on you, would you?"

"Sure," Green eagerly replied. He was a sucker for any GI standing out in this weather, so he gave him his last pack of Chesterfields while eyeing the unusual shape of their flashlights. "Where'd you get those flashlights? Army issue?"

"From a dead Kraut, sir. Might have been an MP just like us. They help in this weather."

"What earned you that bandage?"

"Ricochet, sir. Don't know where the shot came from. Sniper must have hit a rock."

"Do you need a medic? I have at least two somewhere in this column. They'll probably do a better job than what you have now. No offense."

"No, no sir. We'll be fine," the sergeant quickly replied and saluted, backing up as he spoke.

"Alright, keep warm," a surprised Green suggested and returned the salute.

With that, they started off again hoping to come across their new positions within a mile or so. As they moved out, Green noticed there were large white *Xs* painted on two of the trees along the side of the road. Not knowing what to make of it, he passed it off as a lame attempt at remembering where they were. With men in a combat situation for the first time, strange things were expected.

"They were nicest MPs I've ever seen, sir. If you don't mind me sayin' so."

"You know Sergeant, you're right. It's probably the cold. They're finally getting religion."

"They have clean white sheets for camouflage sir. Damn MPs get everything. Hell, sir. Another hour and they'll be the same old grumpy sonuvabitches. I'll still wait and see."

Green then realized his right foot was getting numb and both were soaked.

"House, we're going to have to do a foot check after tonight. Should do a sock change too. My feet have been wet for hours."

"Same here, sir. These boots are not exactly top quality, sir."

"Not much better than the ones I started the war with, except you can lace 'em up a little higher. But the leather still cracks."

After another thirty minutes, Green's feelings of anxiety and frustration were reaching a boiling point. Coming out of another bend in the road, there was a GI standing by the side of the path waving a lantern of some kind, running toward the truck. Instinctively pulling back the retractor rod on the Thompson, Green leaped from the jeep and greeted the anxious soldier.

"Who the hell are you guys?" the young GI yelled, then realizing he was speaking to a lieutenant, "Oh, sorry sir."

"I'm Lieutenant Green with the 590th, what's your unit?"

"We're from the 589th sir. Service battery."

"How many of you are there?"

"About a dozen, sir. Two ammo trucks, empty of course, and one prime mover.

"Shouldn't you guys be north of us already?"

"Don't know, sir. Our trucks got separated from the rest of the column about a mile ago. We were following some trucks from the 422nd. Been running around for almost two days, sir. Then those MPs told us to keep going straight."

"The MPs back behind us?" Green asked pointing towards the end of the column.

"I'm not sure, sir, we just turned left from over there. Came outta that firebreak from the main road."

The young soldier was pointing uselessly into the darkness and away from Green's column.

"What did the MP sergeant look like?"

"The usual sir."

"Size? Appearance?" an exasperated Green begged.

"About your size sir, little more unshaven. Big bandage. That was all I noticed. Oh, and long scar on his face."

An increasingly anxious Green began realizing what was happening.

"How long ago was this?"

"Two hours at the most, sir," the private said, straining to see his watch.

"Two hours? Did you get a name?"

" Heard something like West or something?"

"How many guys did you see?"

"About six, sir. And the Sergeant asked me for smokes, Luckys, even though I saw one of his men with a carton and already smoking. Then another one of his men went up to the trucks and was asking for more smokes. I thought this guy might be selling on the side or something. Gettin' a little greedy I thought under the circumstances."

"Darino!" Green yelled, waving frantically at the truck directly behind him.

Darino leaped from his truck and started over.

Turning back to the 589th private, "By the way, I might have some of your guys in my column. Just give me a second. What is your name Corporal?"

"Perry, sir. Ken Perry. Should I have asked who won the World Series this year or something like that, sir?"

"Don't worry about it, that's hindsight. But by the way, who won the Series Corporal?" Green asked with an all-knowing smile.

Perry was stunned, eyes widened, and gulped. Then he quickly realized he knew.

"The St. Louis Cardinals, sir?"

Green smiled and nodded. "Who did they play?"

"Oh Jesus, ah…the Browns, sir."

"Correct. They lost to the Cardinals. A Kraut wouldn't know who the Browns were anyway. Why would you wanna know, they've always stunk. You passed."

Darino finally arrived front and center.

"Darino, where is Lieutenant Meyer?"

"I think he is at the end of the column with some of the Battalion HQ guys."

"Pass the word or do it yourself, I need him up here on the double. Then get that sergeant from the 589th up here as well. I assume Davis and Greeley are in your truck?"

"Yessir."

"And give one of them a flashlight."

The snow was being blown hard into their faces as they mulled around by the side of the road, shuffling their feet to stay warm. It was almost 0400, but first light was still hours away.

Meyer and Sergeant Goodwin arrived almost simultaneously, both panting.

"Sergeant, just ahead of our column are some of your service battery guys. They can certainly join us, but get them straightened out and join up at the end of the line, okay? Don't stray too far."

"Christ, some of my guys are still roaming around? We are all screwed up. Sorry, sir. I will get this thing sorted out."

After the sergeant trudged off, Green turned to Meyer.

"Look, Charlie, I think those MPs back there could be Krauts. Either that or they are Uncle Sam's Keystone Cops."

"Why do you think that?"

"Those directions he gave those 589th guys were false and probably ours as well. These guys from the 589th ran into the same MPs at another roadblock just two hours ago on a different road. And we both have ended up in the same place. On top of that, I now realize they were the driest looking bunch of soldiers I have seen in a while."

"There's not that many roads to go down. How could we be lost? Did we go too far?"

"I'm pretty sure we crossed the main road but can't be certain. Those MPs are Krauts, I know it."

"Do we want me to go back and check it out?"

"No, I'm going."

"Brendan, you're the exec, you're in charge now. What if those MPs are just confused or something? For all we know those service company guys might have it wrong. It's not worth the risk."

"Lieutenant Meyer, the decision has been made. You are taking the lead. I've had to sneak up on Germans before and no offense, I'm a better shot than most here. Besides, Battalion would never let me hear the end of it if I lost one of their own. Davis and maybe Greeley will go with me. Keep Corporal Darino close, he can probably answer any questions you might have about the guys. Pryne and the rest of the section chiefs run thc battcry anyway."

"But Brendan…"

"Don't worry," he quickly countered with a pat on the back, "try to keep going straight on this road. It's your best bet. If you make it to the Auw road, turn left for a bit, but get across as soon as you see an opening. I took a reading and we're still heading northwest. You already know all the Operations lingo. They've been grooming you for a while. And most of all, take care of my guys. Congratulations on your new command, Lieutenant."

Meyer stood there open-mouthed and getting angry, trying to reply to Green in his usual refined manner. Before he could get the words out, he started to turn away.

"And Charlie, I'm taking your jeep. You can have mine."

Green ran back over to House, told him what was happening and that, until further notice, Meyer was in charge.

"Drive safely, Pete. Precious cargo over here."

"Good luck, sir."

Green took take off down the line of trucks picking up Davis and Greeley along the way. Curiosity and rumors quickly spread down the length of the column. He ran by each truck telling the men they would be moving out with Meyer in charge for now. As Green reached Meyer's jeep, he instructed the driver to hop in somewhere else, and he promised to bring the jeep back as soon as possible.

But T/5 Rutkowski, the driver, was eager.

"Can I come sir? I'm already all the way back here."

"Are you good with that carbine?"

"Did well in training, sir"

"I think you're full of it, but what the hell, get in."

Rutkowski's diminutive stature and thin frame made his overcoat look three sizes too big. His gaunt face stuck out awkwardly beneath his helmet and his soft hands were like those of a clerk, which gave Green pause about accepting the request. Green accepted his plea, but he would do the driving.

"What about the Lieutenant's charts, sir?" Rutkowski asked, referring to Meyer's map overlays and targeting information.

"Take them up to the next truck, and tell one of the guys to get 'em to Meyer on the double, okay? Just mention my name."

Rutkwoski grabbed them obediently and was off. Green knew that Meyer may as well burn those. They were useless at this point.

"Suh, you gotta plan? Whir we fixin' t'go?" Davis inquired.

"I'm working on it now. But I'll incorporate getting back alive as one of its elements."

"Greeley, how's the ear?"

"Lost a little hearing. But no pain. Doc said it'll probably come back real soon."

"Good news for a change."

As soon as Rutkowski got back, Green did a broken u turn without spinning out of control and narrowly avoided the gulley by the side of the road. Then he straightened out while bouncing off into the darkness. The other three men breathed a sigh of relief.

Green quickly stopped again.

"Take the top down."

"Suh?"

"Take the top down. We have to have a better field of vision. Let's go."

Reluctantly, they began roll back their cover and the difference was immediate. The blowing snow descended on them, stinging their faces and most especially, their eyes. Rutkowski and Greeley, stuck in the back, covered their mouths with their gloved hands while trying to keep a firm grip on their carbines.

"Check your guns. Keep 'em dry as best you can."

As the jeep slid from side to side teetering from one set of tire tracks to another, a curious concern entered Green's mind again, albeit a little late.

"Rutkowski, when was the last time you fired your weapon?"

"Well, ah…sir, not too long ago. The officers set up a sort of firing range to make sure we were comfortable with our carbines. I think I did okay, sir."

"Glad to hear it."

This kid is probably not much of a shot, but I have to admire his guts for coming along.

"What did you do up at Battalion? Are you a clerk?"

"Sort of sir, little bit of everything, fire control tech, radio work, clerking, and at Atterbury, I even had some time on a gun crew. I've been with Lieutenant Meyer the last few days, sir. Sort of his unofficial aide. He's a real reggala guy, sir."

"Where you from?"

"Mount. Vernon, New York, sir."

"Hey, I'm from Yonkers," Green eagerly replied, reverting back to his accent, "so we're practically *neighbas*."

"Kinda figured, sir. You sounded like you were from my neck of the woods."

Going back the mile or so was even tougher going the second time around. Exposed to the elements, it was an eternity.

"Now Davis, we are about to approach another curve I think, and should be real close to the MPs. When I slow down, jump out just as we get to the end of the curve. Take up a position just to the side of the road, behind a tree or something. Then try to get closer little by little, but maintain a visual on us. It's dark but they should have some kind of light, maybe their headlights, or whatever. Whatever it is, I will have my headlights on them. Be ready to fire. You're supposed to be my crack shot. I won't drive the jeep right up to them. So that will give us time to react if something's fishy. If we get hit, I want someone to be able to get back and tell our guys."

"Yessuh. So I git the Thompson, suh?"

"Sorry, no. You knew the answer to that. Okay, here we go, I think that's one of the jeeps up there, get out now."

Davis jumped out and bumped right into a tree. Crouching between two fallen trees and nervously staring ahead of him, he followed the progression of the jeep's headlights. As he knelt there, he took out his cigarettes to calm his nerves, but then realized lighting up was not an option. The pack dropped into the snow. He reached down to find it, only to find himself tapping on something very much like a fallen tree. Only in this case, it had dog tags.

Oh shit.

Davis felt around with his now trembling hands and there was also an American helmet lying nearby.

The dead GI had been stripped down to his undershirt with dog tags frozen to his chest; his boots and jacket were gone. Davis slumped down and began panting even heavier. He didn't want to look at the face, ever thankful for the darkness. The urge to jump and yell was overwhelming.

As the others neared the MPs' roadblock, there were no MPs. One of the jeeps had been left with flat tires, but now there was no other sign of them. He began give orders as he pulled over.

"Stay here. Greeley, get ready to take the wheel. Most of all, stay alert."

Greeley and Rutkowski hopped out of the jeep and stood shivering for a moment until they turned to stare out into the darkness. Their rifles were stiffly pointed forward in both excitement and fear, resembling a training photo.

"This is sort of like being in the infantry. Wudya think? The fighting 590th, huh?" Rutkowski eagerly whispered.

"*Shh.* Is your gun ready to fire?"

"Yes it is," he nervously replied trying to look at his gun in the darkness."

" Check it. The damn things jam easy. But point it away from me."

"Full cartridge. Thirty rounds. I'm ready for anything," Rutkowski proudly stated, masking his increasing unease and straining to keep his eyes on the Lieutenant, who wandered away from the light.

"How do you move around in that coat?" Greeley asked Rutkowski, referring to the long dark green overcoats that were issued to the enlisted.

"Well, usually because I'm at the CP, it's never really a problem. I just put it on when I leave. But it's cold out here, I'm glad I have it. You look cold."

"Hell, I am. I just layer and sometimes wear two jackets. When you're on the gun, you have to move fast."

Talking, about anything, can help the nerves. Suddenly, the squishing of slush and mud could be heard. They both froze.

"Hank, it's me, don't shoot."

They looked at each other and turned around to see Davis rushing by, finger to his lips.

"It's only me. Be quiet," he whispered.

"Where is he going? Davis? Shit." Greeley lowered his weapon momentarily in exasperation.

Green had sunk into a mountain of muck, and began clopping his way towards what had been the MPs position. He tried to keep to the side of the path that ran along the hillside, with a shallow gulley in between it and the road. Clumps of snow falling from the trees began hitting him. The other side of the road was heavily wooded right up to the edge, only interrupted by telephone poles, surprisingly with the wire still intact. He also felt that old anxiety, being trapped, only this time he might be caught in a shooting gallery. The pain began gripping his chest and got worse with each step. Visibility was almost nil.

This was not the smartest thing I've done. In fact, this is downright stupid. Hope this isn't Kasserine all over again. Only with snow this time.

The feeling of being watched was overwhelming. He could barely be seen by the light of his jeep now, but wanted to get out of that light anyway. Reaching another one of the MPs' jeeps, he heard steps coming from behind him and snapped around. With Thompson at the ready, he saw Davis emerge from the darkness.

"Suh," he exclaimed in a loud whisper.

"Jesus, what are you doing here?"

"Suh, there's a dead GI o'er there by the tree."

"Are you sure?"

"I felt the dog tags, suh. Body's frozen stiff. Tall, lanky feller. Hey, whir them MPs?"

"I don't know. Let's get back to the jeep. Can't stick around here. Did you grab one of the tags or look at it?"

"No, suh. They real stuck.

"We'll get it on the way. Let's get back to the jeep."

While trudging back to the others, a shot rang out. Green hit the ground and got a faceful of mud. He managed to grab Davis by the pants leg and drag him down into road swill as well.

"Davis, stay down. Who fired?" Green yelled, spitting out dirty water.

There was a momentary silence and then a couple of MG42s opened up behind them. It was obvious from the rate of fire that they were German. The Krauts had been watching them. From the sound of clanking metal, both jeeps were getting hit. They may have been firing into the darkness, but the shots were getting awful close. The bullets' sounds were muffled when they hit the soft ground cutting the mud and slush around Davis and Green. It went quiet for a few seconds. But they didn't stop. Single shots rang out intermittently, teasing the Americans.

Toom... Toom... Toom.

Then the Germans opened up with everything.

"Get those headlights off!" Green snapped, as he contorted to avoid the shots that tore the ground around him.

Spouts of water shot up from the gulley throwing water on both of them. He managed to get on his back, raising himself between the firing and Davis, and spray the Thompson at the trees behind them. He kept firing at where he thought the flashes had come from until the clip was empty, then fell back into the mud. Icy water got into his jacket, running down his back, chilling him once more. Things fell silent again. Green took the inside of his jacket and tried to rub the dirt out of his eyes.

"Suh, you okay? Did ya git 'em?"

"I don't know and keep your voice down. Get up and run to the jeep, now," Green snapped in a whisper and tapped on Davis legs. Then a single shot seemed to pop right near his ear as it whizzed passed.

Without a word, Davis began struggling to get himself up. His feet were sucked into the sloppy mess. So he just started moving on his hands and knees until he gained momentum. Green followed, trying to simultaneously keep his footing and get another clip into the Thompson. They arrived to see Rutkowski, laying in the back of the jeep, gasping for air and gurgling blood after taking a couple of rounds, one in the neck. Greeley was holding on to him, his face sprayed with blood, as he pressed down on the neck wound. Green immediately cut the one headlight that was not shot out.

Davis stood staring and Green hit him firmly on the back, snapping him out of his momentary shock. He pulled out some bandages and a handkerchief, handing them to Davis.

"C'mon Davis, help Greeley. Press down hard on that wound. And keep your head down!"

Rutkowski's gasping became louder and blood was spewing everywhere, drenching the floor of the jeep and coating the back seat. He pressed forward with every gasp, unable to speak. He was staring straight ahead, seeming to know what was about to happen to him. His eyes starting to roll back in his head. Green tore open Rutkowski's jacket, to reveal blood-soaked shirts. Ripping them away, the belly wounds were found. One was a small slit, almost like a shaving nick, and another was a large round hole. That one had probably collapsed his lung. Each gasp was squeezing out more dark blood. Green tore open what was left of his bandages, pressed it to the belly wounds and then grabbed Davis' hand.

"Press down as hard as you can, but take your gloves off. The wool might infect the wound. And raise his legs!" Green shouted.

He anxiously glanced out into the darkness for an enemy that was all around them. Suddenly more shots hit the jeep from two sides.

"We're outta here! Hold on!"

Green got in the driver's seat and slouched down to avoid the firing. Slamming the jeep into reverse, he practically put the clutch through the floor. There was a momentary spinning of the wheels, until they started moving backward. The other headlight was hit and some of that glass splattered on the hood and then the windshield crashed in on them. Glass was blown everywhere. Davis was hit in the back of the neck as he was leaning over Rutkowski. Several rounds hit the radiator and it began to hiss.

Despite flooring the gas pedal, going backwards over the half frozen tire tracks and mountains of mud was slow going. But he managed to find some tire ruts, and get around a bend in the road. They stopped to check on Rutkowski. Greeley, finally coming out of the shock, was telling him to hold on. A dark puddle had formed behind Rutkowski's head. His coat was soaked completely through. Davis had found another wound in the shoulder and was working on that when Rutkowski's breathing became even fainter. The gurgling began to slow. Green got the jeep going forward, and sped off into the darkness.

Green felt around on the floor for the flashlight, but kept dropping it due to his blood soaked hands. He was finally able to wipe them of his jacket and get a grip. Then he stuck it through the broken windshield, flashing it on and off with his right thumb. After a few more minutes, there were headlights up ahead with shouts to 'hold it up.'

Green stuck his Thompson out of the driver's side at the GI.

"Whoa! Hey Mack, what are you doing? What's going on back there? Heard shots."

"Who are *you*?"

"Are you Lieutenant Green? Lieutenant Meyer asked me and some of the headquarters guys to wait up for you, sir."

"Yes, and I have a wounded man here," as he pulled in the Thompson and jumped out.

"Medic!"

"Raise his legs more! Come on."

"We need a medic now. This guy is dying."

"Fisher! Where the hell are ya?"

They heard nothing from the gravely wounded man. No gasping for air. No gurgling. Greeley just stared ahead, frozen in place, cradling the kid as tight has he could. Rutkowski now had the gray pallor of a ghost. All life had seeped out of him. His bowels loosened. Green turned away for a moment, afraid he would vomit from the putrefying stench. After a quick breath, he turned around.

"Greeley, look at me," Green commanded as he tapped Greeley's face. Davis helped pry his buddy's fingers off the wound.

"Come on, Hank. We got him," Davis said, almost in a whisper as he grabbed Rutkowski under the arms and away from Greeley. Green and Davis carefully turned the body around and laid him across the back of the jeep.

Blood, glass and bullet holes were everywhere. There were streaks of blood running over the sides of the jeep. The metallic smell of blood was only penetrated by the semi-sweet aroma of the shot up radiator, its steamy hiss beginning to wane. As the ambulance finally came up, a medic jumped out only to see a body. He looked at Green, who shook his head. The ambulance driver came around and they began lowering him onto a stretcher. Before covering the body with a blanket, the medic reached to check the dog tags. He quickly jotted down the name and number, writing them on a paper tag. One of the dog tags would be pulled off later.

"Wait a second."

The medics looked perplexed as Green leaned over.

He reached down and removed Rutkowski's bent glasses. After folding them, he carefully slid them inside the kid's coat pocket so they would be returned to the family. Then he nodded to the medics.

Flashes of a similar scene long ago ran through Green's mind, along with the guilt. There was no elation of being alive, only a feeling of failure. He had brought these guys into trouble because of what he told himself was a sense of duty. He was lying to himself, trying to assuage the guilt that was to come. This was personal. Repeated warnings during training of not to let your personal feelings interfere in the performance of your duty had been conveniently forgotten. His lust for revenge had now led to the death of a man under his command.

Davis and Greeley now stood silently by the side of the road, awash in Rutkowski's blood and some of their own, coming to grips with what just happened. Green turned to see the familiar look of first-time combatants: a sort of stunned, tight-lipped, empty stare. The shaking hands holding cigarettes were testament to the adrenaline pumping through their bodies. They had survived shellings. But those bullets were meant specifically for them. In their first direct encounter with the enemy, they had not only been shot at, but seen a man die an agonizing death in their own arms.

"Davis! You and Greeley give us a hand over here," he said as matter of factly as possible."

Green then turned to the sergeant, "Can we get a ride back to A Battery, wherever that is?"

"I'll do my best sir. We seem to be all bunched up in the same area. Sir, what happened back there? Who's the fella who got hit?"

"German patrol," Green replied cautiously, knowing that was not exactly the truth. "The guy's name is Rutkowski."

"Didn't know him, sir."

"I figured you didn't. Never found out his first name.

"Everything seems to be gettin' screwed up, sir."

"If only Division can hear you, Sergeant. Alright, let's get this shot up heap to the side of the road before we take off," Green ordered trying to change the subject.

After taking a closer look, he realized there were two flat tires at the front. But the slick tire tracks would help them push it out of the way. With the sergeant steering, Green and the others pushed the jeep into a trench by the side of the road.

"Sergeant, open it up and grab the battery. Pull off the distributor cap too. Throw them as far away as you can."

The Germans were going to come this way soon and why chance it by leaving anything useful to them.

"Davis, get Greeley and yourself in the jeep. Then, when we find A battery, take him to an aid station. You both need to get cleaned up, and Hank was cut up pretty bad by the flying glass."

"You too, suh. Right under ya eye."

He had not felt the oozing that came from his cheek. But when he put his hand up to his left eye, the blood was still flowing down his face. That would also explain the metallic taste in his mouth.

"I'll be okay. Take care of Greeley."

Green took out a handkerchief and pressed it to the wound before hopping in the jeep. They managed to work there way past some broken down trucks and slowly work their way back.

"Sergeant, you're with HQ?"

"Yessir. Sort of a runner. Guess I'm the Battery agent for whoever needs one.

"So where are we heading?"

"We've been told to set up positions just on the side of some hill. There's some kind of open field that can fit all of us. Once we get back across the Auw road, we'll head into another beat up excuse for a road. Then it'll be to our right just a little ways in. There's a stream that should be in front of our firing positions."

"That's going to be tight for four batteries."

" The 423rd is supposed to digging in a few hundred yards on the other side and getting ready to move on Schonberg soon."

"That's a tall order to ask of those men now."

The 590th had just enough for one good covering barrage. Even if they got into Schonberg, holding onto it would require a lot of help. Rumors of the 7th armored coming to the rescue were still circulating. Many thought they were waiting for them on the other side of the Our in Schonberg. Some could swear they were hearing the loud radial engines of Shermans making their way down the road.

On the trip back to their positions, confusion was evident. Sitting in the jeep for more than thirty minutes going only five miles an hour, was starting to lead to even more frustration. Trying to veer around the traffic and abandoned vehicles was agonizing, as the temperatures had not yet reached above freezing. What angered Green most was the sight of a gun, intact, lying by the side of the road, stuck. It had been just left there.

"Let's pull it over somewhere about there," Green grudgingly ordered, pointing to an area busy with ammunition haulers. He thought he noticed Darino's skillful parking methods.

As he left the jeep, a captain called out to him, surprising Green, causing a delayed salute.

"I'm Captain Hardy, with M Company, 423rd. You're Green, right? I heard you ran into a German patrol."

"Word spreads fast, Captain. Not exactly a German patrol," Green replied, looking around for eavesdroppers. "It was a group of MPs that I believe were Krauts. But I can't be sure, sir. Did not actually see them again."

"What makes you believe that Lieutenant?"

Green proceeded to retell the story of column's escapades and his subsequent ride back to confront the possible phony MPs, including losing a man and Davis finding another.

"Where is your CO? Peters, right?"

"Was hit pretty bad, sir. I'm the exec, so I guess I'm now in charge.

"Okay, well, I don't have to tell you to stay alert. I'm guarding the rear. So if the Krauts are back there, they'll run into us first."

"Is your company at full strength, sir?"

"No, I've lost at least one platoon. Some got scattered. The others are casualties. I've picked up some engineers to get us up to full strength."

"Well, good luck sir."

"You too. And take care of that face."

"I will."

"Hey, I have to ask. Where you did you get the Thompson? Not standard issue for you guys, is it?"

Green, taken by surprise at his inquiry, had to think quick. The Captain could very well take it from him.

"Found it, sir. Better than those damn carbines. And it came in handy back there sir."

"I bet it did. Stay well."

After a quick salute, they parted. The Captain gathered his ragged men and trudged off into the unknown.

Green now turned to looking for his men amidst the frenzy of activity. Everywhere there was the uncoupling of guns, and the sounds of men, many still in their long overcoats, pushing and pulling on their howitzers to get them unstuck. Green watched this unfold with both pride and sadness. One diminutive soldier had climbed completely onto the barrel trying to make his weight pop the trails out of the muck. Shouts of 'let's go' and 'move it' as well as 'put your back into it' from the section chiefs reverberated all over the field. He could see Biels running to the front of the guns with the aiming stakes. Most discouraging of all were the empty ammunition carriers that lay parked at the end of the field.

The wind was dying down as the first remnants of daylight appeared, piercing the remaining the snow clouds, providing a break from the usual onslaught of precipitation.

"Lieutenant, sir." Darino, still as energetic as the day they landed, called out as he ran over. "We're getting the guns set up, sir. I think almost all of the sections have uncoupled and are prepared for set up. Only one got stuck, sir. But we got it out with Lieutenant Meyer's help. It's a miracle."

"So my guns are all operating okay and in one piece?"

As he listened, the state of his Lieutenant's appearance shocked him. The long gash on his unshaven face along with all the grime, gave him a sinister look. Fingers of dried blood had stained his face. The wet and dirty clothes were nothing new, but this time his pants were almost black.

"Yessir."

But as Darino spoke, his lieutenant was hurting. It was all too obvious.

"Are you alright, sir? Heard you ran into trouble and it looks like someone took a knife to you sir."

"I'm okay. We ran into some Krauts back there. My face caught some glass. The jeep was a total loss. I saw a gun back there by the side of the road. Whose is it? Do you know?"

"No, sir. I saw it. But was already there when we passed by. Do you want me to send some of the boys over, sir?

"No, not now. I'll find some others to disable it. Stay with the guns. But anyway, things are going well it looks like? As good as can be expected?"

"Yessir. Low on ammo, not much food left, but I hear the cooks are still setting up somewhere, sir."

"Got an exact count on the ammo?"

Darino took a deep breath and hesitated to answer. He didn't want hear it himself.

"Five rounds, sir."

"Okay, that's what I figured."

" Lieutenant, I saw Davis walking Greeley away and they both looked beat up. Hank was limping badly. Len said the guy from HQ died on the way back. How is Greeley, sir?"

For the first time, he had heard Davis called Len, instead of that '*hillbilly*,' '*cowboy*,' '*country prick*' or any of the other terms of endearment that had become commonplace between the two odd buddies.

"He's not too bad. More shock than anything. Think he'll be fine. Davis and Greeley handled themselves alright."

"How many Krauts were there?"

"Don't really know. But they had a lot of firepower. Hey, show me what's happening. And where's Lieutenant Meyer?"

"Sir, we got this alright. Why don't you grab some chow and dry off."

"Maybe later. Gotta make sure we're ready."

The concerned Darino reluctantly acceded to the request.

"Whatever you say, sir."

17

December 19, 1944, 0830 hours, just west of Hill 575, southeast of Schonberg.

PARTS OF THE FIELD NOT occupied by vehicles and howitzers were still covered in snow. All the traffic suddenly furrowing the virgin field had created another quagmire. As the low clouds and mist began to lift, the tenuousness of their position was obvious. It was like being at the bottom of a bowl. The field was surrounded on three sides by a crown of steep, tree-covered hills, not exactly the bird's eye perch they so desired.

The gun sections had been placed near the tree line. Everywhere men sloshed around the puddles and mud trying to get their jobs done, if just to keep warm. The section sergeants yelled orders while every section's number one was test setting range and deflection, peering through his quadrant with determination. Others fused the remaining shells. The futility of the situation was not lost on anyone, but when you have been drilled relentlessly to do a job, procedure becomes habit.

Approaching the battery, Green tried to take stock of the men's expressions. The young soldiers had become hoary-looking veterans. There were looks of growing resignation mixed with anxiety of what would happen next. Some of the men peered at the grim, blood streaked face of their Lieutenant walking along with his wet and filthy clothes; they pretended not to notice. Green thought of all the aphorisms about military strategy that the Army had thrown at him over the years none of them seem to matter much now. Leading seemingly beaten men was not one of them.

A makeshift command post had been set up in the back of an empty ammunition carrier. New radio equipment had been placed on some old ammunition boxes with piece of tent on top to keep them somewhat dry. It was a vain hope that any line of communication would remain open. A couple of crates, acting as a table, held the charts. Meyer turned around to see Green coming and was shocked.

"Brendan, what the hell happened back there?"

"The Krauts opened up on us, but we never saw them. It might have been the MPs and it might not have. But more than likely you know the answer to that."

"You face is cut up pretty bad. Anyone else hit?"

Before Green spoke again, he looked around, took a deep breath, and began to speak in a lower voice.

"I hate to tell you this…I lost Rutkowski. I'm sorry."

"Shit! How? What was he doing there? Did he *volunteer*?"

From the tone of Meyer's voice, Green felt like the accused. Then he realized that this was a first for Meyer, and let it go, answering back sternly.

"He asked if he could come and I figured an extra man would help."

Trying to ignore the awkward silence, Monahan turned and tried to get his radio working.

"Brendan, may I ask how he was hit?"

"I'll put it in my after-action. Look…

"Well, you got your pound of flesh alright."

"Charlie…"

"In case you don't know it, this is not your own personal war. You can't go off half-cocked trying to be the hero again. What do you want, another medal? You're an irresponsible son of a bitch, you know that?"

The shouting began to attract the attention of the men standing around. Green began shaking with anger. His eyes narrowed as his fists clenched. Meyer knew he touched a nerve, and he stepped back, lowering his voice.

"Where is he?"

"The medics have him. What's happening here, Lieutenant Meyer?" Green said through gritted teeth.

Green wanted the subject dropped, but Charlie Meyer had to have his say.

"That poor kid had no business even being in the Army, no less overseas. He told me that he had been turned down twice by the doctors and then last year he gets a clean bill of health. He couldn't even walk a straight line half the time."

Despite his rage, Green held his tongue, giving his friend a second to compose himself. He knew the look and what was going through Meyer's mind. What hurt so much is that Charlie was right; this was not Brendan Green's personal fight with the Third Reich. The rage that had been boiling within him that last year had now manifested itself as a thirst for revenge, costing the life of a man dragged into the fight.

Green continued to glare at Meyer, who continued his blank stare into space. Finally, he inhaled deeply and straightened up. Then without emotion, turned back to his map.

"From what I have heard, two battalions of the 423rd will be assembling down the slope of Ridge 536 here," Meyer stated rather matter of factly, albeit somewhat weakly. "At least one company has passed through here already on the way up there.

There'll be stragglers all day. We're here, just behind them. Canon Company is also moving further down the valley."

"Where's the Regimental CP?"

"Cavender's supposed to be moving to the back of Hill 504, so he'll be with 3rd Battalion."

"Where's the 422nd?"

"North of us, somewhere. But their exact position is unknown. Probably parallel to the Andler-Schonberg road, scattered in those hills."

"Have patrols been sent out toward Schonberg?"

"Not sure. I hope so. I did hear that a company tried to use the main road and ran into a whole bunch of Krauts. The Battalions are still trying to coordinate a line of departure. The cutoff is now full of dug in Krauts."

"This is crazy. Are we supposed to just burst through the town and somehow get to St. Vith? Or are we meeting up with other units once we take the place?"

"From what I understand, we still have to get through the town and make our way to St. Vith. Hey look, at the very least we're taking some of the pressure off of St. Vith."

"We'll be fighting all the way. Taking our guns with us is not an option. Are the men in good enough shape to do all this?"

"We're all tired and hungry. Ammo is a problem for all of us. I spoke with some of the infantry guys who came through. Couple of them only have a clip each for the rifles."

"You know Meyer, you're not helping my mood any."

"What's new? Colonel Lackey came around before he left and asked how we were. He's on his way to meet with Cavender again. There is supposed to be some conference up at Regiment. He ran over asking about you. Rumors are spreading."

"Rumors about what?"

"About those MPs, stuff like that."

"That's the least of our problems. Do we know exactly how close the Germans are? And worst of all, does anyone above Battalion realize we have five rounds left?"

"Just pick a spot on the map, the Krauts are bound to be anywhere you point. As far as ammo goes, Lackey knows we are scrapping the bottom of the barrel. Cavender knows too. What can they do? Orders are orders."

Then Meyer suddenly looked up from the map, as if being suddenly reminded of something. He had his own bad news to convey. Waving Green away from Monahan for a little privacy, he began speaking in hushed tones.

"Peters is dead. One of the guys up at Battalion Aid came down and told me."

Green tried not to look upset, despite the sickening feeling in his stomach. He knew he should not be surprised. Now he had to try and look as composed as possible. Meyer knew the bond that had been created between the two men, and having to pass on the news that he had lost a friend, tamped down Meyer's anger as well.

"How long did he last?"

"Not sure. I assume it happened last night."

"Knew he would not be back here, but I was hoping he might make it home."

"You've been the boss since Saturday night. Nothing changed. So if you can get to St. Vith, they'll probably make you a captain. As if you really wanted that incentive."

"I'm not interested. Don't congratulate me, please. So what about the 589th and Colonel Kelly?"

"He's run back and forth several times desperately seeking his battalion. But not much is known. He looked angry when I last saw him. I don't think Division has any idea what is happening."

"That's obvious. We're in some serious shit here. Be prepared to do whatever you need to get out in case we get overrun. I hate to say this, but that could happen anytime. You can hear that firing going on."

"I know. I'm curious to hear what Lackey says when he gets back."

"If he gets back. We need plan to get out now."

The two men paused, realizing Monahan had big ears and that the others were close by as well. Green could feel the blood oozing down his face and into his shirt collar. His heart felt like it was going to burst through his chest.

"Look Brendan, we have some time. I gotta go talk to the each Battery CO for Major Meadows. Then I'll be back to help. The infantry has to climb that ridge to get in position, it will be a couple of hours at least. Go get cleaned up and dried off. You're freezing. Besides, you might be scaring the men," he said with a smile, his anger appearing to have waned.

Green's teeth had a slight chatter to them when he was standing still.

"Are you giving me an order, Lieutenant Meyer?" Green mockingly stated to the still youthful looking officer.

"Well, it's a strong suggestion. You look a mess, if you don't mind me saying so. There's a medic around somewhere. I even heard the cooks are making the last of the hot chow before they destroy the field kitchens."

"Sort of a Last Supper?"

"Maybe. Then I hope the cooks can shoot straight."

"Look Charlie, in all seriousness, talk to Fonda and the others. Find out if they have any other plans. And if you meet with Lackey or Meadows, try to express my opinion strongly, as only a staff officer can. We're running out of time. Let's break the hell outta here. If we're gonna make it, we have to get organized."

"I'll try."

"And look, I am sorry about …"

Meyer put up his hand.

"Don't worry about it. We got these guys to worry about now."

"Let me get you a driver. That way you have an extra hand."

"I got Reed from HQ to come over."

As he walked away, Green saw him take out his .45, and check the clip before he forcefully slammed it into the chamber. Once at the jeep, he then reached in for his carbine, placing it on his lap as they drove away. It was as tense as he had ever seen his friend.

"I stowed your gear sir, in one of the trucks over by the road," Monahan chimed in.

"Much appreciated."

He was tasting the blood now as he scanned the field once again. Davis was back from the medic, without Greeley. Prynne was having the usual animated conversation with Darino and Mixon.

"Hey Pryne!"

As he approached, Green finally saw the physical toll the last few days had taken on the first section's leader. Like the other section chiefs, he had performed above any expectations. The senior section chief had become a de facto commander on a chaotic battlefield. Sleep had been almost non-existent; his bloodshot eyes were a testament to that. It was the shuffling in his walk that concerned Green the most. Every step looked painful.

"Sir? How's the face?"

"Forget about it. I'm fine. Now listen, I want you to grab five men. Get them as much ammo as possible. I want to extend the perimeter or at least find out how close the Krauts are. I want the men to get up to that firebreak running above us. Have Davis lead the squad and include Del Valle as well. Questions?"

"Sir, the Krauts are hot on our heels. For God's sakes, they might be right up the goddamn road. I could tell ya that."

The sarcastic response was not a surprise. Everyone had their breaking point. Letting off a little steam might be the best thing for him right now.

"I know, Sergeant. But we have to do what we have to do, right?" he replied in a rather fatherly tone.

"I'll get 'em armed to the teeth. Would you like me to go, sir?"

He saw that question coming.

"No, I need you here. We still have ammo left. Have Davis see me before they take off."

"Yessir."

Before Pryne could leave, there was another worry.

"Have you checked your feet lately, sergeant? You're walking a little funny."

"Yeah. They're okay."

"You're sure?"

"Yessir. I would never lie to the Lieutenant."

A wry smile came over Green's face. He folded his arms and took a deep breath.

"That's a lotta crap and you know it. At least change your socks. I'm heading to the Doc, you should too."

"Yessir."

He just nodded and began sloshing back to his men, already barking orders before he got there. The wobbling in his gait meant escape for him was out of the question.

Surprisingly, as Davis approached, he looked almost chipper; it seemed as though he had no scars, mental or otherwise from the past few hours.

"Suh, you wanted t'see me?"

"How are you feeling? How's Greeley?"

"I'm right tired, but I be okay. Ol' Hank's doin' good. Minor wounds. But I think ya should git checked out, suh. That gotta hurt."

"In a minute. Are you ready for a little more action?"

"You got it, suh. What you fixin' t'do?"

"Pryne is gathering some of the guys for you. I want you to lead them up that hill behind us. Try and make visual contact with the Krauts. If you do, don't engage. Send a runner back or whatever. Keep your ears open. They could be anywhere. There might be men from the other batteries out there too. So be careful. Give yourself no more than an hour and then get right back here. The snow is still fresh as you rise up that hill. Might be tough going. Sorry about that."

"Don't you worry. We be okay."

"Looks like it's clearing up a bit."

"Best day yet, suh."

"One more thing. If some reason while you're up there…," he hesitated, wondering how to phrase his thoughts on their predicament, "well, let me put it this way, if you see us get hit or overrun by the Krauts, and you can make a break, do it. You're in charge of this little patrol. So as far as I'm concerned, every man in this outfit is authorized to get out. Understand?"

"Yessuh. But them armored boys gittin' to us real soon, suh. Jus' wait an' see."

"Believe what you want, but be prepared."

"See ya in a bit, suh."

If he had his way, he'd call together every man in the battery and tell them to make a break for it immediately. All he kept wondering was if he was the only man in the Battalion, or the Division for that matter, who believed the 7th Armored was not coming.

"Monahan, I'll be back."

Green first went to get some water to wash his face before he went to the medic. After taking a cupful of water from the tank and splashing it on his face, he wiped some of the grime away. The temperature was so cold, that the water felt warm. He found a mirror in his bag to examine the cut. He did look like hell. There were minute shards of glass still in his face. Removing them stung, and with each pull, a little more blood began to trickle down. The biggest gash extended down his left cheek, running parallel to his old scar. He would have to see the medic before he did anything else.

The medics had begun setting up an aid station by one of their jeeps for the time being. It was a muddy, low-lying area, not far from the stream but it was as far from the guns as possible. Green lumbered over holding pressure on his face with a fresh bandage. The medic seemed happy to have a customer that he could actually help.

"What happened, sir?"

"Cut myself shaving." Green retorted as he dropped his hand to reveal it was more than a razor cut. "What's your name, Corporal?"

" Kiley, James J., sir. *Ooh*, nasty slice there. Might require some sutures. Let me get a better look at it. This might sting, sir."

Kiley's hands were cold. Between hunger, Kiley's cold hands and the pinching of the wound, he didn't know what was worse.

"You have pretty funny beard growth, sir, if you have to shave at that angle. And it looks like you've done this before."

"Truth be told, Kiley, I ran into some Germans who were not happy to see me."

"I figured as much, sir. Lots of glass hit you it looks like. Word has been getting around."

"You guys are all in the wrong line of work. Intelligence might be your calling."

"Everybody knows you, sir."

"Alright, can we get going on this thing, Corporal? I'm starved."

Kiley began to reach into his satchel. "Sir, if you don't mind me saying so, you should have changed your clothes too. You're freezing."

The sound of his teeth chattering could not be hidden.

"I know Kiley. But I figured this could get a little bloody and what would be the point."

Kiley began by reaching for a small vial of brownish-looking liquid, which he snapped the top from, spilling a few drops. It's strong odor was immediately apparent. He then proceeded to rub some on Green's cheek, which caused him to almost leap off of the box from which he was sitting.

"Shit Kiley. That burns!"

"That's why we use iodine, sir. It cleanses. Trust me."

"It stinks too. If you ever run out of smelling salts, you could always use that stuff."

There was now a big brown, circular stain on his cheek. After that, he sat as still as he could as Kiley slowly stitched his face together. There was no topical anesthetic, so feeling the silk thread through his face didn't add any pleasure to an otherwise awful day. Intermittent shells rumbled overhead, falling harmlessly into the hills above them. Green spoke without trying to move his mouth very far open.

"So tell me Kiley, how long you been with the outfit?"

"Met up with you guys at Standish, so basically just before we left for overseas, sir."

"This is a hell of a start for us, Kiley."

"Yessir, I didn't think I would see this much action with the artillery."

"Sorry we haven't had time to talk and all."

"Don't worry about it, Lieutenant. I've been up at Battalion most of the time."

"How many medics do we have here? Seems like we have a surplus right now."

"Besides myself, Jersey and Alden, we have a guy from the 589th. Think his name is Fisher. He just wandered over. Not sure how he got here. Krauts overran an aid station that was set up in some barn outside of Schonberg. And he couldn't get back. There's also a medic from the 423rd, who brought over some wounded and is sort of stuck here too. He ran into some Krauts on the way. They stopped the ambulance and let him go. Either the Krauts have a heart or figure they will see him later. Looks like that little path between us and regiment is full of them."

"I think we ought to stop talking about anything until these stitches are done, huh? All this talking may throw off the stitching process."

"Yes, sir."

Trying to not think of the stitches or the Germans, he stared down at the Ihrenbach stream, as it peacefully flowed passed their perimeter carrying with it chunks of ice and snow. Vehicles left by the 423rd were strewn in and around the water. Some were still smoldering. They had discarded them during their retreat the previous day. The smell of gasoline lingered in the air. Tiny patches of oil skimmed the surface. An overturned jeep had its gas tank and radiator shot out. Soldiers had shot it out like a cavalryman would shoot his wounded horse. It now lay as a testament to the frustration and chaos that unfolded for the past three days. As his eyes came back to the scene around him, a couple of other medics were rushing over to help set up. The low-lying area was a less than ideal spot for an aid station, but it gave them room to work in case of a heavy load of wounded. Kiley finally tied off the stitch and stood up.

"Lieutenant, I have to give you a couple of shots before I send you on your way."

" Forget it. The iodine was enough. Just give me a couple of packs of sulphur."

"But sir, I have enough to..."

"You heard me, save it for the real wounded. Let's go, Kiley."

"Alright, sir."

"I'll take some extra bandages, if you can spare them."

"No problem."

Green got up, feeling a little woozy.

"Well look, Kiley. Take care of yourself."

"Keep it clean, sir. Don't want infection. And go get a change of clothes."

"Is that Doctor's orders?"

"Well, sort of."

"I'll come by to check on you guys later."

"If anybody asks sir, just say you met Joe Louis in a dark alley."

"More like Max Schmeling with an MG."

Green hurried back to his gear. Much of his clothes were in poor shape but was able to find some relatively respectable wool pants and a cleaner field jacket. After grabbing all his Thompson ammo and two emergency ration bars, he began trudging back to the new mess area.

From behind came a shout.

"Lieutenant!!"

It was Darino.

"What's going on Corporal?"

"Socks, sir. Lieutenant Meyer told me you were in need. I had a stash. Don't worry, I had all sizes." Green was touched by the offer. Having extra socks these days was like having spare cigarettes. No one ever turned them down.

"Much obliged, Arthur."

"So how is everything? Trucks, guns, et cetera."

"Everything seems to be working, sir. Guns are ready to fire, if we had ammo or targets. Mixon is working on one of the trucks. Him and Pete House wanna disable the trucks, sir. They say they're useless now."

This was a moment of validation he could not let go.

"Let them do it. Tell Pete and Vernon to have at it, per my orders. Don't make a big show of it. Keep one truck and one ammo carrier working. Listen, stay close. I may have to give the order to disable the guns real soon. Got me?"

"Yessir."

"And make sure you all have a weapon. Rifle, *.45*, whatever.

"Consider it done, sir."

"By the way Darino, I am sorry I just called you Arthur again."

"You are the only one allowed to do that, sir," Darino replied with a smile.

"Alright, make sure everyone grabs something to eat. I'm doing the same. Get going."

The kitchen truck was set up not far from the medic's station. From the smell, he could figure out what that they were serving was eggs and something else. The cooks had very little, so they borrowed several cases of K rations to supplement their breakfast. They broke out all the eggs and meat, then passed out the biscuits. He was so hungry, it tasted like steak. One last hot cup of coffee was savored.

Green decided to take a look around the woods himself when he realized, to his amazement, he had left the Thompson at the truck. A pocketful of clips, but no gun. He considered the *.45* that he carried, useless, so having the men see him walking around with that weapon, wouldn't inspire much. Thankfully, he found the gun next to his gear. Scanning the gun line, he saw Private Biels wiping his boots off.

"Biels!"

The bespectacled private obediently ran over. Behind those glasses were tired eyes, almost hollowed out. He had not slept in a couple of days and it seemed his dedication was hurting him more than the Germans were. As he stood, he could barely keep from falling over, rocking back and forth.

"Hey, where's your rifle?"

"Sorry sir. I left it with my gear. Been busy."

"From now on, keep it close. "

"I promise."

"How are the men?"

"I think okay. Itching to do something."

"A decision is coming. Either by Battalion or myself. Until then, take a load off, that's an order. I know we have coffee left."

"Thanks, sir."

Biels just smiled weakly and took off again.

The lingering grayness had now given way to a somewhat clear sky; just a few patchy clouds lingered. It was still freezing. Any escape would require a tortuous run up hill. His old claustrophobic feelings came to the fore again, and began to envelop him. One good shelling and his men were through. Enraged at his predicament, he ran back to the CP.

"Monahan, what's going on?"

"I got one transmission from Regimental. Pretty garbled. Said to standby.

"Standby for what?"

"Not sure. But sir?"

"What's the problem?"

"Some guy from Battalion, Reed, I think, just drove over here about Lieutenant Meyer."

"Why? He was supposed to be with Meadows."

"He said he was driving the Lieutenant back to a meeting at Regimental when they ran into a bunch of Krauts who opened fire. Reed slammed on the brakes and threw the Lieutenant from the jeep. He was okay, but waved him on. Told him to back up and keep going, while he limped over to side of the road. As he put it in reverse, he saw Meyer return fire with his *.45*. But that was it."

"That was it? Where's Reed now? Did he go back and get him?"

"Yessir. He was wounded, but Ray Brown and Krause jumped in with him and took off. I haven't heard anything more."

Monahan finally saw a look of complete despondency on his Lieutenant's face as he took a deep breath and removed his wool cap. After rubbing his forehead a couple of times for no particular reason, Green composed himself. With all that had happened over the past three days, he was still shocked at what he had just been told. He started to run towards the road, only to realize it was fruitless. There was a battery to run.

Monahan felt compelled to say something.

"Sir! We might have orders any minute!"

After one last long look up the road, he turned around. At worst, Meyer was dead. At best, he was captured, with the former being the most likely occurrence. There had been no time to grieve for Captain Peters and there was no time for grieving now. Green found two men on his way back, asking them to grab the .50 caliber machine gun and set it up at the edge of the road. Now, his feelings of helplessness turned back to rage.

The Battery was useless as a field artillery unit. Their only hope lay with getting organized into fighting platoons and try to get out on foot. He came back to what he considered his laughable CP, and grabbed his maps, throwing them on the ground.

"Monahan, burn these. And destroy your radio equipment. Do it now."

"But, sir."

"What now?"

"It's the old man, sir. He's over there."

Looking down towards the other end of the field where it met the road, was Colonel Lackey, speaking with Captain Fonda.

It was now time to cash in any chips he may have built up with the brass. At times like this, his less than conventional ways of approaching problems in the past did not help.

"I need to talk to the old man."

"Sir, I'll hold on to these maps."

"I gave you an order. Get it done. And the radios too. When I get back here, all I want to see is you, your rifle and a large burn pile. Understood?"

"Yessir."

For the first time, the almost inexhaustible radio man became truly worried about his new CO. He stood up from the crate he was using as a seat and nervously lit up the last of his pack while watching Green stride defiantly through the slush.

As Green headed down to the Colonel, kicking up water and mud along the way, he went over in his mind what he wanted to say. They heard him before they saw him. Both men looked over to see a man whose face was telling a thousand stories and ready to speak his mind. Startled by the sight of his bedraggled, bandaged officer, it was not what they expected from their Silver Star winner.

"Sir," he began solemnly with a salute, ignoring the Captain.

"Green," Lackey quickly returned the salute. "How you holding up? Looks like you were in a bit of a scrape," he asked in his refined Southern manner.

The Princeton-educated lawyer from Tennessee had a disarming quality about him, and was well respected by the men. Much of the deference came from his age. He was over forty, so his worldly nature made an impression on the mostly twenty-somethings of the Battalion. He was not a big man, but he carried himself with an air of authority even higher than his rank.

"Sir, may I speak freely?"

"If I said no, would that stop you?"

The comment actually broke the gloomy mood for both men. Green smiled nervously. Even Fonda braced for what was to come. Green drew a long breath, wanting to appear as calm as he could before stating his case. His body was trembling and he moved his jaw from side to side.

"Sir, this position is untenable and I'm just about out of ammo. I can hear the Krauts approaching. I'd like to form the men into provisional squads in an attempt to break out."

"I'm fully aware of what's happening, Lieutenant," came his terse reply. The exasperation of the last few days was evident in the response, the question having been posed before. "But we still have to support the attack on Schonberg. I have not heard much, but I will be speaking with Colonel Cavender momentarily."

"Sir!" his anger now laced in an almost mutinous tone, "we won't last that long. Cavender's guys are all over the place. By the time they get in position we will have had it. I have maybe five rounds left, two of them smoke. Just listen, sir. Those are German machine guns and tanks rattling around up there. Again sir, I ask respectfully," Green slowed down for emphasis, taking a deep breath, "permission to break out."

"Brendan, you're out of line," Fonda interjected.

"No, I am not Captain!"

The confrontation was now attracting attention to the embarrassment of the Colonel. Several of the men around them had stopped what they were doing while others just pretended to be busy. They wanted to hear their fate.

Quiet fell upon them. Both stared at each other. Lackey became pensive, trying to quickly mull over how to handle this deteriorating situation. Never one to handle insubordination lightly, this was the first time he had to deal with it from an officer. There was hesitation as he thought of a way to placate his angry young officer. He stood ramrod still for a moment.

Having appeared calm over the past few days and even in their few conversations since Saturday, Green felt Lackey had handled himself well.

"Permission granted," he responded dispassionately.

Then moved closer and began waving his right finger for emphasis.

"You do what you have to do. Just don't let those guns fall into enemy hands without disabling them. Is this understood?"

Despite the admonishment, Green was visibly relieved.

"Yes. Thank you, sir."

As he answered, Green instinctively stood straighter. He regarded Lackey's acquiescence as perfunctory. The decision had been made a long time ago. It was escape, or die trying.

"Oh, and Green," Lackey now lowered his voice,, "you've done a hell of a job since Peters got hit. And you've performed exactly as we thought you would. All the men have. I don't know if we'll meet again, but I just want to say thanks, to you and your men."

The Colonel then extended his hand.

Compliments from a superior officer were like curve balls, one never really expected them. Green stuttered for a moment before deciding what to say.

"Sir, I'm sorry for being a pain in the ass," he said with a smile

"Every unit needs one."

"Sir, I'm sure you know about Charlie Meyer."

"Yes, I just heard. He'll turn up somewhere. I'm sorry, Brendan. There's nothing we can do."

Before he could leave, Lackey had one more question.

"What would you have done, if I said 'no'?"

"I would've explored my options, sir."

The Colonel just smiled and raised his eyebrows.

"Get going and good luck. Put your helmet back on too."

With one last look at Captain Fonda, Green nodded and turned on his heel.

18

Expecting to smell the burning maps, and see smashed equipment, Green instead saw Monahan diligently trying to get a signal.

"What are you doing?"

"Sorry, sir. Some infantry captain called just now. Trying to make contact with someone. Said he may need a fire mission."

He allowed Monahan to stay on air for a little bit longer. It was just after 0900. But just as quickly, an order to stand down came over the radio.

"Monahan, destroy all your equipment immediately. I don't care if goddamn Eisenhower calls."

Finally giving into the inevitable, he turned off his set.

"Doing it now, sir."

The silence was then shattered. Bullets began ricocheting off trees and mortars began landing near the guns, churning up huge mounds of earth. Mortars hit the last remaining trucks. A hurricane of shrapnel swept through the field. Shouts of 'incoming' and 'scatter' were shouted. Two loud explosions were heard almost simultaneously. The remaining ammunition and a fuel truck had been hit. Purple flames shot up into the sky and debris began raining down. Dense smoke swept over the battery. As the section men tried to put out the flames, they were fired upon from up on the hills.

Green was now down at one of the lowest points in the field where the fourth gun section had been set up. Darino had crouched just next to the first gun, carbine at the ready, waiting for anything at which to shoot. Others scampered under the trucks. A few had even taken cover behind an upturned ammunition carrier. The firing had slowed. The mortars stopped and for a few seconds there was silence except for the moaning of the wounded. Shouts of "Comaraden Kaput" could be heard echoing from the Germans over the hill.

One of the section sergeants from C Battery ran over to say they were surrendering and to destroy your weapons. Green grabbed him.

"Who gave that order?"

"Sir, the captain has been hit bad and I lost three other men. Half my men are walking wounded and we are out of ammo. Two guns are now out of action. I think the aid station got hit too."

"Before you do anything, Sergeant, get those guns disabled. Understand?"

"Yes sir, unless the Krauts get to us first."

"Do it now!" he angrily retorted, his bloodshot eyes now bulging. "Don't let that happen, understand?"

"Yes…Yessir," he nervously nodded, before carefully taking a few steps backwards.

Green did not know what to say to his own men. He could see his section noncoms remaining by their guns trying to gather their crews. Crawford had a shrapnel wound to his shoulder and was bent over one of the guns, still shouting orders. Others had begun smashing their carbines into the ground after hearing the sergeant. Shouts of "medic!" were reverberating around the field again. Several men had run over to ask what to do.

Looks of fear and confusion appeared on the men's faces. Some stared ahead in a stunned silence. Many coughed from the acrid smoke billowing over the field. Others continued to hug the ground. Blowing on his hands did not help much, but it was all Green could do while trying to formulate a plan. A secondary explosion shook him from his thoughts as one of the burning trucks' gas tanks finally blew.

The guns were still in working order. If they surrender now, they would be no time to disable the any of them. The Thompson was with him, but that would be the last to go. Bullets began whizzing by again, whipping up the dirt around them. Some of the men hugging the ground did manage to blindly shoot off a couple of rounds from their carbines.

Davis and Darino were still at their gun, crouched down behind its shield. Seeing this, Green headed straight for them, dodging bullets and his own men. Mortars began falling anew, blasting the trees behind them and sending deadly wooden shrapnel into the gun positions. Green dove down as he reached the first section.

"Jesus Christ, sir," Darino shouted, "these Krauts are gonna kill us all. Are we really surrendering?"

"I'm sure some have already. Did you disable this gun?"

"I was about to sir, but was unsure."

"It still kills me to say this, but do it now. What about the others?"

"They're all still usable, sir."

"Where's Prynne?"

"He's trying to get his arm patched up, sir. That last blast threw some shrapnel his way."

As Green scanned around, he spotted Prynne, helmetless, trying to wrap a bandage around his left arm while sitting against one of the trees. Even from that distance, he could see a dark redness coloring the bandage.

"Davis, run over and take care of that firing pin on two or get someone to do it. That goes for the others as well. Then you and Darino step away from the guns and move back toward the trees. Keep your rifles on you, then wait for me."

"Sir?"

"Get it done. I'll be right back."

He scanned the hills above them looking for his enemy. Finally, through the haze, a group of German appeared dressed in their long, gray coats and coal scuttle helmets. They brazenly milled around at the top of the hills, seemingly unconcerned about the Americans. Their comrades were slowly closing the ring.

Darino and Davis hurriedly went about the disabling of the guns. They were masters at speedily disassembling the firing lock mechanism and that came in handy now as they pressed down the front end of the sear to remove the firing pin holder. Once the cotter pin was withdrawn, they unscrewed the pin bushing and they were done. The pins were either shoved down into the dirt or thrown far away into a snow bank. Just to be on the safe side, they also shot the tires out of a few of the guns.

After one last mortar round harmlessly landed in the woods, things began to get quiet. Green finally reached Prynne, who said he was fine. But the blood pouring from underneath his bandage told another story. He ripped open a sulphur package and sprinkled it on the wound. Then took one of the bandages from his pocket, and began to tie it around the wound while Prynne grimaced.

"Sorry for the blood, sir. I pulled a piece of shrapnel out and it just started flowing."

"Don't worry about it. I'm not exactly a doctor, but you should be fine. Look, I don't know what is going to happen in the next few minutes around here. Take of yourself. If it looks like we're done for, try and get out. But I understand if you don't feel up to it. Okay?"

"Sir, I don't want to be a POW either. I'll try and talk to my guys."

"If I don't see you Sergeant, good luck."

"It's been a pleasure, sir."

Prynne grimly nodded and Green scampered off.

The aid station was a flurry of activity. Most had been unharmed by the mortars but the chaos of men diving for cover and knocking everything over caused a mess. Green could see Kiley and the other medics hurriedly getting the wounded resituated. Those men couldn't take much more.

The men who had tried bury themselves in the ground during the shelling began to slowly get up as the eerie silence spread, though no one stood still very long. Occasional bursts of small arms could still be heard coming from the top of the hill. The Germans appeared to be firing into the air but with the haze, no one was quite sure, nor did they want to take any chances. Men ducked at the sound of every burst. Green arrived back at the sections to see Davis and Darino finishing up their work.

"Everything done?" Green asked in an almost pleading fashion, wanting desperately to hear the right answer. Every second was now precious.

"Yessir." Darino confirmed. "What now?"

"Stay alert and keep your weapons close. Watch me."

"Oh crap," Davis snapped. "Hold on, I left my carbine in front of our gun."

With one quick glance around, Davis jumped up and ran to his weapon. Then the Germans began emerging from the smoky haze on other side of the break. They triumphantly strode down the tree line.

"Lieutenant!" It was Monahan, waving frantically to get Green's attention. Green looked up and saw him in the midst of burning their maps and message logs in a pit near the CP. He waved back and nodded.

"Hey, where's Greeley?"

"Aid station again, suh."

"What happened?"

"Shrapnel. Hank b'fine. But it took a nasty chunk outta his leg."

It occurred to him for the first time that he would be leaving men behind; because of wounds or just their position in the field, many men did not have the option of trying to escape. He tried to reassure himself that he had done all he could do right up to the end. Whether his men would admire his attempts at escape or damn him for it, he could not decide.

"Suh," Davis began to ask, "we jus' givin' up?"

"Not yet. Spread out a little."

Green now stood with Davis and Darino at the edge of the forest, the 105mms lined up before them, as they waited for the Germans to pour out of the forest to take them prisoner. In front of them, burning vehicles and equipment were everywhere. Many of the men clustered together in the center of the field. Thick black smoke blew across field, hovering well below the tree line, and temporarily blocking out the gray horde that was approaching. It was a sad end. Green witnessed the dejection and felt the walls closing in on them. The coughing and moaning of the wounded drowned out the guttural shouting of the Germans. Their weapons having been rendered useless, most of the men began to put their hands up in disgust.

Green's chest pounded from both anger and fear. Within minutes, he would be a prisoner. A trickle of men had tried running into the woods only to run back after being fired upon from the top of the hill. The thought of being cooped up by his enemy of the last three years was unbearable. He looked all around and saw some open space behind them, then the tree line. The Krauts could now been seen entering the pocket from three sides, coming down from the ring of hills. Green crouched down behind one of the guns, and grabbed his Thompson.

Darino stared and was confused about what he was doing. "Sir, should I destroy my weapon? Lieutenant?"

Green turned around and stared; his furrowed brow and angry eyes signaled to Darino that he was not giving up. Davis, who was still reflexively holding his carbine at port arms, glanced back at Green, waiting to smash it against the wheel base of the howitzer.

Another group of Germans, more wild-eyed than the first group, began pouring out of the woods from the other side, marching through the open gap between the stream and the trees. They began shepherding the men up front towards the road and lining them up. Some of the more eager of the victors were starting to pull watches from the men or ask for their boots. The Germans shouts of 'Hände oben!' and 'Raus!' began to ring out.

They were maybe twenty feet from the woods and no sight of any Krauts in that direction.

"Darino," Green whispered, "we only got a few feet. No Krauts behind us. I am making a run for it. On my signal, go. Tell Davis and whoever else wants to chance it."

Darino reached over and tapped Davis in the back, making a motion with his head toward the woods behind them. Davis understood with some trepidation, for he was the furthest from the forest. A few feet could mean the difference between life and death. The sucking mud certainly would not aid him in his escape. Biels began to look at Green and figured out what was going to happen, wanting to give a try. Green nodded. The crunch of the German boots got closer and Green's small cluster got noticed by a rotund German sergeant who approached them, pointing and mumbling. Green was hesitating as he stood up. He was awash in guilt about leaving wounded men behind but the will to get out overpowered him.

"This is it, Darino."

Green looked to his left and saw two young privates, one of them was Wallenbach staring at him. The young replacement looked like a veteran now. His overcoat was gone. He kneeled there in just his sweater, dirty face glowing red, and gloves torn to shreds. With strong reluctance, he nodded his head again, giving them the okay to follow. But then from behind him, another German came up and tapped him in the back with his mauser.

"Hände oben!"

Green stunned, turned around and stared into the eyes of a young, diminutive German, whose ill-fitting helmet gave him a comical look. He told him to drop his weapon, shoving his Mauser into Green's chest. The Thompson was slowly lowered as he turned around.

Shit, where the hell did he come from?

The German was wide-eyed with fear; his Mauser shook as he pointed it at Green's chest. The decision was made. With all the strength he could muster, Green grabbed hold of the Kraut gun but the young German would not let go despite the panic in his eyes. A kick in the shins and Green got the rifle. He took the butt and smashed into the German's face, knocking him to the ground.

"Run! Darino! Davis! Go now!"

He threw away the Mauser, but not before he reached down and got his favorite weapon. Green took off running and then made his way into the trees. The Germans fired a few shots in the air. Then they fired right at him but the shots all whizzed by his legs. He kept running, stopping behind a tree to see how close they were, with Thompson at the ready.

"Stop Amerikaner!" the stunned German sergeant yelled.

Wallenbach and the other private, after a moment's hesitation, ran in a different direction, heading towards the stream. But they were cut down before they even got close. Several rounds went right through them. They twisted grotesquely for a second and then fell to rest in a puddle of their own blood.

The German sergeant raised his MP44 assault rifle, and fired several rounds at Davis and Darino. Davis got hit in the legs and back, falling immediately. Darino realized this and instinctively stopped.

"Len!"

Green looked back as he ran, but it was too late.

"No don't… keep going!"

Darino knelt down to help his friend and received several rounds to his chest and head, falling dead instantly. Biels bravely ran in front of his fallen comrades, waving his arms to stop the firing.

"Shit, what have I done," Green whispered.

Then an incensed Prynne pulled away from the medic, tore his bandages, and got to his feet. Immediately he raised his carbine and began firing at the Germans. With a heavy limp, he lunged forward.

"You Sonavabitch!"

One of the Germans cut him down with a long blast of his MP44 and Prynne fell at his enemy's feet.

More Germans came running into the woods, shaking Green from his shock. He fired back, but purposely over their heads to avoid any errant shots hitting the now captive GIs. It was enough to slow the Germans down for a minute or two. Then he turned and ran as fast as he could, dodging one group of trees, than another, with three frustrated Germans still on his tail.

The pursuing Germans could not be seen, but he could hear them. So he spun, pointed in what he thought was their direction and fired three bursts. From the sudden shout and moan, it sounded as though he had hit at least one of them. Then he finally saw three Germans positioning themselves behind the trees just below. Three more bursts of the Thompson and he headed up the hill. He didn't know exactly where he was, nor did it matter. The Germans were all over. The woods were the only salvation. A man on the run has no time to stop and check out the road signs.

Walking east was not an option, that would be just doing the Germans' job for them. He knew the road network at least, but walking due west would put him in between the firing. Other units of the Division continued to hold out to the north and west, though it could not be for much longer. Schonberg was not an option. The forest grew denser to the south, interspersed with large open fields, so he might have to take the long way around. As he ran up the heavily wooded hill, the sounds of firing had almost stopped. He had underestimated the steepness and the amount of snow, which now reached his knees. As he continued, he got a good look at where the men had surrendered. They were being herded to the road, hands on head. Some were being searched while others were cudgeled by the Germans with their rifles. Since his escape, and the others' attempts, he now realized the Germans would treat his men more harshly.

Upon reaching the top, he crouched precariously by the side of a road that ran over the crest. Sweat poured out from underneath his helmet and wool cap. It pooled around his eyes until finally running down his cheek. Steam rose from his body like a boiling steam kettle.

There were sounds of tracked vehicles around. The ponderous clank and squealing gears of a long-barreled German Mark IV became louder and louder until its barrel poked over the crest of the hill. Green dove into a nearby gulley only to be soaked by the melting snow, still managing to hold his Thompson over his head. Splashing around for a second, he rolled himself out of it. Looking around for a direction to go, there was only one option: back into the woods. He leapt into a snow bank, got up and started running again.

19

December 19, 1944, 1200 Hours, somewhere southeast of Schonberg

TRUDGING UPHILL THROUGH KNEE DEEP snow in Army-issue boots was tough, but it was even harder alone, with an entire army surrounding you, ready to annihilate anything in its path. He could not help feel that he was just delaying the inevitable. His boots filled with snow every time he went to take a step. It was like walking in wet cement. Chunks of snow and ice fell from the trees. When a bare spot was found, it was just mud. It seemed as though a dry spot in the Ardennes could not be found. The fall into the gully did not help. His helmet fell off and his boots filled with water. It soaked him head to toe, even his wool skull cap now had icicles forming on it. After throwing away his scarf, he zipped up his jacket further and turned the collar in the vain hope of warmth.

Staying off the main roads was vital. But the woods were getting more and more claustrophobic. Darkness was just a few hours away. A thick, smoky haze hung in the forest from the hours of fighting and burning vehicles all over the perimeter. With every blast of wind, the choking stench of diesel and cordite pierced his nostrils. Trees seem to multiply with every blink of the eyes; everything looked the same. This was not nature's cathedral. A hole in his left glove caused the tip of his middle finger to stick to the barrel of his Thompson. Pulling it off had been painful. He could not even remember when it had happened. Stopping to rest, he began shivering violently. Realizing he only had a few hours before freezing to death, he kept moving.

With a German round having gone through his compass, he took off in what he thought was a southerly direction. Walking parallel to the roads, just out of sight would be risky. There wasn't much choice. Eventually he was going to have to cross one of the main roads, either the Andler-Schonberg Road or the one running north from Bleialf in order to head west. Otherwise, he would be walking in circles. Reaching the Our river was only the beginning, the Germans were not going to let him cross over with just a wave of the hand. There were several bridges, but they would be of no help. Getting wet again was a certainty. Sounds of fighting were still coming from just north of his position. It was the only option for a desperate man.

As he started off again, he looked down to the ground and noticed something familiar sticking out of the snow. It was the rifle butt of a Garand. Pulling on it, the rifle easily slid out. Green immediately noticed the firing mechanism had been damaged. There were a few helmets and a jumble of mess tins. Battle debris was strewn everywhere, a sad reminder of what was occurring all around him. He quickly got moving to escape the reminders of defeat.

The pounding in his chest was excruciating, barely able to take a breath. Despite the cold and wet clothes, his body suddenly felt a surge of heat, almost as if it was on fire. It would not last long, before the freezing wind and precipitation would overcome the adrenaline. Reaching for his canteen, he shook it to break up any ice that may have formed, and took a few sips. Half a Hershey bar was next. The real chocolate beat the D ration bar any day.

The mental anguish was as bad as the bone chilling cold. He kept going, trying not to reflect on the losses among his men. The promises to himself to not let any harm come to them were unrealistic, he knew, but it never got easier. Running from failure as much as he was from the Germans, he had to continue his escape to nowhere in particular.

With the imminent risk of freezing to death, finding a place to stop and dry off was priority number one. There were farmhouses and barns everywhere. Finding civilians who would be brave or foolish enough to help one lone American, was going to be difficult. These people had just come out of four years of occupation. They were survivors. Throwing away all that instinct to help a hungry soldier, even if it was the decent thing to do, was going to be hard.

The woods now began to slope downward as he made his way over fallen trees and the decreasing snow drifts. Shivering resumed as the wind picked up. The steepness of the slope increased and another clearing appeared up ahead. He crouched down as much as he could and took a position as close to the edge of the woods as possible, enough of a vantage point to see a fairly wide path at the bottom of the hill. A fresh odor of burning fuel began to fill the air. His eyes began to well up. As Green quickly scanned the small dirt road, burning American half tracks and ammunition carriers could be seen to his left. He grabbed his field glasses and stared intently at the scene, hoping to see at least one American still alive and waiting for help.

Off in the distance, the thunderous clap of an artillery barrage echoed again, well west of where he was. Finally, he heard the faint sound of German voices coming from below his position. He scanned to the right. Just behind a small patch of trees, he could make out a German half track and officer's car; maybe two dozen grenadiers were milling about. Some were enjoying cans of C rations, while others fiddled with American rifles.

As he counted the troops, he looked to their left and noticed some bodies. They were obviously American; some had on the enlisted man's dark overcoat while others wore just their field jackets. Six GIs in total lay almost side by side. Making out their patch was impossible but a few of the faces had been turned to the side. They were black. At first, Green assumed that they had just been killed in an attack. But there was something strange about the bodies. When men fall in combat, they are scattered all over. Even in a fight among small groups of men, soldiers get separated. These guys were all face down, lined up almost in perfect position along the road a few feet apart and at least a hundred feet from their own vehicles. They had been murdered after surrendering. To add further insult, their boots were gone and he was sure, anything else the Germans deemed valuable. Studying the scene, he followed a small trail of blood that wound its way through the mud to a small frozen patch of snow. He watched it grow increasingly red.

Goddamn it. Those Krauts just sit there and eat.

Any possibility of eventual surrender after a valiant struggle to get out was gone. Being captured alone, or even in a small group means certain death. Gathering himself from his anger, the prospects were even grimmer now. There was a momentary desire for one last gallant firefight. Why not? The chances of getting out of this mess were slim and none.

Let me go out in a blaze of glory and take those murderous bastards with me. I got brothers. They can take care of my folks.......

But logic got the best of him. He became embarrassed by the histrionics of his own inner voice, damning himself for his emotions. Escape was his primary duty, not a one-man war. He had to get to the other side of that road. It was almost dark. If he moved along the crest of the hill another mile or two, away from this band of Germans, maybe he could find an opening to cross the road.

Another uphill climb lay ahead. The sweat was beginning to freeze on his body. Hopefully they could not hear the bass drum pounding in his chest. The tear in his right glove had gotten wider. His socks hung around his feet like wet dish rags. A *squish* could be heard with every step. There was an extra pair of socks in his jacket, not clean ones, just a pair that should be fairly dry again. He was going to try and save the ones Darino had given him till at least tomorrow. The constant state of stress made him reach for his inside left pocket.

I could really use a cigarette right now.

He would have been willing to break his own rules about his men smoking out in the open, if only the three cigarettes in his pockets were dry. His trek back up the slope away from the road began again in earnest. Straining to avoid snapping any branches or banging the Thompson against a tree or the occasional boulder dug in to the side of the hill, he got to the top in one piece. He immediately wiped off a log, sat down and ripped his boots off. Not wanting to look, feeling them is all he could do until curiosity got the best of him. After finally laying eyes on them, they were in better shape than he thought. He squeezed the socks out, put them in his left jacket pocket and reached into his inner pocket, grabbed the drier pair. The one last handkerchief he had was used to wipe the inside of the boots in the faint hope of getting somewhat dryer. It was not fun exposing your feet to the cold, but there was no other choice. The boots had to be wiped dry as often as possible. Having the feet sitting in wet boots for a long period will cause the feet the swell. Once the feet swell to almost twice their normal size, the skin will start to die and turn a dull gray. Then they turn black. A man probably could not feel anything after that. Once the skin starts to decay, it could be just a matter of hours before amputation is the only option.

As he put the wet hanky back into his jacket, he felt something at the bottom of the pocket; it was his mother's rosary. He gripped them tighter.

Forgive me, Ma. I do wish they had been socks. Now shut up and get going Green. Shit. I have to pee.

There were plenty of trees from which to choose, so he tried to pick the biggest one. He had to take his glove off to unzip. It hurt to pull it out, but not as much as when it finally started to flow.

Trying to conserve, he had neglected to drink much the past two days. His pee was dark yellow and it stunk. Finally zipping up after what felt like an eternity, he drank from his canteen.

The noise of what was left of the 106th attacking could now clearly be heard. The sound of an American .30 cal machine gun slowly rattling on was encouraging for a second. It was quickly drowned out by the distinctive thumping of German anti-aircraft guns being used for ground cover. Loud speakers blared something in very accented English, but he could not quite understand it. Although, the word surrender was probably included in the rant.

Within a half hour, the wind died down and the sounds of war abated. What had been a somewhat clear day, was giving way to thickening clouds, and flurries began to fill the air. He heard the sounds of trucks rumbling up a road. That's when he realized he was probably back at the Auw road again. He had been walking east. Deciding to use it as a guide, he tucked himself back into the safety of the trees and turned to his right to begin moving south.

As late afternoon approached, Green decided to stop again and somehow dry off when he heard the sound of boots walking toward him, causing him to crouch down behind the nearest tree. Seeing nothing, he chalked it up to his ever-increasing paranoia, he rose to begin moving again. Then voices came within earshot. He hit the ground and slid his body into a shell hole, grabbing some fir boughs to cover him up. He only wished these fir trees were as expansive as the ones back in the states; underbrush was at a premium. In the distance, he thought he heard German. Snow got under his jacket, shocking him for a second. He was now on his back, Thompson pointing up.

They got me. I'm going out with a bang. I don't care.

Fear, more than cold at his point, made him tremble. A burning sensation suddenly ran through his body. Sweat began stinging his eyes again. His head felt like it was going to burst. Tired of fending off the inevitable, he made a decision. Disregarding the noise, he slammed back the retracting rod on the Thompson and prepared to die. The inner torment of the past two years was finally coming to an end. There was only a sense of relief. As soon as one of the Germans tried to nab him, he would lurch up and start firing. He could not hear any voices now, only the ponderous steps of an approaching soldier. So he drew in one last deep breath and eased his right index finger onto the Thompson's trigger. The boots got nearer and nearer. Suddenly they stopped. Green closed his left eye for better aim.

"Psst, you're American right, so am I. I'm Sergeant Jackson, Emmett J., from the 333rd Field Artillery."

Green heard the deep, panting voice with just a hint of the South, and knew a German soldier could not mimic that. He peered through the boughs and gazed up at a tall American soldier in olive drabs, who really was black. His pencil-thin mustache looked odd on his long, dark face, which made him look older than he was. Two bandoleers of M-1 ammunition crisscrossed his chest, and he was holding a Garand in his right hand. There was a small green satchel tied to his waste. His wide-eyed stare only added to his wild appearance.

I'll be damned.

Jackson stood there with a smile on his face, proud of his find. Then he quickly turned to his right at the sound of snapping branches.

"Get down and keep your voice down too, Sergeant," Green snapped as he tried to sit up.

"Sorry, sir. I saw you from a distance, but did not want to call out," Jackson said, now trying to speak in a whisper.

"I thought I heard the Krauts."

"You did, sir. They were walking right for you but then suddenly veered off in another direction. Lucky for both of us they just had to stop to relieve themselves. I've sort of been tracking them, sir. Then I spotted you. The olive drabs caught my eye. I think the Krauts would be shocked if they saw an American at this point, sir."

For a few seconds, Green pondered that. Maybe he was just lucky.

"I'm Lieutenant Green, 590th Field Artillery," Green eagerly introduced himself as he offered his very cold hand to Jackson. His pleasure at seeing another American was obvious. "You must have really good eyes. Are you alone? Hurt?"

"I'm all by myself. I was hit by a tree blast in my shoulder as I was trying to make a run for it. Knock me down for a few seconds. Guess the Krauts thought I was dead. How did you wind up here, Lieutenant, what happened to your unit?"

"Long story, most them are prisoners now I think, or dead. But we did manage to fight for almost four days. After the first two days, it felt as though we mostly just drove around. What about you guys? How did you get separated from your unit? Are there anymore of you?"

Green felt like he had just risen from the dead. He hungered for information, so badgering the Sergeant with questions could not be helped.

"Well sir, I was in a convoy with some of your other units. Ran into some Germans and all hell broke loose. It was everyman for himself. And I think I'm the only one from my unit to be still roaming around free, so to speak, sir. I was with an observation party in Bleialf when the attack started."

Jackson went on to tell his tale, meeting Lieutenant Wood, and mentioning Due of course. But it was the end of the story that caught Green's attention.

"There was a shout to surrender and I saw from underneath one of the trucks that some of the guys began to put there arms up. I just got up with this M-1 and two bandoleers I found near the truck, then ran into the woods. Don't think anyone saw me. Before I took off, I was high enough to look over the river sir, just past the main drag in that town. I heard a lot of Germans firing and yelling. I looked to the other side of the village and going up a hill was a bunch of guys, obviously GIs. One was ahead of the pack and got to the tree line when I lost him. I would have sworn it was that Lieutenant Wood I met earlier, sir.

"Eric Wood. Well, I'll be damned. Good man. And lucky him, he's on the right side of the river."

"At least I hoped. But I turned and started running. When I first spotted you sir, I thought it might be him. Then I realized that he wouldn't have crossed the river again."

"Maybe we'll get across and catch up with him. How many men were you with?"

"It was a long convoy, sir. Those Germans were not fooling around. They cut some of the guys down real…."

Green put up his hand.

"I guess you can save the details, Sergeant,"

"Sir, at our outpost in Bleilaf there was a Lieutenant Waters. He was leading the squad when the attack began. Real friendly group, sir. He was putting quite the fight. Did you know him?"

"Yeah, I did. West Point guy. Graduated with Ike's kid."

Deciding not to mention the eventual fate of his friend, and wanting to end the grim conversation, he tried to get them both back on track.

"Well, you found me anyway and glad you are armed to the teeth."

"Is that a Thompson, Lieutenant?"

"Yes it is."

"I feel better too. I didn't know the artillery guys got their hands on them."

"Long story. Personal weapon. Beats those damn carbines any day. The only other useful thing I have is this pair of field glasses."

"I also have three grenades, sir and a *.45*. Oh, and these."

He reached into his inside jacket pocket and produced a pair of Army issue field glasses.

"Sticky fingers, sergeant. You're like a goddamned supply depot."

"I had to rob the dead, sir. And I'm sorry about that. Well, sir, what's next?"

"Guess we just formed a new unit. I am not sure exactly where I am. Thought there was another logging road around here somewhere. I realize now that I walked too far southeast. But at least I found a friendly face. Got a round through my compass, you wouldn't happen to have one Sergeant?"

"Yes, I do Lieutenant, yes I do."

"You are a regular quartermaster. I think the Krauts hit every item on my web belt. So let me get this straight Sergeant, you have been roaming around these woods for almost three days?"

"Almost, sir. More like since Sunday morning and the only thing I've seen are Germans driving on the road to Schonberg. I kept wondering if I'd bump into anyone else from the fighting in Bleialf. You guys sent patrols down all last week and your anti-tank outfits were all around town. So I figured some of the others must have gotten cut off as well."

"Unfortunately, not many of those guys made it out."

"Believe it or not, sir, I've been back and forth across that road at least three times. I came back across because I thought I saw some more of your guys still roaming around. All the villages were already full of Krauts too. You guys were on the move but never could catch up. I knew one of my officers was supposed to be with your HQ as liaison."

"Captain Horn, right?"

"Yessir."

"What about your battery and HQ up near Andler?"

"I think they got hit too, sir. 155mms are hard to escape with. Maybe they got out. Hopefully some did."

"I'm kind of short on information myself."

"Anyway, sir, there was always seemed to be Krauts between you guys and me. Was not sure if I should go ahead and surrender, although I heard the Krauts ain't too big on the skin color, sir. Then just a little while ago, I passed a few dead Negro troops lying face down with what looked like bullet holes in their heads. Was afraid to look too closely, sir, but that gave me my answer. Turns out the Krauts were just up the road from me. So it was a close call."

"You did the right thing. I don't think the Krauts want to be bothered with prisoners, especially Negro ones. How did you avoid detection for so long?"

"It wasn't easy, but I just kept hoping I would run into our guys. I know where I was when I had to run. But now, after crossing the road a few times, I am not so sure. I know the Auw road is just behind us, I think. The first night, I found an abandoned dugout just inside the woods near the Schonberg road, and stayed there. But the German traffic became heavy and I left. So I tried to keep a low profile. For a dark-skinned man, sir, it's hard to keep a low profile in the snow, especially with angry white folks chasin' ya."

He finished off his last sentence with a smile.

"Low profile? More like Daniel Boone. Sounds amazing sergeant."

A disconsolate look came over Jackson. His large, dark eyes became sad, and then narrowed into anger. Maybe this lieutenant did not believe he was capable of such actions. After a moment of awkward silence, Green finally spoke.

"I mean no disrespect, Sergeant. It's good to see anyone at this point."

"Even a Negro, sir?"

Jackson noticed Green's eyes narrow, staring right back at him.

"You're an American soldier, Sergeant. Aren't you? That's all I'm concerned with. Understand?"

The tall sergeant stared at this shivering and dripping wet officer, his face now a flaming red. He was taken aback by the fierceness of the response.

I'm sorry, sir. Meant no disrespect. Blame it on the cold?"

"Look, no need to be sorry. We just need to get on with things, I guess.

"I'm sorry again, sir.

"Have you eaten?"

"I have a couple of candy bars, sir. Have not touched the K ration. I came to a patch of dead GIs that the Krauts hadn't robbed sir, and figured I would take what I need. It wasn't a good feeling, sir."

"You did what you had to do. Any water Jackson?"

"Yes, sir, canteen is almost full and not frozen."

"Mine is half full and I have two Hershey bars as well as this nasty D ration."

"Oh, and I have this knife sir, found it on my travels. Looks like it is very fancy. Big swastika carved into the tip of the handle."

"That is a Nazi ceremonial dagger, it came from an officer. He must have been dead because they would not give them up easy. Rob a dead Kraut?"

"No sir, it was lying by the side of the road. I had snuck out to look for more ammo and found it next to a burned out Kraut staff car."

"Lucky you. Well, it might come in handy."

"Are we going to try and get through the lines sir, or just try to hold out in these woods? I would like a chance to kill some Germans."

"Don't know, but I do think we are going to get the chance to kill some Germans for sure. First thing, let's get moving further away from the road down there. Didn't realize how close we are. It will be night soon, so at least maybe we can gain some rest and try to get our bearings. As the two men looked around, a wet snow began to fall. They both turned away from the sounds of non-stop German traffic to their left. Rumblings of artillery began again, and it was not American. The hammering of anti-aircraft guns and the shallow pop of mortar rounds started anew.

"Where's the action going on, sir?"

"It's my outfit. What's left of it anyway. Trying to get to Schonberg."

"That's a tall order, sir. The town is gotta be like a German fort by now."

"I know."

Jackson noticed the extreme chattering of Green's teeth and trembling body. His cheeks looked like someone had taken a blow torch to them. One he warmed up, that was going to be painful.

"Sir, your clothes are soaked. Wool don't dry so easy. I hate to bring this up, sir, but there are more dead GIs just a little ways back whose clothes maybe drier than yours."

"I know, Sergeant. Later. I fell a couple of times and got drenched. If we keep moving, I will stay warm. Just have to keep my feet somewhat dry. You wouldn't happen to have some extra socks, would ya? I already used my extra pair."

"I just put them on sir, but you need them more than I do….."

"Keep 'em on," he sternly answered with a wave of his hand, "let's head north a little while longer and then decide which road to cross before turning west."

As they started off, German anti-aircraft tracers came up over the hill which lay ahead of them. They both stopped, looked at each for a second. After a shrug of the shoulders, they started off walking deeper into the forest in search of a friendly face or just a warm spot to rest.

20

Jackson could hear Green's shivering as they moved. He was amazed that the lieutenant had not froze to death. His pants were getting rigid from ice on the legs. Droplets of water fell from the tip of his helmet. As they reached steep ground, the Sergeant would offer him a hand, only to be waved off by the stubborn officer.

Just before dark, they came upon a trail that ran perpendicular to the Auw. It was one of the many unmarked pathways that were scattered all over the Ardennes. They stopped and surveyed the area, inching their way to the edge of the trees. The left side of the trail curved just out of sight. But there were fresh tracks of vehicles, albeit small, all over it.

"I don't see anything, sir."

"That's probably good news, Sergeant. Maybe the Krauts are just going around areas like these, figuring they'll flush 'em out later. This looks a lot like the path my battalion took to its last position. But who knows, everything is starting to look the same."

They crouched low, intently peering down the road; then they resumed trudging parallel to it. Approaching another curve, something came into view.

"Wait, that's one of those calvary scout cars. Mini-tanks or whatever. You know those M8s."

The M8 Armored Car was used by American Calvary units mostly for reconnaissance missions. It carried a paltry 37mm main gun on a turret along with one 30mm machine gun. When the calvary units had been bowled over in the first days of the offensive, a lot of these had been left behind. It could hold a crew of four and on rare occasions could reach a speed of fifty. Not much defense against a Tiger or any other German tank for that matter. But this one was not going anywhere.

"Can barely see it sir, just the back end or what's left of it, but it's definitely one of ours." It was about 100 yards down a slight incline where the road veered left.

"Yeah, but where are the Germans?"

"Stay here, sir. I'll make a run for it. I think they've gone."

Before Green could respond, Jackson quickly checked his Garand and took off. The road was slushy, and he kicked up a lot of water. His long legs made a lot of noise along the way. Green stayed inside the tree line and slowly made his way forward, trying to keep his eye on Jackson. He ducked behind the bole of a tree as Jackson reached the M8, and took a peek inside. Green waited anxiously, hoping not to hear the crack of a rifle. He slowly crept forward again. Then Jackson suddenly reappeared, scampering back. He was soaked to his knees, but he was carrying another *.45* pistol, tucked inside his pants.

"Two dead sir, troopers from the 14th Cav. The back of the thing has been seared right off. Lots of jagged metal sir. There is some ammo and two partially dry uniforms sir, except for some blood. Found some rations and one of the guys' *.45s* that the Germans must have missed. We have to go for it. You will freeze by morning. One of them is about your size."

Green's distinct averageness was becoming his savior.

"Okay, let's go."

They gained their footing and ran down the road, reaching the wreckage. Its turret had been blown right off. Tank tracks could still be seen leading away from it. This crew had been caught by a Panzer or some self-propelled artillery. The sight of the driver surprised Green. He had seen a lot of dead and wounded, but it had been a while since he had seen such a grotesque sight. The left corner of the driver's side had a gaping hole from a shell. The guy's lower face was practically shot off, but there was an eye left that seemed to stare back at him. Dried blood streaked down the man's face like the delta of a river and bits of brain tissue covered his jacket. With hushed voices, they went about their business. Green hoped it had been a quick death, unlike Rutkowski, who had time to know what was happening.

"He's about your size, sir."

Green hesitated, "Shit, do you have one without that stuff on it?"

"Try the other one then, Lieutenant. You have to do it, sir. He doesn't need them anymore."

"Okay, okay. Now I know how you got those stripes, Sergeant.

"I'll keep my eyes peeled as you change, okay sir?"

After what seemed like the longest five minutes of his life, Green got into dry clothes or what passed for them. The man's boots did not quite fit as well. So he changed the socks and left the boots. Unfortunately, neither of these guys had shoepacs. Guess they figured guys who ride into war don't need them. Snow was falling again, just in time for another cold night.

"You're next, Sergeant. I'm through stealing from the dead."

"But sir, I 'm bigger than both those boys."

"You can at least get his socks on. And save that extra one you have. Please, you are almost as soaked as I am."

Green handed him the pair he had pulled off the dead GI.

Jackson quickly threw away his old pair and got on the 'new' ones.

"Done, sir."

"One more thing, Sergeant. Knock off the "sir" crap. We are just two soldiers trying to stay alive. Got it?"

"Yes, sir, I mean *Lieutenant*."

"Sergeant, what about that food?"

"K rations. Box was already open, Lieutenant."

"Let's go."

As Green made his way to leave, he stopped. He hadn't even checked the dog tags of the dead men. Did he want to know the names of the soldiers whose bodies he had stripped? Curiosity got the best of him.

"Wait Jackson, let's check something."

Green reached into the driver's area and lifted the trooper up and felt for his tags.

"Douglas," Green whispered to himself. "Check the other one Jackson."

As Jackson felt for the other tags, he managed to move his hand over one of the man's wounds. A small hole could be felt on his chest. He must have caught a piece of shrapnel when the turret was blown to bits. It was hoped he died right away, and was not left to freeze to death. But the wound had not hit the heart, so he must have laid there in agony for hours.

"Here it is, Lieutenant, the name is Greevey. Should I snag one of them sir."

"No, leave the tag. We don't know where we are headed. Our guys may retake this area and graves reg will come through eventually."

Suddenly, the sound of a vehicle bouncing its way toward them began to echo. Green snapped around trying to figure the direction. The road was curving at both ends. It sounded like an American jeep. But whatever it was, it probably had Germans in it.

"Jackson. Hey, Jackson," Green emphasized it the second time, but he was still tucked inside the M8 when Green saw the jeep emerge from around the bend behind them.

"Jackson, Krauts! Duck down somewhere. Don't try and get out. They'll see you. Do not make a sound. I got you covered."

Green reached down a grabbed Jackson's sack of grenades and jumped into the woods. The lack of underbrush was a problem but the battle had churned up the forest a little bit. He hoped some limbs that had been blasted from the trees would help conceal him, and still give him a view of the Germans.

The scout car's ripped open back end would be invitation for the Germans to stop. Green was just twenty feet inside the tree line, covered with as many fir branches as he could find.

The jeep came to within ten feet of the armored car. Four Germans, all enlisted, got out and did a quick scan of the adjacent woods. Despite the cover, Green still had a good view of the both vehicles. The German sergeant shouted something and one of the men made his way toward the back of the M-8. It appeared as though the Germans were just looking for some loot. Green could not imagine how Jackson was concealing himself. He stood no chance if he decided to fight it out.

Another one of the Germans made his way to the back of the M8, but after a cursory glance, kept walking around. Green's hopes were raised. Maybe the sight was too grisly. Jackson would have been noticed by now. Then, the sergeant walked over to the driver and began searching him. One of the others trudged into the woods on the other side of the road just out of sight to pee, while another came close to Green before walking back to be near his comrade. With his Thompson within easy reach, he prepared to make the throw of his life.

Raising himself up from his elbows to one knee, he inched a little closer with his left arm raised, releasing the levers as the German reached inside the M8.

Throwing two grenades at a time was not taught in basic training. He had to pull the pin on one, holding down the lever while trying to pull the other pin. With cold, aching hands, it was not easy and he hadn't thrown one since OCS. The pins were tightly secured, and he had to carefully pull on them, without them slipping from his wet gloves. When he got them both set, he slowly exhaled, holding the grenades as long as he safely could. The seconds felt like minutes.

One grenade was thrown near the scout car and the other rolled within an inch of the other two soldiers, blowing up almost simultaneously. The sergeant was killed instantly and the other two were showered with deadly shrapnel. Both were slammed against the M8. One remained unhurt. Green immediately grabbed his Thompson but tripped as he tried to get to the road. He heard a German yell and desperately looked for him as he made his way from the tree line. Finally catching sight of the last soldier, he ran behind the jeep to fire away at him. The stunned soldier ran into the line of fire and was cut to pieces. Bullets riddled his body as the clip emptied. The German's eyes widened as he dropped to his knees and fell forward, blood pouring from his mouth. Green stopped to look down the road. The firing had echoed, but hopefully blended in with the other sounds of battle. There was moaning from one of the Germans as he approached the back of the M8. He heard nothing from Jackson, not a peep out of him. The severely wounded German had a leg practically severed and gushing blood. He lay on his side gasping for breath, while his fingers were reaching out, feigning to crawl away.

Green looked for Jackson and to his surprise, saw nothing inside the armored car except the two dead Americans.

"Jackson!"

Suddenly, one of the bodies began to rise and from underneath emerged the Sergeant, with skeptical eyes along with a weary smile.

"I am glad to hear your voice, sir."

"Great idea. Get out of there and let's go. Grab your weapon."

Jackson emerged still in a little shock. He looked around and saw the dead Germans lying about and still heard the moaning of the other one.

Green now faced a dilemma. He was certain another German patrol would come soon. The German on the ground was still alive, barely, with the gasping getting weaker. He kicked the German's Mauser out of the way and mistakenly rolled him over to reveal the man's grisly wounds to his face. One side had been shredded by the blast. Green looked away and then up at Jackson.

"Sir, he'll be dead in a few minutes. We should just go. If you're worried about him suffering sir, he wouldn't..."

"I'm not worried about that," Green angrily retorted, although not so sure about his sentiment. "What if he doesn't die and the Krauts come along to save him."

"I don't think he saw us, sir. Besides, there's no saving him."

"Alright, get going into those woods," Green ordered, pointing toward the trees on the other side.

Jackson moved out, but as he got into woods, he felt compelled to stop. Looking back he saw Green cock his *.45* and fire a round that finished off the already doomed German. Jackson couldn't tell if it was an act of mercy or rage, though he was banking on the former. Either way, this white lieutenant had saved his life.

Green looked up, saw Jackson watching, and angrily waved him into the trees.

21

THE BLACKNESS OF THE WINTER night had encompassed them, only interrupted by the distant flashes of fighting to the west. Like two ghosts from a vanquished army, they marched in ankle-deep snow for another hour with the brightness of the snow providing some guidance. It felt as though they had walked for miles as their leg muscles burned and sweat poured from their brows. The real distance was closer to a mile at most.

They reached the top of a hill, and tried to get their bearings. The downslope was bare and surprisingly, almost free of snow. It ran down to a road they could not see, though the ominous sounds of idling diesel engines and the Germans' guttural yelling could clearly be heard. Lying around them were some disabled .30 caliber water-cooled machine guns and M-1 rifles laying in what obviously were some abandoned American shelters. Thankfully, there were no bodies this time.

"The Germans must have gone through here already, Sergeant," Green whispered. "These are perfectly good positions. Somewhat covered. Not too much snow. The Krauts will stick to the roads. We can wait here until near daylight and then we can confirm where we are and figure out what to do. No sense walking around in the dark so close to the Krauts."

"If you think so, sir. I mean, *Lieutenant*."

They checked their weapons as quietly as possible and also looked around for tree limbs and branches to add even more cover to the foxholes. After eating some chocolate and taking a few sips of water, they spent a freezing night huddling in those foxholes while trying to remember to keep their extremities moving as much as they could. Falling asleep in their condition could mean the loss of a foot or some fingers. Green ordered Jackson to check his feet as he did the same.

"Sir, did you hear about the order warning that if any GI came down with trench foot, he might be court-martialed?"

"Yeah, I heard. Never found out if it was true or not. I guess they will never be able to measure the effectiveness of that order. Quite frankly, if they want to court martial me when I get back, I would be more than happy to accept. If all I end up with is trench foot after this mess we're in now, it's the price I'll pay."

"Amen to that, sir."

Each of them occasionally took turns leaving the foxhole, either to move around more or for a nature call.

With first light, they realized that Schonberg lay in the distance, its church tower rising above the clusters of white stone houses and rust-colored roofs. The town was still relatively in tact. A glimpse of the Our River could be seen to the left, peeking out from between the houses.

The sloping field in front of them was blanketed with a fresh coat of snow and hordes of Germans. The Germans wore a plethora of uniforms. Black uniformed Panzer crews were meeting off the road. Snow suited infantrymen sat leisurely up on the tanks, eating and smoking. So great was their confidence, that a small group stood around an open fire pit. Feasting on the spoils of war was the priority; some tried on American boots while others were trading in a variety of cigarettes and chocolates. Green and Jackson stared in amazement. The

Germans were now within a couple of hundred yards of their trench. Green was disgusted.

How did we not know about all this?

Besides the Panzers, there were Hetzers, German tank destroyers and the Sturmgeschütz 75mm self-propelled guns, which GIs always mistook for Tiger tanks. But what really troubled them, was the sight of their enemy riding around in American jeeps and trucks.

"Take a look, Sergeant."

Jackson took the field glasses and exhaled as he viewed the onslaught.

"I see some GIs, Lieutenant."

Green snatched the glasses back and peered intently trying to see if any of his men were down there. He could not make out their patches, although it was a good assumption that they were from the 106th. There were numerous medics in the crowd. Others huddled outside a barn that was used as a makeshift aid station.

"I'm sort of back where I started, Lieutenant. If you look just past the town sir, you'll see a small hill on the right side of the road. That's where I thought I saw Lieutenant Wood running from the Krauts."

"That must have been a hell of hike."

"Lieutenant, look off to the side there."

Jackson was pointing to their left. There was a small dirt road leading away from the town just southwest of where they were now. Green followed the road with his glasses until he saw the farmhouse or what appeared to be one, peeking out from between the trees. There were no signs of any Germans near the place. There was another structure behind it that appeared to be some sort of barn.

"Okay Jackson, options?

"You asking me, Lieutenant?"

"Yes I am."

"Well, if we can sneak over to the farmhouse, stay there until nightfall, we could get drier and maybe steal a little food. Then begin our trek back to our lines or just fight it out, sir. Would be easier with a final meal. Besides, we are sort of heading that way. We'll have to try to get across the river soon or forget about it. I think the river bends and narrows a little south of here."

"I like it, sounds grim. But it's a plan."

"You sure that you didn't already know the answer to that question, Lieutenant?"

"Well, I always like to confer with my men," Green answered with a wink.

Jackson just smiled to himself, and like so many others who had served with Green, could only wonder about the man's past and what made him the most unusual officer they had ever met.

22

THEY WAITED ABOUT TWO MORE hours in their foxhole, silently observing German troop movements. It was almost one o'clock. Traveling in daylight and exposing themselves by leaving the Spartan comfort of these prepared positions was worse than risky. It might be suicidal. Both men left that unsaid. Finally, they decided to creep towards the main road. More snow was falling, the wind was beginning to gust, and temperatures were dropping again; hopefully the Germans were too busy keeping warm to notice the unusual duo roaming around amongst them.

After struggling down a small hill, but miraculously managing to keep the snow out, they reached the edge of the Schonberg road, crouching low on the edge of the tree line. To their absolute shock, there were no signs of any Germans coming up or down the road. They had picked the right spot, the crest of a hill. The road from Bleialf rose sharply before dropping down towards Schonberg. It was also fairly narrow and with the mud, no vehicles would be able to move that fast.

"Listen for any engine noise or Krauts."

At this point, neither of them probably needed any reminders.

"Can't believe it, Lieutenant. Where did everybody go?"

"This ain't gonna last long. Alright, here we go…"

"Let me go first," Jackson boldly stated while grabbing Green's shoulder. "In fact, I demand it, sir."

"You *demand* it?"

"I'm sorry, Lieutenant. It came out wrong. I…"

Green laughed.

"No time to argue. Get going. Don't look."

After a quick scan right to his left, Jackson jumped over the large gulley and hit the road running. He slipped only once, and was on the other side. Green did not hesitate, only he fell flat on his face again when he missed the jump. Regaining his footing, he aimed for the tire ruts. At the middle of the road, he heard a truck shift into first gear as it made its way up the hill. Green leaped off the road and landed next to Jackson, who was pointing his Garand down towards Schonberg.

"Move it," he ordered, out of breath, more from nerves than exertion. "Get into the trees. We have to get to the other side of this patch of woods anyway."

They cleared the road and reached the relative safety of the dark forest before the convoy past them. The knobby hill rose higher than they thought.

"I think the Krauts can hear us breathe, sir."

"That's the least of our problems."

On the down slope, the trees went almost right to the road, enough to keep them covered. Calling it a road would be kind. It just seemed to be for private use, maybe a bypass. Both men peered up the path towards the town. Green checked his watch out of habit. It was almost three o'clock, the onset of darkness less than an hour away.

The house they sought now came into full view. It lay just off to their left, with the barn about another hundred feet behind it. As he looked further past the house, it appeared that there was already a little path through the snow leading from the house to the barn. But there were no Germans in sight.

"Sergeant, this time I go first."

"My pleasure, Lieutenant."

With Thompson at the ready, he took off, sinking immediately into the mud. He refused to look up, not wanting to see what might be coming. Finally getting his feet loose, he crept to the side of the house and tried to peer in the window to no avail. Smoke billowed from the chimney, so someone was home.

The house appeared unusual for the area, in the fact that it was almost made entirely of wood construction with some sort of upper story, possibly just an attic. Its foundation was made of stone and mortar. But for that, it looked almost like a typical American farmhouse. He could not help but note the irony that they had picked the one place that looked American. Most of the houses in the region seemed to be almost entirely of whitewashed masonry construction.

He waved Jackson over and the Sergeant made it a little easier using Green's steps. As they were catching their breath, they heard steps in the house.

"Let's go for it now," Green snapped. They sprinted over the slush, pushed the huge wooden door open and immediately grabbed their weapons.

Green peered through the wooden slats. The curtains at the back door moved just before the door opened.

"Get ready for them, Jackson."

Jackson checked his Garand, made sure he knew where his clips were and crawled to a small broken window to look out.

"It's a little girl, sir, and she's coming this way."

"I see that. Let's not scare her. She's probably a Kraut kid. We don't want any screams." Green put his back to one of the doors and waited for her. Jackson stayed at the window with his Garand.

"Jackson, anyone else following her?", Green asked in a barely audible whisper.

The sergeant shook his head.

Suddenly there was a creaking of the door. It opened slightly and a smallish girl, not quite ten, wrapped in a white wool blanket, stuck her head inside. Her large blue eyes met Green's.

"Amis?"

They were at first shocked by her stern voice. There was no fear in this kid.

"Shh, Green put his finger to his lips. "Sprechen Sie englisch?"

"*Un peu.*"

"What the hell was that?"

"I think it's French, sir."

"*Shh*", Green put his finger to his lips. "Joi Americans", Green tried the one French phrase he knew.

"Amis?" she asked. 'Amis' was the local slang for the Americans.

"Yes, oui, yes…"

Green looked at Jackson, "So they speak French?"

Jackson excitedly came over and began speaking in broken French, "Nous sommes des Americains, nous avons besoin de nourriture."

Green stood open mouthed, gaping at Jackson.

A Negro speaking perfect French? What the hell was he saying?

"*Maman ou papa dans maison?*"

"No" the shocked little girl answered.

"Where the hell did you learn French, Sergeant? What did you say? Where are her parents?"

"Just a second, sir. I'm kind of unsure about my French, sir. Sorry, just cover the window. Pousvez-vous nous aider?"

"Oui, je puis. I… know some English. Me Catherine. You stay."

"Parlez-vous Anglais?"

"Oui."

With that, she turned and quietly went back to her house.

"What's going on Jackson?"

"I asked her for help and some food. She is the only one home right now and I think she can speak some English. As you heard, sir, she asked us to wait."

"Yeah, while she gets the Krauts."

"I think we'll be okay, sir."

"Where did you learn the French?"

"It's a long story, Lieutenant. But anyway, at college."

"College?"

"Yes, *college*," he retorted slowly for emphasis, feeling a little disrespected again.

"This area is full of Krauts, why didn't you try German?"

Jackson smiled.

"I don't speak German, sir. And besides, she answered you in French."

"Stupid question. Good call. The cold is getting to me. Well, our lives are riding on this kid."

"Hold on, sir. I hear footsteps in that slush out there."

"Can you see anybody?"

"Nothing yet, sir."

Green pulled back on the retracting rod of the Thompson and crouched at the window. Jackson grabbed his Garand and pointed it at the door. It was now fully dark. Only a flicker of light came from the house. The steps were getting closer, they were too big to be the girl. Finally, there was a knock.

"*Halo Americains, Je suis le pere.* I am father."

Both men shrugged, and gave themselves a look that it was okay. Green slowly raised his Thompson anyway.

The door was opened very slowly. Catherine and her father appeared in the door, then the man quickly closed the it behind them. Even with the darkness, Jackson could see that he probably was in his late 30s, maybe 40, wearing the mostly flannel clothes of a farmer and those oversized boots that they heard. He was just a bit shorter than Green, standing almost eye to eye with him. The always cynical Green flicked off his lighter and turned back to the window to remain squinting into the darkness with hands cupped around his eyes.

"You are *Américain*, I help. I know some English. My name Leo."

"I am Sergeant Jackson and over there is Lieutenant Green. Have the Germans come here?"

"All over. Schonberg many. They stop here. Look in. Keep going. I went to town. Boche, no stop me. I tell Catherine no leave house. She no do."

"Do you think we can make it to American lines? Green chimed in.

"Get to *Américain Armee*?"

Even in the poor light, Green could see the surprised look on Leo's face. It gave him his answer. Leo just took a deep breath before continuing.

"No. I just see more American prisoner come down hill. German general come last night. More Germans. St. Vith bad now. Lots of fighting. Boom, Boom. I see flash."

Leo had become animated, and was now making hand gesture signifying explosions, and pointing to the ceiling.

"You stay here. I give food *et* blanket. I 'ave food in house."

"Okay, for now. We don't want to get you in trouble. They won't come back?" Green asked.

"I don't think so, they check house *et grange*...how you say?" Leo pointed to the walls of the barn.

"The barn," Jackson immediately responded.

"Ah, yes, barn. They see nothing. Keep door lock, *s'il vous plaît*. But I ask, if something happen, no shooting. Just Catherine and myself now. My wife dead."

"So you don't think they'll be back?"

"No, I don't think so."

Jackson and Green just looked at each other and shrugged.

"Thanks Leo. Hey, are you French?"

"Well, me Belgian, from west. My wife Flemish, from Saint Vith. Many here speak two language. This used to be Germany, yes."

"Flemish?" Green was puzzled.

"Lieutenant, they are ethnic Belgians," Jackson relayed.

"Oh, okay. Even now I am learning something new," he replied sarcastically. "I did not read any 'U.S. Army Guide to Belgium', if there is one. You obviously did. Thanks again, Leo. I promise we'll be quiet."

"The village *est très* German. So must be careful. No like war, but they want more Boche. I am friendly with everyone, but you know... *c'est la guerre*."

"Yeah, I know. I did notice some civilians a few days ago looking more than happy that we were retreating. Most just seemed scared. So I guess we picked the right joint to stop at, right?" Green smiled at Jackson.

" I was also a soldier once, in the Belgian *Armee*, years ago. Met my wife on leave in Brussels. I also serve in the *Armee* at start of war. No captured. Came back to farm."

"Say Leo, guy with your skills would be very useful in the underground. Were you in the resistance movement at all? Did you guys even have one?"

"No Maquis!" he answered sternly, after a long pause.

Despite the darkness, they could feel the expression on Leo's face change, his change in tone left an impression. Green quickly came to the realization that he had asked a foolish and very dangerous question. The man had not given his last name either; it was now obvious as to why.

The Belgian underground, known by some as the Maquis, had been aiding the Americans since they arrived in September. Like every other occupied country, fear of German reprisal was commonplace. The *Boche* would have no mercy, even on a widowed father.

"Forget it Leo, you didn't have to answer that. I understand." Leo understood that the chances of these two Americans getting captured were pretty good and the Germans might start asking questions.

"Cigarette?" Leo eagerly asked.

"I had some but they got soaked. Don't smoke much anyway. Jackson?"

"Sorry, sir. The ones in the K ration got wet and I don't smoke either."

"Don't smoke? Sorry Leo, you got two teetotalers here."

Leo nodded politely and turned to leave, then stopped as his daughter ran ahead.

"Lieutenant, I no say in front of Catherine, but I see three *Americain* shot by *Boche* in Schonberg. He was yelling. You know, 'escape, escape..' They line up….."

"I got the idea, thanks," Green quickly interrupted, putting up his hand.

"I am sorry."

"So there were no other Americans who came through here, trying to flee?"

"No. No."

Leo bowed his head.

"I see you soon."

On that grim note, Leo turned and left. They put the boards back against door. There was a moment of quiet and Green felt the need for an order.

"Take off your boots and change your socks if the others are drier, rub your feet too. Check for trench foot," he sternly ordered. "I know I'm a broken record but…"

"Already doing it."

Green quickly unlaced his boots and took off his wet socks, laying them down on a wood board. He felt his feet. They were wet and cold, but the skin seemed intact. The four inches of leather that were sewn into the top of the boot did nothing to keep precipitation out, even when they were buckled. Because of the darkness, getting a good feel is all he could hope for. His Ronson's dim light wouldn't help. Letting the dry air hit his feet for a little while might be better than immediately changing socks again. They would be cold, but keeping them dry is what mattered.

As his eyes adjusted to the darkness, he looked around and noticed six stalls for cows, three on each side in the back of the building; there was a back door similar to the front. Thankfully, it had been a while since the cows had come home; the scent of the manure lingered, albeit slightly. Green then removed his helmet and the wool skull cap he had taken from a dead GI. His head itched and he gave it a good scratch. The curly hair on top was now almost straight and matted down. Steam rose from his head. After a shiver, he put the skull cap back on.

"I think I could use a bath."

"You could say that again, sir."

There were two knocks on the door and Green immediately stood up, pointing the Thompson at the door.

"It is Leo."

Leo had came back with some bread, tea and four Hershey's chocolate bar, obviously obtained from being in contact with the Americans. And most importantly, some clean socks.

"You hungry. This help you."

"Thanks Leo, We owe ya."

"No need, Lieutenant. I 'ave to give you help."

"Say Leo, do you get any other news on the battle, besides what's happening around here?"

There was a long pause by Leo, who seemed to be choosing his words carefully.

"Saint Vith. Fighting bad. But I no know much else."

Green figured that Leo had a radio to the outside world in the house because his answer was not very convincing.

"Please, eat."

Jackson and Green both nodded to Leo to show their gratitude, with Jackson adding a *Merci*.

"There is light," Leo then reached around the door to point out the lantern sitting by the window. "But please no let Germans see anything."

Leo then walked to the back of the barn and reached down for what turned out to be two large green canvas tarps that he had gotten from the American Army. He brought them over to the window close in order for them to understand what he meant.

"Don't worry Leo, I gotcha."

"Merci," Jackson said again in perfect French.

"Très bien, messieurs."

Leo smiled and went back to his much warmer home. The boards were carefully put back. They quietly ate one of the Hershey's and loved the warm tea, saving the bread.

"Maybe we should have a toast, Lieutenant."

"You're right, Jackson. We deserve one. How 'bout to Red Legs everywhere, wherever they may be."

"I second that, Lieutenant."

They both raised their cups of teas in salute.

"With two Red Legs taking them on, the Krauts don't stand a chance, wouldn't you say so, Sergeant?"

"You bet, sir."

They sat silently in the darkness savoring the respite from escape, but the silence was awkward to Jackson, who felt compelled to talk after so many days alone in the woods.

"Sir, I ain't ever seen a barn with a window. Have you?"

"Well, maybe it doubled as a garage. Hell, maybe just to air the place out. It's a little stuffy during the summer maybe?"

"Yeah, but we're lucky. I won't complain."

At last, they had found a friend, even if it was temporary.

23

After hanging a canvas tarp over the window, Green used one of his gem blades to carefully chop the chocolate into eight pieces, four for Jackson and four for himself. They took a chance using a lantern to hold some burning paper they lit up, providing enough light to prepare their 'dessert.'

"Guess we should take it easy on the food, Sergeant. We don't want to be shittin' up a storm when we're on the run."

"I was just thinking that very thing, sir."

"We should save the K rations as long as we can. I wish we had some of those heating tablets for the food."

"I have plenty, sir. Almost forgot about it."

"Jesus, how could you forget about those?"

"Sorry, Lieutenant."

"You were right to save them. Even if it was unintentional. If we have to, we can burn the K ration box."

"Do you think what that man said is the truth?"

"What was that?"

"That we can't get back to American lines?"

"Well, we don't have any choice but to try. I mean we both saw what the Krauts did to a lot of their prisoners. Unless we surrendered in a large group, I don't think we would stand a chance. These Krauts are on a tight timetable."

"I understand, Lieutenant."

"Okay, sergeant. I am going to give you an order. Spill the beans."

" Excuse me, sir"

" Let's have it, the college, the French language skills, etcetera…"

"Never seen a Negro in college, sir?"

"You know what I mean," was Green's stern reply.

Green was now squatting near the broken window, trying to get it covered again with the tarp as the wind kicked it open.

"I mean, where did you learn to speak French? You been out here a while, I figure. And everybody picked up some French while driving across the country, but still. Yours was damn good."

"My mom always wanted the kids to get the best education. Being colored folks, that didn't always happen. But my folks were determined. There were six of us. But we could all read real well. We were lucky, when the family moved to Chicago from Mississippi in '28 I was nine. It was soon after the big flood. My father got a pretty good job at a candy factory. First, as a janitor. Then, because the owner was decent man, think he was Jewish, born in Russia. He gave my dad a chance by letting him work the line. Good pay. The factory stayed open even after that stock market crash. People loved candy and my Dad really liked Chicago. He felt sort of free. We were still segregated, but my folks got to vote. My dad was a big fan of Roosevelt. That was the first Democrat my folks voted for. They been good to us in Chicago. Democrats up north seem to be a lot different then the ones in Mississippi, sir."

"That's what I've heard."

"Sorry, sir. Think I'm talking too much.

"So get to it Jackson, how did you do it? You know, the college, the stripes, etc."

"Okay, I actually graduated from High School in Chicago, '41 and made it into Howard, you know the Negro college in D.C.

"Yeah, I heard of it."

Well, I majored in journalism, thought about being a writer, maybe work for the Chicago Defender. Took a lot of language classes. My Dad had been in the last war in France and I always wanted to go. Then I thought about going to law school, especially with Judge Hastie runnin' the school now."

"Law school? I don't get it. You already finished a couple of years of college but you are not an officer. They have colored officers, I know because I've met 'em."

"Well, Lieutenant, after Pearl Harbor I thought of immediately signing up even with the segregation. They sent a couple of black officers over to the campus to recruit. But a friend of mine said if you want to get overseas, don't become an officer. And I wanted to fight sir, I really did. We thought the colored officers were just for show. Besides sir, a lot you white officers only have a little college, but to be a Negro officer, they wanted you to have finished the college. At least that's what we kept saying anyway. They weren't just gonna send Negros to no OCS willy-nilly."

So after basic training, I heard they were going to form black combat units, not just drivers and stuff. I lucked out and was assigned to an artillery unit, the 333rd. They tested me, said I could become a forward observer. Had I known it was going to be this dangerous, I might have been a little more worried. Been overseas since the summer."

"Some story."

"What about you, sir?"

"First of all, stop the sir."

"I promise, I promise."

"Grew up in Yonkers, my folks were actually born in Europe. I got three brothers. Worked at a quarry on Midland Ave, just a mile from my house. I also graduated high school there. Joined the Guard out of there too. My two younger brothers are not old enough yet for the Army and another whose been in the navy since '43. Turns out he was aboard one of the ships off Sicily when I was landing there, the Ancon. Had a great billet, worked on the bridge. Watching all the Higgins boats and other craft head toward the beach he unfortunately was inspired to get closer to the action. Now, he's a crewman on an LST. The last letter I got from him said he was in Hawaii, training with the Marines. Scuttlebutt said there's a big offensive planned early next year.

"But what about *you*, Lieutenant? Did *you* go to college?"

Jackson was frustrated with the rather understated nature of his new Lieutenant. After a question about himself, he ended up talking about his brothers. His concern was admirable and it gave an insight into the kind of officer he was, but Jackson's curiosity had to be satisfied.

"I went to Fordham University, Jesuit school down in the Bronx."

"I know about that school. I heard of the Fordham Flash, Frankie Frisch. Pretty good football team too. You do have kind of a different accent. Now I recognize it. We had a lot of fellas from up near New York City at Howard," Jackson recalled, reacting to Green's pronunciation of Yonkers.

Green's accent could not always be heard. He suppressed it whenever possible setting up a sort of mental blockade. After he was activated and became acquainted with so many different soldiers from around the country, he tried not to let it out. He wanted to sound as Yankee as he could. But in stress or after the rare night out on the town, the Yonkers kid took over and the accent flowed out.

"Well, I only spent a year there. My Guard unit was activated in my second year. I sort of liked the Army and decided to make the best of it. After Pearl Harbor I got myself transferred into the 1st."

"The First Division? You seen a lot of combat too?"

"A little. Most of it involved getting shelled on top of some hill in the desert. But I had more than anybody else in my last outfit. Thought I had it made because of that too. When they sent me back for OCS, I figured with some combat experience, couple of Purple Hearts, I could be of value for training. Next thing I know I'm off to Tennessee for the 106th. I'm tired of these Krauts. They're probably going to ruin another Christmas.

"Been wounded twice? Whoa, I am glad I met you Lieutenant."

"Same goes for me. At least your over twenty. A lot of these guys are way too young. Just saw a bunch of replacements back in England. They got over here with just three months in the Army. No advanced training, right out of boot camp. And even boot camp was not long enough. I heard they shortened it to something like six weeks. A lot of those college guys been coming over too. That ASTP thing was disbanded I heard. Some real eager, others not so much."

"What was North Africa like, besides hot?"

"It was no ocean of sand like the movies and newsreels. It was a continental size gravel pit. As soon as you hit the ground, it's rock. Millions of little tiny shards of broken stone. The Army should have issued us chisels, not shovels. When the wind blew, that sand felt like it was cutting your face to pieces. I can still taste the dirt. At night, those stones were like ice cubes. Then those damn nomads or Bedouins or whatever they're called just sort of sneak up on you. Whatever, they were scary because they were quiet and smart. To survive out there, you had to be. If you were standing watch at one of the artisan wells, they were able to get an entire group of people and animals right up to you before you heard them. What they wore on their feet, I don't know. Even their goats were quiet. Seemed friendly enough. They were just trying to survive. But it was a strange place for any GI."

"When did you go to OCS, Lieutenant?"

"After Tunisia...sort of. I guess I was selected, in a way. My CO recommended me after what he termed a lengthy process. They had asked me once before back at Fort Bragg and I managed to avoid it. After the second time, I guess you could say I was 'volunteered.' Think my lieutenant felt he was doing me a favor, you know, felt he owed me. Not sure why. I was in Sicily when they put on a boat back to Africa where I got shipped home. I only had a year of college and thought it might be too much. But I got by and here I am. Lucky me."

Green skirted the truth by omitting some of the more juicy details, managing to avoid any more discussion of his past service.

"Your folks from Europe? Whereabouts?"

"My Dad is actually from Germany and my mom is from Ireland, County Claire to be exact."

"How does your Dad feel about the war then?"

"Well...he came here when he was real young, and he's Jewish."

"Ooh, okay sir. I got it."

"And your mom ain't Jewish, I suppose?"

"No, she isn't," Green replied with a laugh. "They were and still are, an unusual pair. My Dad had to promise to raise the kids Catholic in order to marry her. So that's how it happened. But my mother always told the neighbors that he was a non-practicing Protestant."

"That's a better story than mine, sir."

"Maybe."

His thoughts flashed back to his parents often the last few days. He had not written in a long time and when they last met he had not been too talkative, although he had tried. They wanted to know how their eldest son was doing. and he desperately wanted the chance once again.

"Do you think your men are being treated well, sir?"

"I can only hope. After seeing those men by the side of the road earlier, I don't know. How many are still alive? I left a bunch of wounded back there."

Jackson could hear the anguish in Green's voice and Green was happy they could not see clearly enough to look at each other's faces. He knew his face conveyed only despair.

"Lieutenant, I'm sure they are happy that you escaped. Maybe others are roaming around too. I know it."

"I cost the lives of a lot of my men," he added ruefully.

"Lieutenant, I don't think..."

"Hey, get some sleep," he interrupted quickly. "I'm going to maintain the watch by the window. I'll wake ya in three hours. It's almost 2200. If you gotta pee or anything else, do it quietly. Keep a weapon near you and one of the bandoleers. I can't always see everything in this blackness."

Jackson was enjoying the conversation too much to just stop now. It had been the most civilized thing he'd done in days.

"Got a girl, Lieutenant?"

"Are we playing twenty questions? Sounds like you are bucking for a job with *Yank*."

"Sorry, sir. I don't get a chance to talk to white men too often. And I would like to take advantage of the opportunity, if you don't mind."

The profound nature of that statement struck Green right away, and he relented.

"Alright, what the hell. Had a girlfriend while I was at Fordham. She was going to the teacher's program that they had on campus for local gals. But been in the Army so long, that we just lost touch. Met a British nurse in Africa, right after I got there. But again, the fortunes of war. She must think I'm dead. Got out to see the Casablanca nightlife a couple of times. I avoided the whorehouses though. Saw too many guys with syphilis. Nasty stuff but the treatment was worse. So technically, I don't have a girl."

"Think you have nine lives Lieutenant."

"Let's hope so. If I do, I've reached the ninth. At this point, I just wanna get back to Yonkers and I'll be okay."

"What do you think is happening out there, sir? You know, at the front? I still don't know how big this battle is."

"Well, I hope by now that the Brass have realized what is going on. They certainly did not see this coming. Although I'm sure they will try and say they did. I know my guys all assumed they would counterattack, but it did not come soon enough for my men. Kept hearing about air drops being on their way. But those intelligence guys really let us down this time. I think they hit us with everything they had, probably all over the entire front."

"Well maybe we can take the war to the Germans ourselves. You know what Napoleon said sir, 'Every soldier somewhere carries a Marshal's baton.'"

As jaded as Green was, he admired the idealism and enthusiasm that Jackson still had. It was an odd combination for a combat veteran, and he couldn't remember meeting anyone this optimistic since basic training.

"Wow, now that's inspirational," he half-mockingly replied, "but I'll say this, you would have made a great officer. Unfortunately, Sergeant, my outfit met its Waterloo. Right now, I don't have any grand plans, so let's hope we can get back to our own guys first. Then we can take up the fight again. Our chances would be greatly improved."

"I know, Lieutenant. Just thinking out loud." Jackson became a little embarrassed at his own enthusiasm, so he changed the subject. "Any thoughts on what you will do after the war, sir?"

"Maybe go back to Fordham. Discovered a knack for some skills I didn't think I had since entering the artillery. Not sure."

"Play any ball, Lieutenant?"

"High school. Little bit at Fordham before I was called up. I wasn't bad."

"My friend Due was awesome. The battalion had their own team and we beat everybody. I only wish he had got out with me."

"Can I ask, how do you spell that name, Sergeant?"

"Oh, it's spelled just like *due date*. Due Robinson Turner was his full name. Probably my best friend in the outfit."

"Kind of an unusual name."

"Believe it or not, I knew another Due growing up. Guess you haven't been around a lot of Negro folks, right sir?"

"Yes sergeant, you could say that. But why the name?"

"Heard a lot of reasons. But Due would always say that he got that name because so many people were asking his mother when the baby was due. But I'm sure that every kid named *Due* tells people the same story. I never saw his service record, but I wouldn't be surprised if his real name was Duvall or something like that.

"Your first name is Emmett? Correct?"

"Yes, sir. No story there, I had an uncle with the same name."

"How long were you with this guy Due?"

"Almost since landing in June, sir. I mean, our survey team had a lot of different guys, but we were the only constant members. We helped lay the guns in most of the time. Don't know what happened to my lieutenant. He didn't make it back in time."

"Six months is a long time these days."

"Due was a character and smart as hell. Despite all his mean words, he always said, *'I don't hate nobody.' No one at all.'* He just wanted some recognition. I got out of the South when I was young but he was there his whole life. Chicago wasn't easy, but it a whole sight better than Georgia or Mississippi. To see him cut down like that. Those Krauts must have put twenty, maybe thirty shots in him. Could even see the blood pouring out of him before he fell. I mean he kept standing after like a dozen hit him. Then he dropped to his knees and took more shots.

Just wouldn't go down. It seemed like it was all happening so slow. But it must have been maybe a few seconds."

Jackson's voice began to break a little. Green let Jackson keep talking. It became a eulogy of sorts.

"Due talked big, but he had a good heart. I knew every time he said something to me about being a '*Tom*' or going to college, he really meant it toward some white man who had insulted him. Problem with Jim Crow is that they keep us all together and we can't say anything back. I mean, they only allow us to talk to each other. So we have to take it out on each other. Nothing gets explained to us. Always doing the shit jobs, sir. Even the Goddamn Kraut POWs could eat in the mess hall at some of the camps when we couldn't."

"I can honestly say, Sergeant, I've never thought of it that way."

"See sir, out of sight, outta mind."

The moments of silence were getting more and more awkward, and Green was actually getting warm from just being inside. Sleep was coming on fast.

"Okay, let's hope we can stay out of the Germans' sights for now. One of us needs rest, and this time, it's you. Remember, if you have to get up, be careful. We don't want to make a lot of noise. I'll blow out the light."

"I will, Lieutenant. Good night." Jackson pulled the blanket Leo had given him up to his shoulders and tried to get warm enough to sleep.

After a minute, Green broke the silence he had been seeking.

"You know what, speaking of getting up, I have to go to the bathroom, to put it nicely."

"I'm glad you said it first, sir."

"Me too. But let's not do it inside this place. Out of respect anyway. So if all you have to do is pee, just step out through the back there and get your business done quick."

"Yeah, all I have to do is pee, at least for now. I'll try and get this back door opened."

"Do it quietly. Hold on, let me peek through the window here."

Green slowly moved aside the sheet that covered the window. The cold air blew against his face but no sign of the Germans. There were just the distant sounds of burp guns and artillery echoing in the valley.

"Okay Jackson. Real quiet."

The Sergeant slowly raised the wooden latch on the door and laid the board down on the floor. As he tried to push the door open, it would not budge. Then they both realized that there was huge snowdrift against the door. It would have to be the front door or nothing.

"So I guess we don't have to worry about the Krauts sneaking in the back way, huh?"

"You got that right, sir."

Jackson began making his way toward the front through the darkness when there was a crash. Jackson had stumbled in to Leo's gardening implements, receiving a rake to the shins. To Green's immense relief, Jackson managed to hold his tongue. He could not see Jackson's face, but could imagine the pain.

"Are you alright?," he whispered.

"Yeah, yeah." Jackson was panting from the pain. "I'm sorry, sir."

"Don't worry about it. He didn't know we were coming or I'm sure he would have picked up. Just hurry up. I might beat you to it. Step out quietly, and make your way to the side of the house. If you think you hear Germans, knock twice on the side. As faint as possible. Take a weapon with you, but don't load it in case it goes off accidentally. Keep the clip in your pocket."

Green sat by the door, Thompson at the ready. He had already made the decision to fight despite the protests of Leo; he prayed it would not come to that. If the Germans found them in here, Leo and Catherine were dead anyway. He would go down fighting.

Jackson managed to finally get outside, carrying just his *.45*. He looked around at first, still seeing quick flashes of bright light against the western sky. Low rumblings of artillery echoed everywhere. But no sound of German voices or vehicles. His aching bladder brought him back to the task at hand. Slogging his way to the edge of the drift, he relieved himself. Fear gripped him. Because of the noise it was making, he could only think of blundering into capture because of a loud pee. With steam still coming from the snow, he quickly went back inside.

"Hear any Germans?"

"Sir, they are probably as cold as we are and huddling up somewhere."

"I'll be back and I will have to cover up our footsteps out there. After I've frozen my ass off, of course."

He then took off his gloves, figuring it would be better to keep them dry and clean.

Green didn't have a shovel to cover up his business, so after he laid his Thompson against the wall, he just dug out a small hole in the snow and took care of things, trying not to let his butt touch the icy edges of the hole. It was hard to relax and just let it happen. After near death experiences, the only other thing that can focus the mind like survival is going to the bathroom. Five minutes later he was finished, he scooped up a bunch of snow and filled it. As he tip toed back to the barn, the rumblings and flashes increased. He felt like a spotlight was shining on him with every flash. One particular sound got closer and closer. Green stopped dead in his tracks and dropped to one knee. There was the sound of some kind of tracked vehicle getting closer. Headlights were coming from the road. He did not want to be caught entering the barn, so he knocked twice on the side of the barn, reached for a clip and cocked his Thompson. Then he jumped behind the snow bank.

He tried judging the distance to the trees, which in the pitch blackness was impossible. Quickly, he turned his gaze back to the road as the engine noise increased. From his left came a German halftrack, with its distinct V-shaped body plates It was immediately followed by two armored cars. They sped through the mud heading towards the main road with their light blaring. At this point, they had no fear of air attack or of the possibility of any other Americans still hanging around. The long lines of prisoners from the last couple of days had imbued the Germans with the confidence Hitler had hoped.

Green waited another minute, popped the clip from his Thompson, then jumped over the snow and ran back to the door. Hopefully, that was it for the night.

"Jackson, it's clear. I'm coming in," he whispered while tapping on the door. He was afraid that because of nerves Jackson may let a round fly.

"I heard the trucks, sir. What was going on?"

"Three of them. One halftrack and two of those small armored cars."

"Maybe they can't see the barn."

"They can see it. Even in this blackness, the snow is silhouetting everything. They were going pretty fast. Thankfully."

"I'm good for the night."

"Me too, Lieutenant. Good night, sir."

"Get some sleep."

Green let out a deep breath and plopped into the corner of the barn near.

He could not let his true thoughts about their plight, and the chances of getting out of it, be known. His emotions had been ranging from fear, to panic and a renewed bloodlust, which was still being driven by guilt. Wanting revenge was understandable, he knew. But Meyer's admonishment rang out over and over in his head. Revenge was incompatible with escaping from his present situation. And it was no longer all about him. Jackson was now one of his men too and getting them both out was his only chance for atonement.

Jackson dozed off and Green sat peering through a broken window, trying to stay warm against the blowing draft. It was still cold, but they had a roof over their heads, and that was always better than a snowy foxhole. They had real food too. Sleep was coming on even faster now. He had started to itch from getting warm. As his eyelids got heavy, he finally gave into the exhaustion.

24

THEY WERE BOTH STILL ASLEEP when Leo came knocking at the door. It was almost light, and Green reflexively grabbed the Thompson.

"Lieutenant, it is Leo."

"Shit, what time is it? Hold on Leo, let me get this crap out of the way."

Once the boards were gone, Leo opened the door and had even more tea and bread.

"Sorry Leo, we were exhausted. Let me wake my staff up," he sarcastically added.

After finishing the bread and tea, Catherine ran over and had two more Hershey bars. Her cute smile bringing an odd touch of humanity to an otherwise inhuman couple of days.

They continued eating in silence, aware not to overdue the indulgence. The quiet was only broken by their shivering. Jackson could not stand it any longer.

"Lieutenant, are we just gonna hide out here? Do you think we can check the woods out a bit or...."

"Yeah, I know," he quickly interrupted.

He knew the question was coming, but still struggled with the uncertainty of their plan.

"I don't wanna sit here all day either, even with its accommodations. But we don't want to get them in trouble. You keep asking a lot of questions, Jackson."

"Sorry. Again sir, I don't get a lot of deep conversations with a white man."

Green started to say something but then thought better of it.

"Point taken."

Green felt as claustrophobic in this barn as he had in those woods. His anxiety forced him to constantly peel back the sheet and listen for the Germans. He took one last bite of the chocolate as the wrapper flew out the broken window.

Green rose and peered out the back of the barn through the slats.

"I figure we have, what, maybe another forty or fifty feet to the tree line. The snow will slow us down a little. Just checking, in case we have to make another run for it."

"Have you noticed sir that the woods around here seem almost clean?"

"You mean not much underbrush or old growth."

"Yeah, other than some long branches and tree trunks."

"We'll have to stay further away from the roads then I wanted."

"Have you been south of here, Lieutenant?"

"This is the first time I've been on this side of the road for any length of time. Never looked like much on the maps," Green answered as he reached into his jacket for a map before continuing.

"I can't tell you exactly how much cover we'll have between here and the American lines, wherever they are. There are lots of woods but I saw long stretches of clearing, which might not help us much. I do know that along the road between Schonberg and St. Vith, there are two large stretches of woods on either side of the road. Then just before St. Vith, there's a large patch of empty ground to cover. Not sure if it matters. With all the fighting, we'll have to stay far away from there."

He now moved closer to Jackson, to show him the map.

"Heuem and Setz have certainly been taken by the Krauts. So there go our other crossing options. Urb is here to the south, some distance away. We could use that as sort of a boundary about how far south we want to go. Depending on how the river bends, we'll be traveling either south or east of the river as long as we can. There's no way we can cross the Our at this time of year unless we find an extremely narrow spot. We'd freeze in a matter of minutes. Maybe there's a section with some boulders or something we could use."

Jackson viewed the map intensely noticing that it had been drawn in pencil but looked professionally done.

"Lieutenant, where did you get the map. Is it an officers' issue or something?"

"I drew it from a copy of another map," Green hesitantly answered.

"Are those markings on there yours as well?"

"Yeah, possible gun positions for my outfit. At least, they were the positions we wish we could have had. Found it in my pocket. Thought I had lost it."

"That's pretty good. Do that a lot?"

"Once in a while. It's easier to carry than the Army issue, and whenever I couldn't sleep I just got my pencil out."

"Might come in handy considering our present situation, sir."

"While we're on the subject, let's go over what we have again, ammo, weapons, et cetera. Make sure they're clean and ready to go. Use the rags Leo gave us. I say we head out by tonight at the latest. It'll only be tougher if we wait."

The decision had been made. He had not even thought about that last sentence. It seemed to just come out. Something told him to get moving. Leo would not like it. Their chances of getting caught before they made it to the river were great, but there was no alternative.

Green took the time to show the eager sergeant how to work the Thompson. It was a heavy gun, just over ten pounds and holding it steady for a novice was difficult. Sometimes the action lever sometimes stuck, so Green had Jackson slide the retractor rod on the right side of the gun back and forth. Then he had him put a clip in and then out. One had to make sure it was secure to prevent jamming. Firing in short bursts was the best way to use it.

As Green began cleaning the Garand, Leo came out to chop wood. He slowly got into a rhythm and the sound was almost comforting, a sense of normalcy intruding on war.

They tried to resume their lesson, until they heard the whine of a vehicle changing gears, coming down the road, struggling through the sloppy road. Jackson jumped to the door and Green grabbed the Garand, lifted the curtain slightly and waited nervously for his enemy to appear. The sound got closer. Then it appeared, just past the house. Leo now stopped and calmly looked up. It was a German staff car with four occupants, one angry looking officer and three enlisted soldiers. At least one sergeant was in the group.

"Oh shit," Green whispered. "Jackson grab a weapon and your bandoliers. Check the door. Don't bother with the boards now, they'll hear us. This guy is SS."

An officer jumped out wearing a gray-green camouflage jacket and pantaloons, his cap jauntily tilted to one side. The tunic collar was now clearly visible, showing the unmistakable Runic double *S*. The enlisted wore a variety of camouflage smocks and jackets, one was even wearing American boots.

Jackson snatched the Thompson, the closest to him, and tightened his boots. Seeing this, Green reached in his pocket and tossed Jackson a clip for it. The sergeant then returned the favor by throwing one of the bandoleers over to him. There was no time to get touchy about weapons. He would have to use what was close.

The SS man grabbed Leo, waved his Luger at him and signaled his men to look around. The sergeant went into the house and came out with Catherine. The Krauts were getting reports of escaped troops roaming around and his orders were to check all the locals. Not that they needed a reason to terrify anyone.

"Have you been helping enemy troops?" the officer said in perfect French to Leo. "Have you been helping the Amis?"

He quickly responded in broken German.

"*No, no, bitte. Ich habe eine Tochter.*"

Green, still at the window, tried to understand what the German was asking.

"Jackson, could you make out what he was saying," he asked in a hushed tone.

"Something about enemy troops, sir. I heard the word '*Amis*'. They know that Leo is helping us somehow."

"They also knew his native tongue was not German."

The two German privates began nervously searching the property. One started walking for the barn, but stopped halfway. He looked young and scared, not really wanting to find anything or anyone.

Green, heart now pounding, automatically checked his Garand again.

8 shot clip, four Krauts. And I got Jackson. But it has been a while since I used one of these.

The SS captain was now shaking Leo and the bulky sergeant had Catherine tightly by the arm. She was crying and yelling '*Papa.*'

"Emmett, we gotta do something. Where are those grenades? Looks like we'll need them. We're gonna have to break out of here."

"There in that sack behind you," he reflexively answered, although he was still startled by hearing his first name.

Nervously, Green grabbed the sack and tossed it over to the Sergeant. Then he moved the window tarp slightly more to the left, just enough to getting a clearer look. He slowly moved his left hand out over the sights for a quick adjustment.

"They're gonna kill 'em, Sergeant. I have a clear shot on the SS guy and the sarge. Got them zeroed. You gonna have to take out the other two. As quietly as you can, move those boards."

Jackson gingerly moved to the door and picked up each board, placing them on the floor.

Green continued checking the sight on the rifle, trying not to move the tarp much, but zeroing in on the sergeant, who now was holding Catherine by the coat collar.

The young private came right up to the door, then suddenly stopped. He had noticed something on the ground, and reached down to pick it up.

"Herr Leutnant, American chocolat," he yelled over.

Now Leo's interrogator had proof.

" So, no Amerikaner?" he shouted at Leo, as he motioned for his men to search the barn.

"Oh, crap," Green whispered to himself, "what a dumbshit I was."

"Jackson, let 'em open the door," Green barely audible, "take him out with the Thompson and you are gonna have to get the other one too. He is just to your left. I still have a clear shot on the officer and sarge. Remember, short bursts with that thing and be fast. Watch Leo and the kid. That thing has quite a kick."

Jackson positioned himself just to the right of the door, that way he could get the other German right inline. As the door opened, Green moved the tarp aside from the window, squeezed the trigger and took out the Sergeant first. He fell immediately as the bullet went right through his chest. The shot echoed. Catherine screamed. The SS captain turned around stunned. Green quickly dropped him, hitting him in the face, just below the left eye. Blood and bone matter splattered all over Leo. Catherine had now grabbed on to his leg.

Jackson hit the first private with three quick bursts, which seemed to cut the young German in half. The light from the Thompson was blinding and the sound deafening. He automatically turned on the other private to his left, who was stunned, and could not even raise his Mauser Kar98k before he too was cut down. Jackson let out a primal scream as he kept spraying bullets from side to side until the clip was empty.

Pututututut…click…..click …click.

"Jackson! Jackson! Stop!" Green yelled and finally grabbed his arm.

All that could be heard now were Catherine's sobs and the clicking of Jackson still pulling back the trigger of the now empty Thompson. The look on Jackson's face told a story: revulsion at what he had to do, but somehow a strange satisfaction. An artilleryman did not often have the chance to see his target and touch it. The war had now become personal for both of them.

"We gotta get outta here," Green shouted as he ran over to the corner of the house, looking down both ends of the road. He assumed the Germans must have heard the commotion, particularly the Thompson.

"We gotta get the hell out of here," Green yelled, scooping up Catherine and pushing Leo away from the house.

Leo was trying to wipe his face clean.

"You can't stay here. Do you have somewhere close to go? We have to move. The Krauts must have heard all of this."

"In village. *Oh mon Dieu*."

"Pare', Pare'" Catherine screamed.

"Look Leo, I'm sorry. But they were gonna kill you, I have no doubt. Believe me. You should know. They have been here a lot longer than us."

Green pushed Leo toward the barn as he continued to carry the nearly hysterical Catherine. Jackson was in a trancelike state, still staring at the dead Germans.

"Sergeant, let's go!" Green yelled, as he stood glaring at him to no avail. "Pick up your weapon and grab the grenades. Check those two Krauts for any food, drag them to the barn and head into the woods. Emmett, you heard me, let's go!."

Jackson turned to look at Green. Hearing his first name again seemed to bring him back to his senses. He began searching the closest German. After dragging the bodies into the barn, he grabbed the sack, the bandoleers and plunged into the knee deep snow following right after the others. Green felt a hundred pounds heavier in this cement-like snow especially with Catherine. He stopped and got her back to her father's arms.

"Keep going. I'll be right there."

Green ran back to the house. He was uneasy and had to check on the bodies in the barn. He noticed the officer still breathing and took out his *.45*. There was a slight gasping and his chest heaved. Jackson's German knife lay on the floor near the officer. A gunshot would attract too much attention. He put his *.45* back in the holster and knelt down. Reaching down, he picked up the knife and plunged it right into the man's chest. But the *Leutnant's* eyes suddenly popped open. An arm came up to Green's throat, gripping it tightly. Their faces were inches apart. The German's blue eyes had a glass-like quality to them; they were empty, devoid of any feeling. He just kept staring as Green held onto the knife. After his initial surprise, Green pushed the knife in deeper, then turned it. He could hear the tissue tearing. Blood now poured out, coating both men. Then the *leutnant* fell back just as suddenly. After one last gurgling breath, death came.

Shaking with rage, Green yanked the knife out and threw it to the back of the barn. He threw the tarp over the body and then moved hulking German sergeant to the back of the barn. This body was the toughest. Green's arms and legs burned. Sweat began pouring from his brow. Stopping to catch his breath, his mind ran wild with thoughts of hundreds of Germans chasing him. He did not want to be responsible for losing Leo and Catherine.

About a hundred yards into the woods, Green found the group, and asked Leo where he and his daughter could go.

"I 'ave people in village."

"It's crawling with Germans."

"I know a way."

"Well, we have less than a mile to town. Where in the town is the house?"

"I will show you. But Catherine…she is very cold. I have…"

"Here, hold her Leo."

With that, Green took off his somewhat dry field jacket and wrapped Catherine in it. It was snowing again. Green would be only wearing his sweater.

"You okay, honey?" She shook her head still shivering.

"Alright, I'll give you back to your Dad, your Pare'."

Just as they moved on, the ominous sounds of tracked vehicles could be heard back toward the house. The distinctive guttural shouts of the Grenadiers echoed through the woods as they began ransacking Leo's house. Green and Jackson both looked back and then at each other. They knew their tracks would be seen.

"Jackson, throw me one of the bandoleers."

"Lieutenant, there going to be on top of us real soon. I can delay them so you can keep moving. Six grenades, the Thompson and I have the three clips you gave me, sir."

"No, keep moving. The snow might cover our tracks."

"Sir, they will see where we are going and find that house."

Green stopped, looked back and then looked at Leo. The one thing that had to be done was getting Leo and Catherine into Schonberg and then get as far away as possible.

"Sir, I'm bigger and won't move as fast as you guys will. Besides, a Negro running through the snow is gonna be spotted a little bit easier. Sir?"

Jackson smiled as said that last part. Green knew this was not about being faster or better camouflaged. The sergeant wanted a fight and there was no time to argue. Still he felt compelled to argue the point.

"You're bigger than I am, you carry the kid and …"

"Sir, I don't want to disobey an order, so please don't make it one. You go and save that family. I will be along. The grenades and Thompson will slow them down long enough for you guys to get clear. I will catch up. But let me fight some Germans. They have to walk in this stuff too. On the way back, we'll meet up halfway."

Jackson was not negotiating, he was demanding.

Leo now chimed in.

"Sergeant, you must come."

"Forget it, Leo. You're not in the Maquis, right?"

Leo went to speak, but thought better of it. His participation in the underground was an open secret and it was obvious to the two Americans.

"Sergeant," Green suddenly paused, feeling the urge to make it more personal, "Emmett, stay hidden. They'll be on you in a few minutes. I will keep walking with them until I can see the town. I'll be back as fast as I can."The crack of Mausers was then heard. Bullets started ripping through the branches.

Toom, toom,, toom.

Green pushed Leo on, aimed his Garand and fired a whole clip, eight shots. Catherine cried and put her fingers in her ears. Jackson then set up behind a couple of fallen trees about fifty feet away up to his ass in snow. Artillery blasts had turned the pristine woods into a mess of tangled limbs and blasted trunks.

"Toss those grenades high Jackson. It'll spread the fragments around and get some branches and other shit on top of them, like mini tree bursts." he yelled.

"Go sir," he yelled back with a wave of his hand.

More shots were coming his way.

He managed to catch up to Leo and Catherine. The little girl begged her father to let her run on her own but the exhausted father would not let her go.

"Leo, see if she can run too. You look beat."

Green tried to keep looking back. He heard the Thompson.

He had really learned how to use that thing.

25

TWENTY MINUTES HAD GONE BY and Jackson's tenuous defense was beginning to give way. With one grenade left, and dwindling ammo for the Thompson, he had to plan an escape. Shots ripped the bark from the tree near his head as he dove back into a small depression. Every time he let out a short burst, he took a few steps back. The Germans were coming up on his flanks. He could hear their voices right near him. Just to his left, a gray, wool cap emerged from behind a tree, silhouetted for just a second by a distant flash. Jackson instantly turned the Thompson and fired, but missed him. There were now Germans visible all around him.

He pulled the pin, counted to three, raised his right arm just enough to get it over the trees and tossed it. As it left his hand, a shot got him in the wrist. He ducked down and waited for the explosion. Branches came raining down on him followed by lots of snow.

"Shit," Jackson groaned.

Blood was streaming from his firing hand. He could handle the Thompson with his left if he braced it against his body; he would have to stand up though. Grabbing a handkerchief, he tried in vain to tie it around his wrist to stop the bleeding. Getting it tight enough was impossible. His hands were too slippery to hold anything, and metallic odor of the blood began to penetrate his nostrils. Random bursts of machine gun fire struck all around him and he could hear their boots crunching the layer of frost that was forming on the snow. Exhausted, he rolled onto his back and waited for the inevitable.

Green, Leo and Catherine heard the frantic battle, but kept moving. The village then came into full view.

"Which one, Leo?"

They stood on the knob of a hill, looking almost due North into the village.

"Lieutenant, we must go this way," Leo carefully whispered as he pointed below to a concealed area just to their left.

The slope was a sloppy mess with a half-melted, dirty snowdrift at the bottom. Leo had been trying to interrupt him many times but the impetuous officer would never let him get a word out. Never wanting to show anger in front of his daughter, he let Green take charge, waiting until the moment was right. This was his land, his town, even if occasionally there were language barriers.

"Duck down. Stay right here," Green demanded, using his finger to point to the ground, which surprised Leo, who rolled his eyes. If the lieutenant found out how good his English really was, he would be surprised.

Green took on a quick reconnoiter, and slowly worked his was to the edge of town, hiding behind one of the two-story white stone houses. He felt like an even bigger target, silhouetted against its faded stone wall, until he realized how close the other house was, providing him with some cover. The house formed a long alley with its neighbor. He could not hear any German voices, only vehicles idling, though it still felt like a thousand eyes were fixed on his position. Jackson's struggle with the Krauts was still echoing in the forest. As he stood leaning against the cold, wet stone wall, suddenly one of the shutters on the long, narrow windows creaked open slightly. Green instinctively wheeled around with his Garand.

Two beady eyes stared back at him. For a few seconds, they just stared at each other. Then the shutters were cracked a little wider. It was an old woman and Green lowered his rifle, letting out a deep breath. He put his index finger to his lips, trying to signal her to be quiet. Assuming she was a German, he figured his attempt at concealment was now in vain. To his astonishment, she did the same, even cracking a smile. After a nod, she quietly closed the shutters again. Green was alone once more.

Slowly peeking into area between the houses, he knew he needed to make it up to the street corner find where the Germans were. The street was a mix of cobble stone, gravel and dirt. Garand at the ready, he made a run for the front of the house, trying to stay on his toes as much as possible. The streets were bare and he was worried his steps over the gravel would echo. He reached the next corner, and looked carefully up toward the center of the village. From the loud rumbling of the diesel engines, he knew what he would find. Several Germans stood at the back of an armored personnel carrier enjoying their American cigarettes, and inexplicably savoring K rations. When he swallowed he felt as though he had pushed his heart back down to his chest. With the onset of darkness, everyone would be inside, except for the Germans. Looking down the street in the opposite direction, there was nothing but a couple of wrecked jeeps and an ammunition hauler.

He stared at the wrecks a little longer and lifeless forms of three GIs came into view, laying face down in between the vehicles. They were stripped of their boots and jackets. Making out who they were without getting closer was impossible; not knowing was probably better anyway.

Green, still faintly hearing the far away shots of Jackson's fight, struggled up the hill, back to Leo and Catherine as fast as he could.

"I saw no one on the street. You should be okay. Try to go straight in there and avoid all that snow. I have to get back."

"Lieutenant, please, let me show you the house."

"No, I can't see ya again. It's for your own safety. The next Americans they find...", his voice trailed off, not wanting to finish the sentence in front of Catherine.

Leo shook his head.

"I'm sorry for the trouble. You probably saved our lives."

" No, *Merci*, Lieutenant. Please help Sergeant Jackson and be safe."

"Bye Catherine. Your daddy will keep you safe."

"Your coat, *Messieur* Green."

Green hesitated. Leo told him she would be fine. The house was close. Leo helped Catherine with the Lieutenant's field jacket. She then reached into her pocket and gave Green one last thing, another chocolate bar.

"Thanks, kid. I'll see you guys after the war."

Green zipped up, put a fresh clip in the Garand as quietly as he could, and took off in the direction of the shooting.

Jackson was now getting weaker. His adrenaline was now giving way to lagged movements, almost slow motion. He had managed to crawl to a mound of underbrush at the base of large fir. The Thompson ammo was gone. He had used it trying to retreat. There was a blood trail that led to his new position. He knew he needed to run for it. The darkness was his ally, but he was too disoriented to know which way to go. The slow progression of shock was setting in and so was frostbite. His left hand began showing the first signs as his fingertips were swelling and two of them were already blistering. Melting snow began to fill his boots with water. If the Germans would stop and listen, the sound of his chattering teeth would lead them right to him.

Green's whole body now burned with exhaustion. Because of his soaking wet boots, he felt as though he were barefoot. He could hear and see the firing. The flashes led him right back to Jackson's previous position. The Germans seemed to be firing from three sides. Errant shots ripped the branches right next to him; deafening were the sounds.

Toom, toom, toom. Brrrrp, Brrrp, Brrrrrrp.

There was a moment's hesitation as he knelt down to get his bearings and ponder whether it was worth jumping back into the fight. The chances of Jackson having survived the onslaught were slim. Obviously, the Germans still thought he was alive or else they would have stopped firing. That gave him his answer; no one was being left behind this time.

"Emmett! Emmett!" Green whispered as loud as he could.

Jackson tried to raise his hand and wave, but it was too dark. So he fired off a round into the air hoping Green would see the flash.

"Lieutenant!" Jackson said with all the breath he could muster. He realized now that there was another wound in his leg. Blood was pooling around him.

Green knelt in the snow and began crawling to where he thought the now slowly dying sergeant may be.

"Jackson," Green whispered as low as he could. He heard heavy breathing and thought he could feel the heat of a body. He was close. Suddenly a huge hand reached up and grabbed Green's left calf, only to let go for lack of strength. Green snapped around and looked down on the bloodied, but still hulking figure of the Sergeant, whose body now lay half under a fallen fir tree.

"Jesus, Emmett. We gotta get the hell out of here," Green quickly retorted in as loud a whisper as possible.

"Sir…"

"Stop lying there. Get up. They have stopped firing which means they are getting closer. If you stay here, you die."

"I'm numb Lieu…," the sergeant's voice trailed off.

Green shushed him quietly. He heard a German voice and then footsteps.

"Amis, Kaput!"

"Wo sind Sie?"

Green lay on top of Jackson and could feel the oozing from one of his wounds. When his hand reached around the sergeant's back, it was soaking wet as the blood pooled.

"Emmett, are you ever going to stop bleeding on me?"

His mind raced. He tried to sound stern, then tried humor.

I must turn him over to stop the bleeding. But I'll be exposing him to the cold even more and the inevitable shock. It'll kill him just the same.

While searching for the source of the bleeding, the Germans got so close he could smell them. Their poor diet and rotten tobacco left a unique scent. Now one could be heard breathing heavily right in front of them. Green tried to push himself under some tree limbs. He heard two steps and suddenly a German voice called out from right next to him in a weird sound and Green could feel something hit the tree.

'Schulte, wo sind sie?'

He looked up, and a gray-coated grenadier landed right in his lap. The soldier had tumbled right over and on top of the pursued. Jackson moaned slightly from the extra pressure but Green realized that this was it. With the stunned soldier still trying to get up, a desperate Green leaped on him, grabbing the German around his neck. But he had too many clothes to do any damage. The Kraut regained his senses and took his Schmeisser smashing into Green's shoulder. Stunned momentarily, he then took hold of the German's arms, flipped him over and put his knee right in the small of his back. With the soldier twisting furiously and the Germans shouting in the darkness, he quickly took hold of the Grenadier's head, forcing his face into the snow. Green finally was able to grab the Schmeisser from him and maintained his grip on the German until he stopped moving. One down, and many more to go.

With trembling hands, he now searched for the German's long-handled grenades, known to the GIs as 'potato mashers'. He found three in a bag attached to the soldier's belt.

'Strom, seien sie ruhig!'

Returning over to Jackson, Green listened for a breath. Nothing.

"Emmett, get up."

Jackson was dead. He was talking to a ghost, and he knew it. Feeling like the only American around for a thousand miles, he did not want to admit it. Denial was a powerful driving force. Dead or alive, the sergeant was his only company.

"Jackson, stay with me buddy. We got the Krauts beat now. We've scared them off."

With a split second to figure out how to use the Kraut's gun, he just stood up and began spraying what the Army would term covering fire. The only problem was that the covering fire was for him and he should have been moving somewhere. The gun had a full clip, so this could buy him some time, a few minutes maybe. He crouched back down, reached for the grenades, pulled the cork-like pin and began throwing them: one to the left, one to the right and the last one straight ahead. The last one hit a tree just a few feet in front of them but managed to bounce in the opposite direction.

"Halt schießend!"

The frantic Germans recognized there own weapons and thought it was just a case of friendly fire. As the masher went off, Green grabbed Jackson under the arms, and began dragging him as far as the forest allowed. When he got stopped, the way blocked by dense trees, he leaned Jackson against a tree in an upright position, turned around, squatted with his back to the Sergeant's stomach, and tried getting Jackson up by pulling on his arms from behind.

"Okay, Emmett. This is it. Just a bit more."

"Wake up, c'mon."

The snow was providing enough silhouette that they occasionally came into the sights of the Germans for just a split second. The Germans were now firing blindly. Green managed to get Jackson up on his back one more time and drag him a few more feet before falling. He then lost his helmet on the way down, knocking his head against a tree. Jackson's weight added to the pain.

"Damn it." Fuck!" Green started to yell out and caught himself.

As he rose again, three rounds ripped into Jackson's back. One had penetrated far enough to hit Green. After a few more feet, there was a slightly warm feeling down Green's pants. A sharp pain rose up in his side. He dropped Jackson to the ground, reached around to his lower back. The hope that it was Jackson's blood and not his, faded fast. Blood was dripping down the inside of his pant leg. The warm oozing only added to his panic. He had to find the wound.

"Amerikaner!"

Green dropped Jackson, stared at the lifeless body of the sergeant and finally accepted the fact that he was dead. Ripping off a dog tag would mean acceptance. He put aside his own worries, knelt down and reached inside Jackson's shirt, pulling off one of the tags. With his pain increasing, he placed a couple of tree boughs over the body, reflexively making the sign of the Cross. Green began to stand up slowly, and move out. Where, he did not know. The Krauts were right on top of him. Capture would mean torture. They would shoot him right away or maybe just let him freeze to death for their own enjoyment.

He was now light-headed and weak. The adrenaline that he had lived on for so long, was gone. He clung to a tree that felt as though it was swaying.

Maybe I'm close to the town. If I could find a house. What if I don't? Will someone grab my tags? Cover my body? Who will tell my parents?

As Green summoned one last ounce of energy, he pushed away from the tree and as he did, his legs went out from under him and he began to tumble down another draw head over heels, coming to a stop only after most of his body was stuck in the snow drift. Thankfully his face lay upright to breathe. But a blackness was coming over him. He began to hear a voice, maybe two.

A hand reached out and violently grabbed him out from under the snow.

"Don't you guys know I'm dead?" Green slurred, with all the energy he had.

Before he faded into blackness, he thought the voices he heard were not German.

26

A SMALL GROUP HUDDLED AROUND the American soldier lying on the butcher block table in a damp, cold and windowless basement. It reeked of rotting potatoes and assorted vegetables. There was a dark flannel sheet dividing the basement in half, adding to the claustrophobic environment. Everyone had to stoop in some way. A delirious Green could not understand the whispers of German being spoken.

"How is he, Doctor?

"Not good."

"Is he going to live?"

"We hope."

"We are going to get in trouble for this. Let the Germans have him. They have doctors. *Mein Gott*, they are treating some of the *kriegsgefangene* here in town and they have American doctors there."

"*Seien Sie ruhig.* It is too late for that. They will shoot us. And they would let him die."

"Doctor, his breathing is labored, but getting better," the nurse matter of factly stated.

Green, in his fever-induced haze, stirred about from all the voices.

Did I hear German? Am I alive? They sounded sort of German. This must a German hospital or Hell. All that shit we went through just to get caught anyway. God I'm freezing.

His tortured body began to awaken him further. He was constantly shivering from the cold and when his fever rose, it got worse. The constant fever still made the doctor fear possible infection of the wound. When Leo and his brother yanked Green out of the snow bank, they had not immediately seen the wound, but saw the pool of blood. By the time they traced the bleeding to the source, his lower right back, he was on the verge of shock. That was three days ago. Hypothermia had set in. Another shrapnel wound was found in his left leg. His feet were slightly swollen. The top bit of a left finger came off and it was still swollen as well. His wool uniform had been cut off, evidenced by the strips of olive drab now laying all over the floor. They put a nightshirt from the doctor's collection on him, with part of the back cut out. Blankets were then thrown on top of him.

"Doctor, he is moving again."

"Lieutenant, can you hear me," the doctor said softly, in perfect English, as he turned his ear down to Green's mouth.

He had been falling in and out of consciousness; a sort of delirium had come upon him. Very realistic dreams would turn into nightmares as the faces of comrades lost appeared and called out to him. They would strain to hear him mumbling the names of the men. Then he would break out in a sweat. Visions of Kasserine and the Ardennes took hold. Fields of snow turned blood red. The sounds of war reverberated in the dreams. The falling rounds of artillery, the crack of a single sniper's bullet and the slight muffled sound of a round hitting a soldier. Then he would try to scream. Doctor Henin's nurse struggled to keep him quiet.

Visions of his youth and then his parents came to him. The sight of his mother's face the last time she saw him and her constant question, "How's my boy?" echoed in his mind, but just as suddenly he would wake him up to his predicament, all alone in a freezing, stinking basement. The times he did open his eyes, the only thing he noticed was his breath. Every labored exhale brought a lingering cloud of hot air. Sometimes the sounds of people walking above was the most frightening, particularly the boots stomping all about, which would shake dust from the ceiling.

How long have I been out?

Green finally became conscious of the many pairs of eyes staring down at him. Barely audible, he mumbled, "Who are you?"

He began to raise his right arm, but the pain was too much. Any movement of his right side pulled on the sutures.

"I am Doctor Henin," he carefully whispered, "you are in Schonberg among friends."

"Don't tell him your name," said a voice in German, whose sternness was undeniable.

The doctor ignored the glare and the advice of the portly, red-faced Ernst Sohn, a Belgian citizen of German descent. His detractors, of which there were many, called him 'little Goering', because of his uncanny resemblance to Hitler's obese confidant. Although, he was much more rumpled than the Reichsmarschall and slightly less overweight.

Many of these ethnic Germans had assisted the *Wermacht* before the invasion by passing on information to their intelligence units, but not *Herr* Sohn. Despite his reputation, he liked Schonberg and its people. He had resided here since the end of the Great War after coming home disillusioned from the Western Front. This was his basement and the doctor was his renter. But fear gripped him, and the others could see it on his face. It might tip him over the edge. He also had a family to worry about, a wife and two sons, both of whom were just a year or two away from being of military age. Leo did not trust him, even going as far as hatching a plan to kill him. But he could never bring himself to murder his own brother in law. Family was family, even if his sister married poorly.

"Hey Doc, what about Jackson?" Green asked in a barely audible voice.

Henin looked perplexed and turned to the nurse. She shook her head admitting ignorance of this man. Sohn piped up and said that he had heard Leo speaking of another American, a dark one, the *schwartze*, maybe that was him. They were going to try and look for him.

"Of course, he cannot be as lucky as this fellow. He is probably dead or captured by now."

"Sohn, please keep your voice down."

Ernst Sohn just harrumphed and carefully went upstairs to converse with the many Wermacht troops that sat in the living room recovering from their wounds.

All those involved in helping the Americans knew that Sohn would have to be watched. Everyone feared he was reaching the point where he might just turn them in. Besides, the Germans could decide they need the building for something other than medical care and start searching. That would mean a quick execution, probably by firing squad.

The Doctor turned once again to his patient.

"I am Doctor Henin, and this is my nurse, Marta. You are recovering from some very serious wounds. It is important for you not to move too much."

Green laid there for a few seconds and thought about what he had just heard. Not moving, with the exception of shivering, would not be problem. Everything hurt. Slipping in and out of consciousness helped keep movements to a minimum as well.

"Okay," Green mumbled, as he let out another labored breath. "Any word on the other soldier, Jackson?" Green asked again.

"I am sorry Lieutenant, nothing."

"I know he's dead but..," the Lieutenant's voice tailed off as the doctor laid his hand on Green's shoulder.

"Please Lieutenant Green, someone will always be here with you. I have to go upstairs for now. You are safe here."

The doctor then asked Marta in German, her native tongue, to watch Green's fever and alert him of any trouble.

"Lieutenant," the doctor then whispered, "you must be as quiet as possible. The Germans are right above you. Okay?"

Green let that sink in for a minute, not knowing what to say. For some reason, it had not brought on any more fear.

"So I'm not a POW?"

"No. We will protect you. But you must remain quiet."

"Okay, Doc. Gotcha," his voice began to tail off, catching his breath was painful.

"Try not to speak, please. You are getting better."

For the time being, Green would have to wait patiently. Whether he was waiting for death, rescue or capture, only time would tell.

27

"*Joyeux Noel*. Merry Christmas, Lieutenant."

A surprised and somewhat more alert Brendan Green sat up carefully on the now padded table to see Leo coming through the curtain, standing there with a tiny tree with a small cross on top.

"Leo?" he asked weakly.

"*Joi*, Lieutenant." Leo whispered, and gestured with his finger to his lips.

"Where exactly am I? What time is it?" Green softly asked. "I can't tell the time of day in this crypt you got me locked up in."

"It is morning and you are in Schonberg."

"I know that, surprisingly I remember the doctor telling me that. But whose house is this and how the hell did the Krauts not see me?"

"No worry, Lieutenant. You hungry? Do you want your… how you say? *Déjeuner*? I don't know word."

Green saw Leo make an eating gesture to jog his memory.

"You mean breakfast?"

"Yes. That's the word."

"Yeah. I guess."

"Good. I will tell Marta."

"The Krauts are still all over the place, aren't they?"

"*Joi*, Lieutenant. But it is okay, you are among friends here. The Germans here for years. We know how to, how you *Americain* say, take care of them?"

Green realized that the less he knew, the better. That way, he couldn't name names if and when the Krauts got him. Although, he already knew too much. The shelling he had been hearing subsided, but the unmistakable sound of American fighter bombers hitting the roads around the village was encouraging, albeit scary. The Air Corps figured everybody in town was a Kraut. He could hear the Germans yelling *Jabos*, which he knew was their slang for the P-47s.

"I hope so, Leo. What is going on in the war? How many days have I been here. Is it Christmas Day?"

"I am afraid it is December 30th, Lieutenant. No see you in long time. The battle is still going on. We hear about the Boche stop somewhere, but after that, nothing."

"That's something. Look Leo, did you find the Sergeant, you know Emmett?"

"I am sorry, Lieutenant. We could not go. He is out there? No?"

"Yeah...," Green started, but then let out a visible and still painful exhale, "his dog tag was in my pants pocket. Where are my pants? And what the hell is this thing I got on?"

He then felt for his dog tag again.

"Much blood. No good. But some things in, how you say poche?"

Green furrowed his brow, until he saw Leo putting his hand in his jacket several times.

"You mean pocket?"

"*Joi*. No worry. We make new soldier clothes for you. Marta save your things."

"Thanks Leo. *Merci*."

As he spoke, he was interrupted by the drone of a radial engine overhead. It was another P-47. It dove and two rockets suddenly tore through the air. Seconds later, two thunderous explosions blew apart a convoy of trucks just up the road, making the house rumble. Plaster and sawdust rained down on them. Leo threw his body on top of Green as a choking dust covered the room. Bits of masonry had been ripped from the sides of the houses and were clanging against the Germans' vehicles. The Germans began shouting and running from the building upstairs. Engines started up everywhere. Leo knew they would probably be bringing in more wounded today and had to get out of this basement before it was too late.

Although still a little woozy, Green started to feel better, noticing the difference in his hands. The swelling was still there, though the color was getting better. There was still a burning sensation in his feet as well. He had been off them so long he was afraid they wouldn't work right. All his toes were saved, except for a couple of toenails. His feet hung over the end of the table, hidden not only by the blankets, but several bandages that were wrapped up to his ankles

"Hey Leo, where's Catherine? Safe and sound, I hope."

"Oh, yes. With family."

"Well, tell her hi."

"I do not want to say anything to her about you, Lieutenant. Because..."

"I understand," Green said weakly. "If I'm a threat to you, Leo..."

"Lieutenant, no worry. If the Boche find you, all will die. No let happen."

"Jesus, these Krauts," Green's voice trailing off.

"I have to get back to help the doctor. Marta will be back. And remember, be quiet. The Germans right above you." He finished his sentence with a finger pointed toward the ceiling as a visual reminder to his patient of the dangers only a few feet above them.

"Don't worry, I can hear their boots and their moaning. That's worst than anything."

"I know."

"Are there other Americans here? POWs?

"*Joi*, yes. I saw a few the other building. Some barn near town. There is American doctor with them."

"Shit, the one free American, sort of, in Schonberg. What a title. Were there any others with my patch," Green asked, pointing to his shoulder to give Leo a visual reference. "You know, the one with the lion?"

"I no see. It is hard, many no have clothes."

"Sorry Leo, should've thought of that."

"*Monsieur*, you are weak. Time for rest."

"Hey, do you get to talk to the Americans at all?

"The Germans do not like us to speak to them or give them anything. Please, you must rest. Would like a priest, Lieutenant?"

"Well, I am Catholic, but don't have one risk his neck for me. I'm sure I can get one to grant me absolution after the war. But thanks."

Green finally laid back down and stared at the ceiling.

"Stay well, Leo."

"A rvey."

Leo nodded, stooped and quietly walked up the stone steps, softly opened the creaking wood door, locked it, and went into the kitchen area to rejoin the efforts of Doctor Henin. Despite their best efforts, blood stains covered the tiled floor, collecting in pools at the corners. The kitchen area was separated from the dining area by a small corridor. The dining and the living room area connected to make one large room. It was now the waiting room for the more ambulatory wounded. Several German soldiers were still waiting to see the doctor or having done so already, were waiting there for orders. In one of the bedrooms, several litters of wounded Germans were spread out.

The rugs that were scattered around the floor squished with dampness from the wet boots and blood. An aroma of human waste still lingered, even though the Germans were now taking there more serious cases down toward Bleialf and Prum. Green occasionally got wet as blood and other body fluids soaked through the wood floor right onto his head. He learned to turn fast despite the pain.

To the relief of all, the Germans never noticed the basement door. Most of the walking wounded who wandered in were patched up quickly and sent on their way. The officers would not let them rest for long. Leo was making a sort of carrot soup and would hand it out to the Germans with some biscuits as they sat in the waiting area.

The Germans had not caught on that it was Leo who owned the house where the SS officer and his men, had been cut down, nor had anyone else in town given it away. Despite Leo's activities being an open secret, they blamed it only on the Americans. For now, Leo was hiding in plain sight, his daughter securely tucked away at his sister's. Doctor Henin conveniently called Leo his 'assistant.'

During the next few days, Green felt better, although still weak. His feelings of claustrophobia were coming back in droves though. Being in this basement was like being buried alive. He couldn't fight his way out. Not only was he stuck in the basement, he only technically inhabited half of it, with his portion divided from the rest of the room by two large, white sheets and some boxes. He begged to be allowed upstairs, even for a minute, but there were always Germans around.

The odor of the place was bad, it smelled worse than the barn. But it was the sounds of war that bothered him the most: the screams; the creaking of the floor as the heavy German boots went to and fro, the clanking of tracked vehicles plodding through the morass of muddy roads. He had faced the enemy before; now he was in the middle of it all, almost eavesdropping on their lives and plans, powerless to do anything to stop them.

28

The New Year came and Green gradually regained his strength, buoyed by Marta and Leo visiting as often as they could. With his health improving, he became crazed by a desire to get out and see the world again. Quietly pacing the floor every morning, he counted his steps, pushing himself to go further. Marta had noticed the dirt on the bandages and socks, castigating him for trying to do too much.

A radio was out of the question. They had a couple of magazines that the GIs had left behind along with some really old dime novels. Getting any kind of light with which to read was nearly impossible. There was a candle for light, when he was allowed to use it. Despite the windowless environment, tiny strands of light along with a lot of cold air filtered in through boarded up vents and small cracks in the foundation. The minute strands were not much help for reading, but when he saw them, he knew it would be an entertaining day; the Allies would be flying that day.

Too much on time on one's hands, gives a person time to think. When the memories are not good ones, even a short time is too much. There was at least a writing tablet and pencil around. So he tried to write down the names of every man that served under him, even in the dark. What the point of this recitation was, he could not answer. Somehow, it just made him feel better. He went over and over in his head what he would say in letters to the men's families, but could never bring himself to write any of it down.

Hope had sprung though. There had been word about the Americans holding out in St. Vith. Leo passed along wild stories of an American fighting alone in the woods harassing the Germans as they moved west. He wanted to believe it, wondering if Leo was just saying it to make him feel better.

Marta was coming in more frequently now. First, it was to help him shave, then later it was therapy; she would move his legs up and down to stave off atrophy. The therapy had even gotten him kind of excited. It was comforting to know that some things still worked right. And she was pretty. Despite her lack of English, he still tried to engage in conversation.

"What's your last name, Marta?," Green asked, forgetting once again the dangers of knowing too much. She understood what he asked, hesitating to answer. After a little more prodding, she told him.

"Recht."

"Wreck?"

"*Recht*."

She laughed quietly, putting her finger to her lips.

Shhh.

"Kraut name? Hey, you smiled," challenging her as she rolled her eyes.

Sometimes during the visits, she would occasionally take her gray headdress off and he could see more of her light brown hair, although it was kept demurely in a bun. With her height only about 5'2", she didn't have to stoop that much. Her age was a mystery. She looked older than she really was because he had only seen her in the nurse uniform, which usually showed the gruesome signs of caring for wounded men. Despite dealing with men on a daily basis, she remained shy with Green, their eyes almost never meeting. Getting a glimpse of her pale green eyes was a struggle. She did not seem the least bit curious about her patient until one day there finally was an inquiry, albeit with some difficulty.

"*Leutnant Green, Haben Sie Kinder*?"

"Huh? Kinder?"

"*Enfants*?"

She now switched to the French for the word children, only to get a more quizzical look from Green. Finally, she decided to show him by folding her arms and rocking them back and forth. He got the message.

"Oh, you mean babies. I got ya."

She smiled.

"Ja, babies."

"No, I don't have any children yet."

"E'pouse?"

"Wife?"

She nodded, and pointed to his bare left ring finger.

"No, no wife."

That got a smile.

He kept trying to walk on his own throughout the first week of the New Year, both for himself and for Marta. Impressing her everyday became a pastime. He would venture out from behind the sheet on his own, needing to be ready to jump back quickly if he heard the door. The ever present stomping German boots walking above him reminded him of that.

Mentally, he agonized about what his parents had been told, if anything. Did they get a telegram saying he was missing? There was some comfort for them in that. All he wanted to do was get word to them somehow. It was so strange to have recent days missing from one's memory. Since he did not remember Christmas day, Marta brought him another small tree to put up in the basement. There had not been many updates on the war.

The Germans were still passing through, but with a lot more wounded being shipped to the rear. The occasional clatter and squeal of tank treads could still be heard, whether they were coming or going was hard to tell.

By mid-January, word began trickling down about a massive Allied counterattack going on all over the front. The Allies might be here in a few days or a week. There had been clear skies for almost three days in a row and the constant sound of planes, both bombers and fighters, droned overhead. Shelling echoed from far-off. Hearing American artillery, no matter how distant, was like being at a symphony for a trapped GI. He began walking without holding on to anything and was wearing real clothes again; they were mostly patched up olive drabs along with some local civilian attire. It was better than nothing. Leo had managed to get him an Army field jacket that was like new and he had no idea how they did it. He felt it might have something to do with the makeshift hospital in town that had held wounded POWs. Obviously, Leo had been putting some things aside. The jacket would be saved for his last day stuck in Schonberg. He had been able to sneak up into the house for a few minutes just to look out the window, for about a week off and on. German soldiers were not stopping by the house with any frequency. The retreat was on and Green had a ringside seat. There was a nasty history of destructive retreats by the Germans dating back to the last war, so everyone held their breath.

New rumors swirled everyday about where the Americans were. Driven by this hope and with his strength increasing fast, he ventured upstairs without Marta's help and against the Doctor's wishes. It really amounted to Green just peeking through the door, and if the house were completely devoid of any Wehrmacht, there was the occasional stroll through the kitchen to the back door. He tried to look as Belgian as possible, with his dog tags hidden beneath a dark green wool shirt. A nervous Marta watched him carefully. Her main task was making sure the energetic lieutenant did not get himself seen or heard. Besides the worry of blurting out something in English within earshot of any of the *Soldaten*, it was the creaking of the floor and the squeaky basement door that caused much of the unease. She would scan the house before letting him past the stairway door, making sure all the curtains were pulled, and if he was there, check with the Doctor. When the Germans moved the American wounded out of the makeshift hospital, it left more room for their own. So they ordered Doctor Henin to help out over there. Now, it was mostly just local villagers who stopped in at the office, as Marta was left in charge.

Before letting him up, Marta always gave him a hat to wear, and a typical brown workman's jacket. If their enemy did burst in on them, she could quickly say he was an injured logger or something, then send him downstairs. Of course, as soon as he got to a window, he moved the curtain enough to reconnoiter the streets. All in all, the little adventures went well, except for one day when a Grenadier suddenly stopped in front of the kitchen window, did a quick look around the house and decided to have a smoke right outside the back door. Marta had seen Green's excited expression turn to a mild fear, then to anger. She then peered through the curtain and with her heart in her throat, grabbed the lieutenant by the arm, pulling him to the basement door. The gentle nature of her care was gone with a shove through the door, nearly throwing him down the stone steps.

"Behind sheet, Lieutenant, please."

"Jesus Marta, what happened to my favorite nurse?"

"Soldaten. No see?"

"I see, yeah. Don't worry. I won't do anything to hurt you."

"Lieutenant, you mad. I see."

Marta pointed to her eyes for emphasis. His venomous look had frightened her.

"Hey look, I want another crack at those guys. Honest I do. But I know when to fight. And now is not the time. I promise."

She never did understand his colloquialisms or for that matter, much of what he said at all. Still, his pleadings seemed to put her at ease somewhat. Immediately grabbing his left arm, she gently pushed him down the stairs.

"You stay. No more up," pointing to the ceiling for emphasis. "Soldaten go soon."

Green just gave a nod and a smile.

"I've been gigged by a nurse."

"*Was*?"

"It's nothing."

Marta softly, but securely, closed the door behind her. Then he heard the harsh click of the lock.

29

As THE LAST DAY OF January dawned, Leo arrived with news that most of the Germans had cleared out, including the wounded, and asked Green to come up to the kitchen for something to eat as sort of an honored guest. The Americans could now be heard just beyond the river. Their infantry and tanks had been closing in rapidly throughout the night with German resistance waning. Green sat at the table, anxiously waiting to strip off his Belgian clothes and wear olive drab once again; his dog tags were still carefully hidden underneath his three shirts. A more cautious Leo begged his friend to wait until they walked in the door. Stragglers from the retreating Wehrmacht continued to make their escape east through the village. Some of the villagers prepared to meet them out in the street with bread and hot tea hoping to placate their desperation. Despite the severe cold, the skies seemed to be clearing enough for Allied airplanes to roam the skies uncontested once more.

Doctor Henin came in from his office with Herr Sohn, who had probably come by to get the doctor to start paying rent again, as soon as the Germans were officially gone. Henin's goal was to eventually try and move to St. Vith after the war. But knowing the fate of the City, patience would have to be the norm. It had been practically destroyed. Schonberg had been hit hard too, with its stone bridge over the Our blasted away. An acrid haze still hovered over the town and it was increasing as the battle was reaching a climax. In the kitchen, bits of plaster and dust, which had been shaken from the walls and ceiling from all the shelling, lay over everything.

Marta was pouring the last of the coffee and had made what looked like biscuits. Before sitting down herself, she pulled the increasingly worn curtains again, as they began to huddle around the table with hushed voices. The mood was light despite the ordeal they had all been through, although it would be a while before the fear of German retaliation went away. The Doctor and Leo got a laugh when he compared his 'imprisonment' in the basement with being a mouse to which you would occasionally give some cheese; he was also a pet that got his temperature taken every day. Sohn, who had stopped asking about their American guest weeks ago, actually smiled at Green and asked in his thick accent, how he was doing. For Green, that was the equivalent of an embrace from a guy like Sohn, whose dark, narrow eyes were almost hidden by his bushy eyebrows. He acknowledged the man with a smile and a 'Thank you'.

Ever restless, Green forced his way to the windows to look down the small street that ran alongside the house. Several inches of snow had fallen overnight, but a hint a sun was trying to break through the high, patchy clouds. There was still that abandoned American jeep and weapons carrier, both with tires removed, lying across the street. Thankfully, the bodies had been removed. German vehicles were gone as well, although the clank of a tank's tracks could be heard off in the distance. Two small boys had ventured out and there was no sign of any soldiers. Half the village's inhabitants had fled. After a tap on the shoulder by Marta, he sat back down to the relief of all.

As they ate, Sohn spoke in both English and German about what he expected the town to be like after the war. There was a hope to return to the days of the peaceful Ardennes, the idyllic vacation spot. They all had theories on what the Germans would do. Leo seemed to have the best reports on the American counterattack. The sounds of small arms fire got closer, with Green even hearing the pop of an empty M-1 Garand clip. For the first time in weeks, Green did not have those terrible feelings of anxiety that gripped him since December 16th. Gone was the pain in his chest, the dry mouth and the headaches. He was so happy to be out of isolation, he could care less what was wrong with him.

"Hey Leo, what is your last name?"

"My last name?"

"Yeah. You're Leo what?"

"Willems."

"Will...what? It sounded like Williams."

"You are right. It is very much like your Williams."

"Is that French? Don't sound it?"

The sound of Sohn snickering filled the room.

"It is Walloon."

"But you speak French?"

"Yes, because I born around Liege. My mother speak French. Father from Limburg. He speak French, Walloon and luckily, a little German."

"You Europeans are very confusing."

That made everyone laugh, except for poor Marta. She would smile once it was translated.

"I must leave," Sohn announced.

"But Ernst, it is still not safe," the Doctor begged in Sohn's native tongue. "Your family is safe. Stay here."

"*Nein*. I promised them I would be home tonight. And I must leave before dark. And Leo, your sister and your nephews are asking for you, it is time for a visit."

Without looking up to view his brother in law, Leo responded tersely.

"Tell her I'll be there soon. As soon as it's safe to travel."

Sohn was used to Leo's very cold shoulder, so he left it at that. All Green could do is watch their facial expressions as the two bantered in German, which to him was a scary language no matter what they were saying. Regardless of his untrained ear, Leo's German sounded better than expected.

As Ernst got up to leave, their peace was rocked by the sound of the back door bursting open. In came a short German officer and his much taller sergeant, both in their white parkas and distinctive bluish-gray, wool caps. Their mud-splattered, white pantaloons hung low, ballooning around their ankles. Schmeissers hung over their shoulders and their helmets, which were attached to their belts, clanged against their sides. With their faces gaunt and flushed, showing several days' stubble, they stood in the doorway, guns pointed at the table. They stared at the inhabitants. It was a nervous stare, and the officer's bloodshot eyes darted from side to side as he scanned the room. Sohn, thinking quickly, was the first to speak, making a universal offering, food. For the high-strung German, it was not easy to act so nonchalantly.

"*Was ist dieses? Wir haben Speise.*"

Food seemed to always placate a soldier.

"*Ja*," the officer stated gruffly. Sohn stole a look at Marta, who immediately jumped up and ran to the stove.

"*Kaffee?*"

"*Ja*"

Dr. Henin slowly stood up and asked if they needed care in his almost perfect German.

"*Nein*," he said with a wave of the hand.

Noticing the gash in the Sergeant's hand, through the poor bandaging, he decided to press the issue until they relented. Marta was back with bread within seconds, then poured them each a cup of coffee. The men began voraciously gnawing at the bread, then took a sip of coffee and held it in their hands. The sergeant had wrapped a blue scarf around his head underneath the cap to protect his ears, but had nothing to protect his lips, which were chapped and bleeding. He would winch every time the hot liquid lingered on his lips.

The warmth of the food seemed to bring them back to life. They no longer appeared worried about the others in the room, with the exception of Green, who the *Leutnan*t continued to watch with a wary eye.

The Doctor, wanting to quell the Germans' fear, offered to take a look at the man's hand again. But the mercurial officer declined once more. The badgering continued.

"*Medizins*? "

"*Nein*!

Then in an immediate change of mood, befitting the chaotic situation, he relented, much to the relief of his sergeant.

"*Ja, verbände*."

Marta said she would get the bandages and asked if she could close the door. It was becoming quite cold again. The Germans just nodded as she brushed by them.

"Is there anyone else here?" the *Leutnant* asked suspiciously, as he smugly walked over to the leg of Sohn's chair and kicked the mud off his boots.

"*Nein*," replied the doctor.

Leo and Green sat passively at the table trying to ignore the men and hide their obvious fear, sipping at their own coffees and nibbling on the biscuits. Green now realized that with all his spare time in the basement, he should have picked up some French and German.

What would have been the use, my accent would be a dead giveaway.

Sohn tried to keep a conversation going by asking the obvious qucstions.

"Where are you heading," he asked nervously.

He ignored the question to begin his own interrogation.

"What part of Germany are you from?" the officer asked. Are you a German?"

Sohn was desperate to show his bona fides as a true German, even dropping hints about his past service in the last war.

"*Ja, Gerolstein. Ich kämpfte im letzten Krieg.*"

He now turned his attention to the doctor.

"*Arzt*?"

Having treated German soldiers for weeks, he knew how to handle any questions that were posed about his origins. The Belgian doctor spoke five languages and did not want to be perceived as disloyal or ungrateful. So he decided not to mention his medical school training in Germany.

"*Nein. Ich habe gerade studierte Germanistik.*"

Marta arrived back with the bandages and gently handed them to the sergeant. She then took her place by the stove, standing nervously, and ready to kill the men with kindness.

The two drained their coffee and peered outside. The thunder of more guns got a little closer. The *Leutnant* walked to the stove, brushed Marta aside and grabbed more biscuits, which he stuffed in his jacket. Leaving one on the tray, he smiled at Marta as he walked back to the door.

"*Mehr Kaffee*?"

"*Ja.*"

He began to stare again at Leo and Green. The American's hands intrigued the officer, for they obviously showed the scars of a man who had a desperate fight for survival. Green's twenty pound weight loss was actually working to his advantage. Despite many GI complaints about Army food, they ate better than the average European and their size would show it. Green's slight gauntness, gave him more of a native look. The floor creaked as he slowly made his way around the table, stopping at Leo.

"*Was ist Ihr Name*?"

Green understood the question, but as it was asked, he immediately realized that Leo had not given him a fake Belgian name to go along with the native attire. Leo did his best to cover up, answering carefully, trying to sound as simple as he could.

"I am Leo and this is my workman, Albert."

Leo used his patois German, the local dialect, but the officer made it clear he was not interested in Leo.

"*Ich spreche nicht mit Ihnen*!"

The *Leutnan*t took his Schmeisser and gently poked Green in the back, who turned around and smiled. It was all he could think of doing.

"Or should I say that in English? You are scared, *ja*?"

The sadistic German's command of English was almost flawless, which significantly added to the unease. It felt as though someone had punched him in the chest. His heart skipped a beat. Green had seen that look before: it was a combination of desperation, fear and hate. Both Germans had been getting the shit kicked out of them for weeks. They marched in a month before as conquerors once again, trying to recreate the victories of 1940, but now they were retreating in shame. If anyone got in the way, a little more killing really would not matter. At this point in the war, everyone was going mad.

"Does Albert speak?"

Everyone in the room suddenly held their breath. Marta pretended to heat up more coffee, all the while biting her lip so hard hit bled. Even Sohn didn't know what to say. After a few seconds, Green looked up once again at the *Leutnant*. His *Feldwbebel*, still by the door and looking even more frightened than the others, raised his weapon a little higher. With the precarious protection of the Siegfried Line just a few miles away, it was time to go. The officer prodded Green a little harder this time.

"Speak, Herr Albert."

Leo interjected that they were making Albert nervous and that he was a little sick in the head. He twirled his finger near his temple to indicate what he meant. The Doctor took Leo's lead and seconded the diagnosis, stating that Albert was really a very ill man. Marta could only look away.

The *Leutnant* drew a cold stare at Leo, while he tapped his index finger on his forehead.

"Maquis? Walloonie? Flämisch?

The sergeant was growing restless, bordering on panic. All in the kitchen could hear the firing and shouts of American voices.

"*Leutnant, Wir müssen gehen. Es ist die Amerikaner*!"

Sohn, the native son, spoke to them as their father.

"*Bitte verlassen*," Sohn begged, and finally turned to the sergeant in desperation.

"*Bitte, Feldwebel*."

The panicked soldier just shook his head.

The *Leutnant* ignored them, transfixed on 'Albert.'

"Are you an American, Herr Albert?"

Green continued to stare at the German, taking a deep breath. Their angry eyes were now locked in vengeful glares. Leo, sitting just to Green's right, saw the German's shaky finger on the trigger. He glanced at Green, touching his arm, mainly to stop the staring. Then sudddenly, the harried Feldwebel spoke up again.

"*Bitte ist er nicht gut. Leutnant, die Amerikaner sind hier*!"

The wind had picked up and all could hear it begin to whistle through every crack in the house. It grew colder inside, everyone's breath hung in the air. Just several hundred yards away, the shallow pop of American mortars was heard.

"*Dies ist eine Arztpraxis, bitte...*"

The German laughed.

"What do you say, Albert?"

Green would surrender if it would save the lives of all present, but he knew it would be a fruitless gesture. They would kill all of them anyway. Remaining quiet was his only option. The officer continued to stare at Green while he spoke, alternating between German and English, gauging his reaction.

"What do you think, Sergeant?"

The vibrations of tanks, and the squeak of their gears veraberated all over the village now.

"*Leutnant,* Amerikanisch Panzers!"

Sohn yelled that he had been in the German army in the last war and expected some courtesy. His fleshy jowls shook violently as sweat poured from his brow. The officer was shocked that someone would speak to him like that and he began to shake. The *Feldwebel* opened the door and began to back out.

"How come you did not come back to Germany to help us now? Because you now help the Amerikaner? Warum Herr Sohn?"

"*Ich habe junge Söhne. Bitte.*"

He took the schmeisser and smashed Green in the back of the head. Marta screamed. The Doctor reached out to help and stopped as the German's weapon was pointed right at him. Green began to raise his head again. Blood ran down the back of his neck as he turned to his tormentor. Leo reached up and grabbed the officer, who shoved him back down, then backed away.

"Goddamn it! Stop!" Green gave a muffled yell, more out of pain than frustration, barely able to lift his head.

"You are Amerikaner, yes?" he asked, eyes narrowing with rage.

"Yes I am. Leave these people alone." Green wearily replied.

"Hands up. Alle!"

The German slowly backed himself up to the corner of the kitchen, leaning up against the square metal sink. Green slowly raised his arms as did the others, all except Marta, who grabbed hold of the doctor.

The Feldwebel was now hyperventilating, his panting drowning out everything else.

"Leutnant, die Amerikaner!

"Look, these people have done nothing but help your own men out for weeks. This doctor is a good man. I'll go, just leave them out of it."

Suddenly, he turned his attention to Leo, who he grabbed by his wool coat.

"Maquis! Maquis!"

Then he shoved him near the others, who now gathered at the stove.

The ominous *click clack* of the retractor rod on the Schmeisser was now heard. Everyone's eyes rose toward the ceiling as shells began to fall on the town again. The Feldwebel raised his left hand at his commander, and stepped between him and the others.

"Leutnant."

"We must do our duty!"

He quickly stepped back and raised his gun at the others too, gazing back upon his superior officer with disgust.

Green's eyes went back and forth, watching the terror in the Feldwebel's face, the *Leutnant's* crazed stare and the looks of terror on the faces of the others. Marta just buried her head in the doctor's arms. He spoke up in the vain hope that it would keep him alive a little longer in order to have a remote chance of escape.

"I don't have any weapons on me. Look, at least do this outside. Not here. There's been enough blood in here. Please."

"Be quiet!" The German's eyes bulged as he sought to continue his invective. He began to sweat and shake. The house shook from the artillery and a cloud of dust filled the air. Pots hanging over the stove knocked together like tolling bells.

The *Leutnant* took a breath, and raised his gun. Then a loud burst and flash of a machine gun exploded in the room. The German lieutenant went down just as he shot off a few rounds into the wall next to Green, who was able to flinch enough to miss them. His own *Feldwebel* had cut him down. The officer fell against the sink and slid down, mouth wide open, staring right at Green. A slow trickle of blood started to drip from the corner of his mouth and down past his chin. Soon his white parka turned a dark crimson. There was one last gurgled breath and it was over.

The sergeant nervously raised his gun at Green, who remained standing with hands raised. The others raised their eyes to look in stunned silence at the slumped figure gushing blood, which began to pool at his legs. Staring for a moment, the sergeant then slowly backed towards the door, before turning to Green.

"Stay here," he said in flawless English, to the surprise of everyone. "I won't kill you. Must go. I am sorry, I hated him."

Then in an odd farewell, he turned to Marta with a small bow.

"Ich bin für dieses sehr traurig."

Green turned to him and opened his mouth to speak, but nothing came out. Finally, he was able to say "*Thanks*", but not before the sergeant was gone.

Everyone remained still, except for the Doctor, who instinctively rushed to the man, confirming his death. Then he peered through the curtain to see the German sloshing down the village road.

Green dropped to his chair, slumped forward, head on the table. The excruciating pain in his head came rushing back. Blood still oozed out. He could not only feel the blood, he could hear it mat his hair as it left his head.

"Sind Sie in Ordnung?" Marta cried as she ran over to his side.

He struggled to catch his breath as it hurt to inhale. All he could do was nod ever so slightly.

A shocked Sohn, stood staring at the body, until the doctor approached.

"Are you alright, Ernst?"

"I hope this madness is finally over."

"Ja, me too." The doctor then locked the door and ran over to Green. Leo came back with two sheets.

The Doctor begged Green's forgiveness for the pain, but he had to closely examine the blow to his head. Marta then gently helped him to the other room.

"Leo, help Ernst move the body, and then watch the door."

"Where?"

"In one of the bedrooms."

As they picked up the body, blood streamed out even more, loudly dripping on the kitchen floor. When they finished, Leo closed the man's eyes. Sohn, clearly shaken by this latest horror, fidgeted for his pipe.

"Ernst, it is not safe for you to leave just yet. You are not ready to travel. Wait till the Americans come."

"I have to leave now or wait until tomorrow. You cannot travel at night. I must go. I'm taking a piece of white sheet."

"Danke, Ernst."

Sohn nodded and left through the front door.

30

GREEN'S PAIN BEGAN TO SUBSIDE somewhat after taking a couple of tablets that he thought were aspirin. Once the stitches had been done, he finally could raise his head up, though still woozy.

"I'm sorry to have caused problems for you folks, I really am."

"You did not come to us, Lieutenant, we found you, remember? Besides, I think Marta likes having you around. It was better than taking care of the Germans."

"Well, let's hope my guys are right around the corner like that Kraut kept shouting."

They were interrupted by the *whoosh* of American shells flying over again, a comforting yet still nerve-jarring sound.

Leo yelled from the kitchen that he spotted an American tank down the road. To his relief, it was not firing. They would continue to sit tight until they actually saw the Americans standing in the doorway.

"Leo, put some kind of white sheet outside. My guys won't know the difference between us and the Krauts, believe me."

Leo opened the door to the kitchen, took a knife and jabbed into the wood doorframe. Then he hung the sheet from it, making it clearly visible from far away. Tanks were heard rumbling around the village. From behind the stone house at the end of the block, came a small squad of Americans walking alongside a tank destroyer. Leo also had a white towel, which he waved vigorously. The soldiers, surprised to see anyone, approached cautiously. They sped up as they heard Leo shout something in English and explain that there was an American inside.

The weary, bundled up American troops, some in white ponchos, cautiously walked around the building, peering in the windows. Then a husky sergeant entered with Leo.

"Where is he?"

"In here."

Despite his bleary eyes, Green made out the almost bearded figure standing before him and let out the deepest breath he had had in weeks.

"Hey Mac, what's your name?"

"Green, Lieutenant, Brendan F."

"Oh, you're a lieutenant. The getup fooled me, sir. Sorry. That guy didn't tell me about the clothes. Pretty convincing, sir. Who you with?"

"590th Field Artillery, the 106th infantry" Green repeated softly as he pulled out his dog tags.

"Are there anymore of you around you think?"

As they spoke, more Americans began filtering in to view the curious site of the American, dressed like a Belgian villager.

"I doubt it. I had another guy with me from the 333rd. He's dead somewhere.

"That was the Colored outfit, right?"

"Yeah."

"I don't know what happened to them, sir. Well, you can check with graves reg. Your outfit took a hell of a beatin'."

"Where is the division now?"

"Not sure, sir. One of your regiments might be north of here. Some of the guys floated back to our lines, but I heard a lot got captured."

"I figured as much."

The sergeant then began looking around for his men.

"Hey Munson, get the Doc will ya?"

"How did you avoid the Krauts, sir?"

"It's a long story, Sergeant. But these clothes didn't help much. I didn't get your last name."

"Gates, Francis R. Sergeant Frank Gates. I'm with the 87th., we're part of the I & R platoon. The 4th has already taken Bleialf, we're meetin' up them later."

"Well, Sergeant,. I am glad to see you guys." Green stuck out his hand. "I'd get up but my head hurts like hell."

"Been hit, sir?"

"I think the doctor can explain it. Hey, you got a smoke for me?"

"Sure do, sir."

The Doctor gave a very brief explanation, then directed Marta to see if she could find some American uniforms to put on Green.

"Doctor, do you need anything? We have a whole Army behind us. They can help."

"There is one thing."

He then proceeded to show them the body of the German and tell the more detailed story that accompanied his demise.

Marta rushed back with pants, a dark wool officer's shirt and a surprisingly clean field jacket. Green was surprised to see the Division patch still attached to the jacket's shoulder. Inside the jacket, were a variety of personal effects that she had found in the pockets of his old uniform. Devoid of any modesty after his experiences, he stripped off his native attire right away and got into his olive drabs.

The medics arrived to help Green out to a waiting jeep, but he brushed them aside, choosing to limp under his own power. Henin, Leo and a now teary Marta, all walked him out.

"Put me in the front seat. No stretcher and give me a second, will ya?" Green told the driver. "Hey, Leo. If you find Jackson's body, please tell our guys right away. Okay?"

Leo nodded. "Of course, give your daughter a hug for me too."

"*Promesse*, Lieutenant."

"I will try to get back and see you sometime."

That was all he could think of saying. Truth be told, he knew he never wanted to come back here. Although, he wished he could express his thanks in words to these brave civilians who saved him. Doctor Henin, after one last look at his head, shook his hand and Marta gave him one last, very tight hug.

"Oh, Lieutenant. Please wait," Leo excitedly interjected.

"What's up, Leo?"

"Please." he replied and ran back into the house.

Green patiently waited, inhaling on the last remnants of his cigarette, until finally Leo practically flew out of the house.

"Here!"

They all turned to see Leo holding a Thompson above his head. The veteran GIs all aimed their rifles at him in reflex action, until their squad leader waved them off. Green was stunned by the gesture.

"Is that mine?"

"Well, I don't think so," Leo answered, a little embarrassed, but very proud of his acquisition. "But I find in forest. You take."

The medic, duly impressed with the honor, answered for Green.

"I guess they kind of like you, sir. Gifts and everythin'."

He accepted the weapon, placing it on the floor of the jeep but not before checking the clip. It was almost full.

"It's not easy to keep me quiet, Leo. But you did. Good luck to all of you."

"Au revoir."

Green turned to the driver and waved him on.

"Go slow, okay? My head is still pounding."

"There's no choice, sir. The road is jammed and pretty muddy."

The jeep jerked them back and the tires spun as he hit the gas. The hordes of Americans flooding the road and the sight of the tanks were dreams come true. He was free, physically at least. The impotent feeling of being trapped in a cellar with your enemy right above you was gone.

"Where are we headed?"

"St. Vith, sir. The city is destroyed but we have an aid station there in the shell of a building."

"You're not needed here or somewhere else? I mean, I can wait."

"Oh no, sir. I'm designated as an ambulance and jeep driver for now. We got lots of medics headed this way. You're fine. Try to enjoy the ride. Most of the guys that ride with me are flat on their backs."

"I guess that's comforting. Try to watch the bumps, okay?"

"Sir, would you like another cigarette?"

"Yeah, that would be great." The medic reached in and handed him a Chesterfield.

"We found some Red Cross parcels that the Germans missed. Inside were tons of smokes."

"The Krauts don't miss much, so I guess we were lucky."

The medic, seeing Green fidget around for his lighter, handed him his own cigarette for a light. He inhaled deeply, then let it glide out of his nostrils, wanting to disappear in a pall of smoke.

"Can't believe you made it, sir. We haven't come across any others."

"Yeah, I heard."

He was beginning to lose any energy even to talk.

The skies were almost clear and the air much colder as they bounced along. A hint of sun was trying to burst through the clouds. The driver had to stop several times to get out of the way of the onslaught of American vehicles and men. To the men along side the road, he was probably just another soldier, although there were some curious looks because of the bandages around his head. They could not know of his month-long odyssey.

Surrounding fields were littered with reminders of the battle. Burnt vehicles, abandoned howitzers encased in mud along with the still burning hulks of German Panzers, lay everywhere. Sections of forest were blown apart, the scorched trees stood bare and blackened. The sight of upturned American helmets scattered in the field was a sad reminder of all that had gone wrong. Bodies too, sometimes whole and some in pieces, had been deposited along the road; the smell of burning flesh hung in the air. Many of the German dead lay frozen in place, with arms raised, as if embracing death. The purplish hue of their disfigured faces gave mute testimony to conditions under which the combatants had fought. The GIs stared in sullen curiosity at the strange sights. A group of men had even stopped to eat and were using the bodies as logs to sit on. The bloodied American Army now sought vengeance, inured to the inhumanity around it.

The ride had become an elegy for all the men he had lost. Faces, names and even voices raced through his thoughts. The medic continued to talk and relay all that had gone on the past month but Green barely paid attention. He had become numb to the cold wind and the bumpy ride. As the church tower and the still smoldering ruins of St. Vith's buildings came into view, his mind raced with questions. Do my folks think I'm dead? How were the Krauts treating the rest of his men? Were any still alive?

Then his thoughts turned to Jackson. He lay somewhere in the woods behind him. A man he barely knew a day, but whose example would stay with him the rest of his life. He wanted to shout from the rooftops about what he had been through and the lives of the men it had cost. That would have to wait, for the war was still raging.

Green reached into his inside jacket pocket for another cigarette when he touched something metal.

It can't be.

Pulling it out, he could only stare, not believing his eyes:

Emmett C. Jackson

36365871 T42 43 AB P

What ya got there, sir? Found your dog tags?"

"Um..."

He stuttered. Not in the mood to tell stories, he deflected the inquiry.

"No, some other guy's. We had a lot of casualties at the house. Must have been his jacket."

"Do you want me to take that off your hands, sir?"

"No, no, I'll take it."

"Is he dead, sir?"

"Yeah."

"Make sure you give it to Graves Reg or find his unit to let 'em know."

"I'll do that."

"So sir, do you think you'll make it back to your unit?"

Vapid conversations were not his specialty and he had been unsuccessfully trying to tune out the medic. That very common question brought him back to consciousness.

"Don't know if that's possible, private."

"Yeah, looks like you've had enough, sir."

"I've had enough. We've all had enough."

Green sunk deeper in his seat, took another drag on his cigarette and began to shake. One last look at the dog tag and he squeezed it in the palm of his calloused left hand.

He was a survivor, again.

Prologue

APPROXIMATELY 7,000 MEN WERE CAPTURED from the 106th, most coming in the first week of battle. It is estimated that 180 of those men died in captivity.

However, the Golden Lions did not fade into history after their initial defeat. They regrouped, fighting on during the defense of St. Vith and through the conclusion of the battle. The 424th Infantry Regiment, which remained relatively intact, picked up survivors of the other regiments along the way. Helped by the reconstituted artillery battalions, they contributed mightily to the Allied victory. Total casualties for the Division were 641 killed and 1200 wounded during 63 days of combat.

Lieutenant Eric Fisher Wood of the 589th was one of those casualties. His body was found, along with that of another GI, in February 1945 by local villagers near the Belgian village of Meyerode. Surrounding the two men were numerous German dead as well. Much controversy surrounds his movements between December 17th and the end of the battle. According to the locals, Wood conducted what we would call today, a *guerrilla* war, against the Germans. German soldiers were overheard by the villagers complaining about 'bandits' attacking their convoy around Meyerode. Constant small arms fire was heard to the east of the village, well behind German lines. Despite Army investigations after the battle, no one ever determined what exactly happened. But whatever the truth, Wood fought bravely to the end. Even today, the remaining men of Battery A still speak of him with great reverence, and remember him every December on the anniversary of the Bulge.

The 333rd was overrun on the second day of the battle. A group of 11 soldiers from the Battalion's service company escaped encirclement on the 17th of December and headed west. Northeast of St. Vith, they were taken in by a Belgian family located in the hamlet of Wereth. But a neighboring German sympathizer informed the arriving SS troops that there were Americans hiding in the village. On December 18th, the Germans approached the house and the men surrendered without trouble. That night, after being tortured, all eleven were massacred by the SS. They eventually became known as the "Wereth 11". None of the troops responsible were ever brought to justice. What was left of the Battalion ended up at Bastogne, and made an important contribution to that historic stand.

The Battle of the Bulge was considered officially over by the end of January 1945. The old front line had been reestablished, and many of the infantry replacements brought into the line prior to the battle, were now hardened veterans. For the Americans, the Bulge ended up being the costliest battle of the war with approximately 19,000 dead, almost 40,000 wounded and 23,000 captured. German casualties were said to number about 100,000. The Wermacht was now finished as an effective fighting force. The victory brought renewed vigor to the Allied command. American forces secured a Rhine crossing at Remagen, Germany in March 1945, linked up with the Russians a month later, with final capitulation coming on May 7th.

German General Hasso Von Manteuffel, who led the 5th Panzer Army during the Bulge, commented that the defense of the St. Vith area deserves to be thought of in the same vain as the historic defense at Bastogne. In a letter to a member of the 106th Infantry Division Association in 1970, the General stated, “Here at St. Vith, were all the elements of tragedy, heroism, and self-sacrifice which go to make up human experience at its most acute phase.”

ACKNOWLEDGMENTS

I WOULD LIKE TO THANK John Kline and the membership of the 106th Infantry Division association for their assistance, particularly E.V. Creel, John Gatens, John Schaffner and Richard Ferguson; Carl Wouters, researcher and member of CRIBA, whose knowledge of the Ardennes was of invaluable assistance. He has been a great supporter of the American veteran. Keep up the good work, Carl; Ms. Reta L. Rodgers, managing editor of Field Artillery Journal; and finally to my wife Ann, whose support and patience made this work possible.

Bibliography

I would like to recognize and recommend the following:

Astor, Gerald, A Blood Dimmed Tide. Dell, 1993

Baldridge, Robert C., Victory Road. 1st Book Library, 2003.

Brown, Raymond A., "Diary of Raymond Brown," www.indianamilitary.org

Creel, E.V., Phone interview, October 2005

Dupuy, Ernest, St. Vith: Lion in the Way. Battery Press, 1986.

House, Pete, "My Experiences During the Battle of the Bulge," www.indianamilitary.org

Kelly, Thomas P, The Fighting 589th. 1stBooks, 2001

Lee, Ulysses, The Employment of Negro Troops, United States Army in World War II. Center for Military History, 1994.

MacDonald, Charles, A Time for Trumpets. Bantam, 1984

Ringer, Robert, "My Adventures in Europe in World War II," www.indianamilitary.org

Taylor, Hal David, A Teenager's War. 1stBooks, 1999

Tolhurst, Michael, St. Vith, Battle of the Bulge, St. Vith, Pen & Sword Books, Ltd, 1999

Whiting, Charles, Ghost Front: The Ardennes Before the Battle of the Bulge. Da Capo Press, 2002

Zaloga, Steven J, and Delf, Brian, US Field Artillery of World War II. Osprey Publishing, 2007

FURTHER READING:

For more information on the 106th Infantry Division and the Battle of the Bulge, please refer to these great sites:

http://drizzle.mm.com/user/jpk/

http://indianamilitary.org/

www.criba.be

www.freewebs.com/106thinfantry/index.htm

http://home.planet.nl/~wijer037/Bulge/default.htm

For more information on the 333rd Field Artillery, see:

www.wereth.org/